Pretence

by

Gillian Jackson

A Maggie Sayer Novel

Published in 2013 by FeedARead.com Publishing – Arts Council funded

Copyright © The author as named on the book cover.

The author or authors assert their moral right under the Copyright, Designs and Patents Act, 1988, to be identified as the author or authors of this work.

All Rights reserved. No part of this publication may be reproduced, copied, stored in a retrieval system, or transmitted, in any form or by any means, without the prior written consent of the copyright holder, nor be otherwise circulated in any form of binding or cover other than that in which it is published and without a similar condition being imposed on the subsequent purchaser.

A CIP catalogue record for this title is available from the British Library.

Acknowledgements

Many thanks to my ever supportive family for their help and encouragement, especially my husband Derek, who has to live not only with me but with Maggie Sayer and her many clients.

Special thanks also to an ever patient friend Sean Jackson for answering all my questions about policing and judicial matters.

My gratitude also extends to all those who have read these books and whose positive feedback and appreciation has been a great encouragement.

Chapter 1

It was one of those rare experiences when you wished it was possible to gather up the wonderful sounds and scents, to grasp them like a bunch of wild brightly coloured flowers and store them in your soul forever, to recall and replay when life was not so perfect.

Maggie had awoken to a glorious summer morning, the mellow sun already streaming throughout the house with its shafts of light picking up the dancing dust motes. Birds were singing outside and the smell of coffee brought a smile to her lips as she pictured Peter, forever the early riser, pottering in the kitchen. This was exactly the sort of day when getting out of the confines of the office to see a client at home was really appreciated and the visit being out of town was a bonus. Maggie would enjoy the drive through the stunning North Yorkshire countryside in which she lived. When she eventually appeared in the kitchen, Peter was busy making pancakes, determined to master the American style he had so loved when they visited the States the previous year.

'You'll get more of me than you bargained for if you keep feeding me these!' Mags planted a kiss on her husband's cheek as he set a pile of pancakes on the table.

'All the more to cuddle,' Peter grinned, pouring their coffee as she laughed and began to eat.

'I have a new client this morning who lives a few miles away so I'm not sure how long I'll be,' she told him, 'But all the details are at the health centre as usual and I'll have my mobile on... mmn these are delicious.'

Maggie Sayer worked as a therapeutic counsellor, which in reality was more of a lifestyle than a job and a pleasure rather than a trial. Personal tragedy was the catalyst for this career when as a young woman her first husband, Chris, died suddenly as the result of a brain haemorrhage, shattering her life and plummeting the previously happy-go-lucky girl into a deep depression. It had been a long time before she recovered any sense of normality, clawing back a degree of solace only after a change of focus and career. In dedicating time and energy into helping others Maggie at last found her own peace and became an excellent counsellor with a natural ability to listen and absorb the diverse problems of her clients. Maggie discovered that tragedy had left in its wake a genuine empathy which was an invaluable asset in this type of work and over the years had developed a strength of character, an inner core of unshakable belief in the power of good and positivity which she strived to pass on to each client. Taking things for granted was no longer part of her make-up and living for the day without anticipating tomorrow's difficulties was a technique honed from grief and loss and one she determinedly lived by. Peter Lloyd had come into Maggie's life after several years of being alone, bringing with him a new unexpected happiness for them both and the couple had married two years previously. Peter often worked from home and took such opportunities to make breakfast or dinner and complete some of the household chores to relieve the pressure on his wife and make life a little easier.

****

As expected the drive into the countryside was a delight. The rich green hues of the hills were like a balm to Maggie and the warm air carried rich aromas of peat and newly mown grass through the open car window.

Following the directions of her sat-nav, she turned the car into a wide drive and mouthed a silent 'wow' as the sound of tyres crunching over gravel announced her arrival. The house before her was impressive to say the least and would more accurately be described as a mansion. Three storeys of solid Georgian elegance stood proudly in immaculately maintained gardens, the gateway through which Maggie had driven being sufficiently far from the house to be the best possible vantage point to view the property, a sight evoking the distinct feeling of entering into an entirely different world.

Lydia Armstrong had arranged this visit by letter, the neat handwriting giving nothing away as to why she wished to employ a therapeutic counsellor, which was not entirely unusual for a new client. The address, being unfamiliar had prompted Maggie into a little research on the internet, research which revealed a prestigious home and the fact that Lydia Armstrong was actually a Lady and the widow of Sir George Henry Armstrong. The thought crossed Maggie's mind that here was someone who could well afford a top Harley Street counsellor, a thought giving rise to questions which would hopefully soon be answered.

A small, rather rotund lady opened the door, favouring Maggie with a wide smile which lit up her whole face. A white, starched apron gave a clue to this woman's position in the household and her head bobbed up and down continually while leading Maggie through a splendid entrance hall into a large drawing room where Lydia Armstrong was seated at a small writing desk. Turning at the sound of footsteps, Lady Armstrong rose to greet her with an outstretched hand. A tall slender woman, easily taller than Maggie's five foot six, Lydia appeared to be searching her face as they shook hands, trying to get the measure of this visitor with her own intelligent, soft brown eyes. There was only a hint of a welcoming smile and a polite formality which, Maggie thought, may present a block to an easy and comfortable relationship.

'Tea please, Molly.' The brisk request sent the door opener swiftly out of the room with a few more bobs of her head.

'Please, sit down.' Lady Armstrong gestured to an armchair at one side of the marble fireplace and moved to take its twin opposite. Maggie dutifully sat, smiling warmly and focussing on her hostess while her mind raced to think of the right way to begin a conversation with this seemingly aloof lady.

'You have a beautiful home, Lady Armstrong,' was her opening remark as she took in the comfort and elegance of the room. The comment elicited a slight smile and Lydia Armstrong's shoulders relaxed as she answered,

'Thank you, but please call me Lydia, I have had enough formality in my lifetime and it's Maggie isn't it?'

'Yes, that's right. Have you lived here long?'

'Almost fifty years now, since my marriage to George, but he's been gone for the last ten of those years, which have certainly been the longest.'

'I'm sorry.' Maggie offered the words quietly having read of the death of Lord Armstrong and knowing that it was not a recent event – so therefore probably not the reason for her presence there that morning.

'Would you like to see the garden? It's such a lovely day and the roses are at their best now.'

'I'd be happy to Lydia, but would you not prefer to stay here to talk?'
Lydia answered by standing up and moving to the French windows.

'There is plenty of time for talking later, you will enjoy the gardens, I'm sure.'
Maggie followed through the French windows and out onto a long veranda which ran the full length of the

house. The air was still and the sun warmed the women as they walked side by side to the enclosed rose garden, the scent of which reached them before the magnificent blooms came into sight.

'This is so beautiful,' Maggie gasped. It was far superior to any similar garden she had seen.

'I thought you would like it.' Lydia smiled more warmly now, proud of her roses and pleased to have an audience to show them to. They strolled beneath arched trellises overhung with climbing roses at the peak of their beauty. Maggie couldn't resist touching the velvet petals and stopping to breathe in the rich aroma. Lydia moved purposefully from the main walkway to the side wall, against which was a large orange bush with rose heads the size of grapefruits. When Maggie reached her side, the older lady cupped one of the blooms, informing her guest,

'This one is named after my husband, the George Armstrong Rose, it's among my favourites.'

'It's quite magnificent. I don't think I have ever seen such healthy looking roses.'

'Are you a gardener?' Lydia asked.

'No, I enjoy pottering but that's about my limit. My father is though. He lives in Scotland and relishes the challenge of growing hardy plants which can stand up to the cold weather. He would love to see this, it's magnificent!' She swept her hand around the garden, an open palm indicating the whole scene.

'I can't actually take credit for any of it now. We have a full time gardener, quite a magician really, a man born with green fingers.' Lydia smiled, delighted with Maggie's reactions, the ice had been broken and the beginning of a bond formed between the two women.

Making their way back to the drawing room, they found a tray of tea with a plate of dainty home-made biscuits which Molly had set out for them. Lydia began to pour, while Maggie settled back into the seat, feeling the need to actually begin some sort of session with this lady. She had not come simply to admire the garden, lovely though it may be and was certain that Lydia too wanted more than a pleasant social visit. Maggie accepted the tea before beginning to outline a verbal contract, intended to assure Lydia of the confidentiality of their meetings and the few exceptions to it, which would only be in the event of any concern for the safety of her client or a third party. The older lady waved her hand in a slightly dismissive way.

'Yes, I understand, I have done my research and trust you completely. I've been informed that you are an exceptional counsellor and a consummate professional.'

Maggie felt her face redden slightly at such an extravagant compliment and wondered who this lady could possibly have spoken to to hear this kind of recommendation, but she had made a start and so continued.

'Thank you Lydia but it is important that you know exactly how I work and what you can expect from me. An hour is usually about right for each session, the tea is lovely but please don't feel obliged to make this kind of effort or you will have me thoroughly spoilt! This time is entirely for your benefit, to use however you wish, to talk or not, whatever is most comfortable for you. I may ask questions occasionally, which are only to clarify what you are telling me and confirm my understanding of what exactly you are saying. Anything you do not wish to answer is fine too. I will not be offended in any way and will also not be shocked. I often use the tool of paraphrasing and reflecting a client's words, which is a way to help both of us look at situations and issues from every angle and may hopefully assist your thinking or any decisions which need to be considered. What I really like to do is to empower clients to make choices and move forward with their lives, feeling stronger and more confident. Now, that's enough from me, perhaps you'd like to tell me what has brought you to this point in time?'

Lydia had listened with a gentle smile playing on her lips, not in any way mocking, but a faintly sad smile with eyes reflecting a degree of weariness, as if she had seen too much of life and was now struggling to cope with it. Her posture was erect with hands resting on neatly crossed knees. Maggie noticed how long her fingers were, piano player's fingers, with translucent skin dotted with age spots, still neatly manicured but with a barely perceptible tremor.

'Thank you Maggie, that is all very reassuring and I think I shall actually enjoy our time together but I am unsure of how long our meetings will continue. You see, one of the reasons I wished to consult you is because of a recent diagnosis from my doctor of cancer, and the prognosis is not good.'

Chapter 2

Rae woke up trembling. The nightmare had returned and was, if anything, even more vivid than when it had haunted her childhood. The bed appeared to have hosted a wrestling match, the sheets knotted and damp with sweat. Her heart was beating rapidly as she gasped for breath. The room seemed to hold eerie shadows even after her eyes had adjusted to the gloom. Being alone did not usually bother Rae but the dream had been so graphic that even now, fully aware of being awake, the wet grass was almost tangible on her bare feet.

Shouting and screaming filled the air as her sobbing mother gripped Rae's hand so tightly it made her cry. Blue flashing lights and greedy red tongues of flame lit up the garden, scorching her face as she gazed transfixed at the burning house. Then, as can only happen in a dream, she was no longer in the garden but upstairs in the bedroom, alone and frightened, looking out of the window at the commotion below. Each time she tried to shout for her Daddy, the dry smoke caught in her throat and coughing drowned the words. The flood of tears dried instantly on her face from the unbearable heat. No longer able to see from the window, the child felt tentatively along the wall, back to the little bed and finding her teddy bear waiting there, she climbed under the duvet, sobbing and hugged him close until eventually and silently, the toxic fumes stilled the little girl forever.

Knowing there would be no more sleep for a while at least, Rae went downstairs to make a drink, repeating like a mantra that it was only a dream, only a nightmare. Sitting with a mug of warm cocoa at the little kitchen table she attempted to divert the troubling thoughts to happier things, a task which should have been easy as in only a few hours she would be meeting Sean to visit a venue they were considering for the wedding. Rae wished he was here now. Ringing him was always an option but to say what? 'I've had a nightmare and could do with some company?' No, morning would be soon enough, she would have to shake off the disturbing images alone. Letting her eyes drift from the half finished floor to the stark, unrendered walls reminded Rae that she was living in a virtual building site. Maybe that was it and the unfinished rooms were the trigger for the return of the nightmare? Drinking the milky cocoa and attempting to steer her thoughts away from the dream, she at last felt weary enough to return to bed. Sleep did come, but fitfully and when the alarm clock rang at seven thirty, she climbed out of bed with a pounding headache.

It was a relief to see Sean, his infectious smile and enthusiasm about their wedding plans began to ease the terrors of the previous night, until that is they were completing their tour of "The Bridge." Rae thought she was going to lose it, conscious of a quickening heartbeat and sudden heat rising throughout her body. Trying to breathe steadily and attempting to relax had little effect and the fact that she could not control these feelings compounded them, giving rise to frustration and near panic. This should be such a wonderful time, they were here to plan their wedding, but the persistence of the events organiser was becoming increasingly irritating and she had to either stop this woman from prattling on or get out of the hotel altogether. Sean was oblivious to this mounting fear and a scene was not the way for him to find out.

'Look,' she suddenly broke in, 'I am absolutely certain that I do not want candles!' The words came out more emphatic than intended, causing the other two to stare at her in an awkward silence. Glancing from one to the other it was obvious that an explanation was needed to justify such vehement insistence.

'Sorry, I know that most people think candles are romantic and the open hearth probably does look stunning with them lit, especially at Christmas time, but I simply do not like them.'

'But…' the young woman began once more then stopped abruptly, finally getting the message that this prospective client really did not want candles. Sean's brow furrowed, obviously surprised and somewhat confused at the sudden outburst. Looking at his puzzled expression Rae decided the time had come to tell him about her phobia. Perhaps they could go on somewhere for coffee, it was time to leave now. They had seen all they needed to make a decision.

An hour later Sean folded his long legs under the table in the coffee shop and passed Rae a cappuccino, tilting his head thoughtfully to one side to study his fiancée, who seemed to be miles away, her long red hair forming a curtain behind which she hid, lost in thought.

'Didn't you like "The Bridge" then? I thought it was the best we've seen so far… the views over the river at the back will be fantastic for photographs.'

She looked up and flicking the red hair over her shoulder, focussed her green eyes on Sean and shook herself back to the present.

'Yes, I loved it, but that woman did go on a bit about the candles, she really got to me.'

'Hmm, I could tell, what was it all about love? The poor woman was only doing her job.'

'I know and I'm really sorry if it embarrassed you, it's just that she was so pushy and candles are simply not my thing. Well actually, it's not only candles. Any kind of exposed flame has the same effect.' Her voice had dropped to barely a whisper.

'But we've been together two years now and you haven't mentioned this before.'

'It's not cropped up before and I thought I was over it... but it seems that I'm not.'

Sean, seeing the tears threatening to spill, reached for her hand and Rae was instantly thankful for his love and concern. Rummaging in a pocket for a tissue, she looked at this man whom she loved wholeheartedly, knowing he deserved an explanation.

'When I was a little girl, we had a fire at home. I can't remember it at all, but I used to have dreams afterwards, well nightmares really. From what Mum and Dad told me, the house was gutted and needed to be almost completely rebuilt, so we went to stay with Gran for over a year. The nightmares began when we moved back home and although I had no recollection of the fire, the dreams were so vivid. I'd be standing in the garden with my mother watching as the flames whipped through the house, my whole little girl world going up in flames. Although holding Mum's hand and looking up at the house from below, I was also in the house, standing in the bedroom looking out of the window and crying. You know how strange dreams can be, one minute you're in one place and the next in another, well that is how it was for me and I would wake up screaming, almost feeling the heat from the fire around me.' She paused to dry her eyes.

'Why didn't you tell me this before?' Sean's face held such love and compassion.

'I really thought I was over it, the last time I had the dream was when I was ten or eleven and although I've always avoided naked flames, it hasn't been a problem for years. Just recently the dream has returned, exactly like before, in the garden with my mother one minute then in the bedroom with the fire all around me.' Her voice trembled as she struggled to explain.

'I didn't want to appear foolish and really thought the nightmares were gone forever, I'm so sorry!'

'You don't need to apologise, but I wish you had told me about the fire, it must have been devastating for all of you. Thank goodness no-one was hurt.'

'Yes, but can we talk about something else now?' Keen to change the subject she asked, 'Do you think "The Bridge" is the right venue for the reception?'

'I think it's the best we've seen by far and the price is comparable to the others too. I say we go for it, if the events manager hasn't put you off?'
Rae smiled.

'I think she got the message and yes, let's ring and make the booking when we get home!'

Chapter 3

Kicking off her shoes and padding through to the living room, Maggie found Peter in the office adding the finishing touches to the plans he was working on for the new contract his firm had recently been awarded. Seeing his wife he smiled as she moved closer to kiss him, asking,

'Fancy a glass of wine?'

'Mmn love one thanks. How did you get on with your new client?' He always asked, knowing that Maggie would give only a vague, non-committal answer.

'Fine thanks, have you been busy?' The reply made him chuckle, totally predictable.

'Yes but I'm almost finished now. It's been so good to actually be drawing plans again, I've left it to the others for far too long and have so enjoyed literally getting back to the drawing board.'

'It must be infinitely more interesting than costing projects. I can't imagine anything drearier.' Maggie was speaking from the kitchen, pouring the two glasses of red wine and savouring its fruity aroma. Peter sprawled on the sofa where she joined him. The Lloyds had been in their home little more than a year and had settled into a comfortable lifestyle with Peter working as much as possible from home and Maggie working fewer hours than previously in order to spend more time with him. Their two years of marriage had been fraught with anxieties as Peter struggled to come to terms with a shock diagnosis of Multiple Sclerosis and the frightening possibility of a bleak and restricted future. Presently however, things were much improved mainly due to the prescription of a new wonder drug, Gilenya, which suited Peter and had reduced symptoms of the ailment to a minimum. This breakthrough in treatment was a blessing which they very much appreciated and now, enjoying the magnificent views from their huge 'wall of windows', Maggie rested her head on Peter's shoulder, sighing with the contentment of the moment.

'Jane rang earlier.' he said.

'Good, so are they coming tomorrow?' Maggie was always keen to see her step-daughter and even more so Jane's baby son Robbie and three year old daughter Emma.

'They are and Rachel is too so you'd better get plenty of food out of the freezer, it looks like we'll have a full house.'

'That's great, with Sue and Alan bringing Rose it should be quite a party. Two babies in one day, how perfect!'

Peter grinned knowing how much Maggie enjoyed being surrounded by family and friends. She had formed a close relationship with both of his daughters, Jane and Rachel, for which he was grateful, knowing that step relations, or 'blended families' were often difficult for one reason or another. Possibly the fact that both daughters were already independent adults when he met Maggie had made this second marriage more acceptable and the girls recognised how happy their step mother made him. Since little Robbie Peter had been born, Maggie and Jane had been smitten, the baby being an obvious bond for a closer relationship between them and Jane's older child, Emma was already very attached to her new Grandma.

'It looks like it could be a great day for a barbeque. Did you remember to get extra charcoal?'

'Yes, I did and knowing Sue was coming I bought a couple more bottles of wine to be on the safe side.'

'Oh Peter, you make her sound terrible, yes she likes a drink and did so well not having any through the pregnancy, I think it's a sort of catching up exercise now.'

Sue was Maggie's closest friend. They had supported each other through some difficult situations and were perhaps closer than sisters. Aptly labelled 'ditsy' by most of those who knew her, she was a receptionist at the health centre where they both worked. She and her detective sergeant husband, Alan had asked Maggie and Peter to be godparents to their first baby, Rose, a role they were delighted to accept and one which they fulfilled enthusiastically. Rose had been born only a couple of weeks after Robbie so there were plenty of babysitting duties to keep them occupied. It would be good to see the children together. Both babies were at the crawling stage now and keeping their parents and grandparents on their toes.

It did turn out to be a perfect day for a barbeque and by the time the first guests, Jane, Brian and their children arrived, the sun had made an appearance and the sky was a clear blue, draped over the view from the Lloyds' house like a soft warm blanket, enfolding them all in an almost protective way. Brian immediately headed towards the barbeque where his father-in-law was engaged in the task of igniting the charcoal, leaving Maggie and Jane to catch up on baby chatter. Robbie reached out to wind his chubby arms around Maggie's neck and she readily took hold of him, squeezing the little boy gently as he planted a rather wet kiss on her chin before wriggling to be put down on the blankets spread out on the grass. As his Grandma sat down beside him, Emma took the opportunity of climbing on her knee, vying for attention with her baby brother.

'Why is it that men always take charge of barbeques when normally they would have to be dragged kicking and screaming into a kitchen to make a proper meal?' Jane nodded towards the pair who were resorting to firelighters for their task.

'Must be the macho thing, in the outdoors the hunter provider instinct seems to take over!' As they chuckled at the thought, Sue and Alan pulled up by the side of the house and began to unpack their offerings of wine and salad whilst Rose slept peacefully in the car seat.

'Are we early?' Sue asked

'Not at all, come and join us, we're just getting fired up!' Maggie grinned as Sue glanced at the barbeque and Alan, as if to prove a point went straight towards the other men. The outdoor space at the Lloyd's home consisted mainly of a large courtyard garden, shielded on two sides by a high stone wall with a lower wall and gateway for vehicle access completing the boundary. The small lawned area along one side had been a later addition, with baby Robbie in mind who was now happily exploring a selection of toys which seemed to miraculously increase in number on each occasion he visited. Ben, the family dog, waddled over to see what Robbie was up to and sat beside him, patiently allowing the youngster to pat his back, his tail thumping occasionally on the rug and nose twitching as he picked up the scent of the barbeque, knowing that food would soon be in the offing.

Maggie and Sue brought dishes of potato salad, rice and pasta from the kitchen, leaving them covered until the meat was ready. When everyone had a drink and Rachel had also arrived to immediately begin happily playing with her niece, Maggie and Sue found themselves alone together, both having sought out a patch of shade from the mid-day sun.

'Does it bother you Mags?' Sue asked tentatively.

'Does what bother me?'

Sue looked around at the cosy family scene, sighing.

'Well, it's none of my business but I often wonder how you feel about not having children of your own? You would have made a fantastic mum, it's so sad it never happened for you.'

Maggie was usually pragmatic about such things but looking at the scene in front of her did elicit an unusual pang of regret.

'It is so much easier to think of what I do have rather than what I don't. Naturally children of my own would have been more than welcome. When Chris and I married we talked constantly about a family assuming, like everyone must, that we had all the time in the world...' She stopped, momentarily overcome at the memory of her first husband.

'Oh Maggie I'm sorry, I didn't mean to upset you, me and my big mouth!'

'No, really it's okay, there are times when I think of what might have been but I'm far from being alone in this predicament, there are so many other women who would also have made excellent mothers but for some reason that privilege has been denied them. I've had clients with this problem and I have to say that in trying to help them come to terms with childlessness, it's helped me too. So, I shall stick to being a glass half full person and enjoy what I do have. Which is not to say that I won't be borrowing Rose from time to time and Jane is really generous about letting me look after Emma and Robbie.'

'Well of course she is, we might love our offspring to bits but there will always be times when we're at screaming pitch and need a little break. Just don't let me put on you Mags, if it gets too much you must say, I'll understand.'

'Thanks Sue, but I can't see that spending time with your gorgeous daughter will ever be too much for me! So, shall we grab some food before it's all gone?'

****

'When you know you are going to die it puts a completely different perspective on the time you do have left.' Lydia spoke in flat, even tones as if discussing the weather. Maggie had reached this same conclusion after her first visit to Lydia's beautiful home, having wondered herself if it was preferable to know of your own impending death or not, or for your loved ones to know they would be losing you soon. In her own experience when Chris died, Maggie remained undecided whether knowing in advance would have helped. On one hand there would have been time to say goodbye and do all those important things you assumed you had a lifetime to do and to prepare in practical ways. But would such knowledge taint the precious time you had left? Would fear of the unknown paralyse you and those around you? She had reached no firm conclusion on which was the better option and now faced a woman who was living with that knowledge and from what had been said during their first meeting, there was only a very short time left indeed. Lydia had made the decision to cease all treatment, treatment which had only served to make life distressing and painful and was not the way she wanted her precious last few weeks to be. The only medication now was strong pain relief which helped enormously without the usual concerns as to the long term damage it would do to her kidneys.

'If the doctor is right I should have another two months at most, perhaps only five or six weeks, so you will forgive me if I rush you Maggie?'

'This is your time Lydia, you can move at whatever pace you wish.'

'Well, let's skip all the exploration of feelings shall we, I have come to terms with my mortality and in many ways will be ready to go. There are specific areas of my life however in which I am not quite prepared and it is those matters for which I need your counsel.'

To Maggie this sounded as if Lydia was seeking advice, something she had thought to have explained as inappropriate during their first visit, so as her client paused, she took the opportunity to emphasise again that she could not offer advice.

'Yes, I do remember, perhaps I phrased it badly, what is the correct term? I need you to empower me to make my own choices, is that it?'

Maggie smiled, nodding. Lydia's body may be failing but her mind certainly was not and she was obviously keen to move on.

'I have two children, Patrick the elder and his sister, Elizabeth, both in their thirties now and long since married. Patrick has even provided me with a four year old grandson, Nigel, a sweet child who I don't see often enough but his parents are always busy, the way of the modern world I suppose. No one has time for what really matters these days,' Lydia lowered her eyes and began to study her clasped hands resting in her lap.

Molly, the housekeeper, chose that particular moment to enter the room with a large tray of tea and biscuits. Bumping the heavy door open with a well padded rear, she turned, smiling and placed the tray on a table beside Lydia. With bobbing head she then left the two to their tea and conversation. Lydia poured for them both before her thoughts carried her back in time.

'Growing up during the late nineteen forties and early fifties brought mixed blessings to my childhood. As the daughter of a

farmer I was shielded from many of the tragedies and depravations which other families faced. My father had tried to enlist but was refused due to poor eyesight, a disappointment which spurred him on to do the work of three men on the farm as well as supervising a small group of land army girls who were billeted in our home. If he had been recruited, I may never have been born as my appearance into the world was not until the summer of nineteen forty. As a little girl I was surrounded by an extended and loving family. There were always at least two, sometimes as many as five, land army girls living with us who fussed over me to the point of spoiling me, which for the first five years of my life I assumed was normal. The farmhouse was continually busy from dawn until late at night, a bustling anthill of industry usually filled with happy chatter and girlish laughter. Of course there were times of sadness. One of my earliest memories is of the anguished sobbing of a young land army girl, Mary, who was a particular favourite of mine and who allowed me to follow her around constantly to 'help' with the daily chores. The arrival of a telegram ended those happy times as Mary learned of the death of her fiancé, a young pilot in the RAF. Too young to understand such intense grief, I was only aware of the change in Mary as she withdrew a little more each day, as if her very spirit had died with her sweetheart.

The end of the war coincided for me with my early years in school, a huge change in every aspect as the world began to return to normal but to my young mind became very strange. Gone were the girls who I had played with, who dressed me up and came to my pretend tea parties. The farm became a quiet shell of its former self, with only my parents, me and a young man from the village who came daily to work in the fields. I had chores to undertake now too, not that I minded but I missed my playmates and the noise of their chatter. For my parents the end of the war brought relief tinged with sadness as both of mother's brothers did not return home. I would never know those two young uncles, who like countless others had been far too young to die. Mother grieved in her own way, never showing any emotion whilst I was around although such deep unhappiness was apparent and occasionally I found her concealing silent tears.

My parents were good people and our lifestyle slowly improved as rationing eased a little and father was relieved of some of the pressure he had been under during his working life. The farm began to prosper and two more labourers were employed to assist with the workload. I loved school life, becoming an attentive and enthusiastic student in the small village school where there was only two teachers and therefore just two classes of mixed age groups, something which looking back on worked well. The older students were an example to the younger ones and there was a wonderful family atmosphere which suited we country children. Life was uneventful and I was content, a happy child with a very simple outlook on life. The only real excitement I can recall from those years was during the winter of nineteen forty seven, one of the worst winters of the twentieth century. For two nights most of the pupils were snowed in at the school house and had to rely on the kindness of villagers to provide us with hot food and blankets, which initially seemed so exciting. This was perhaps the biggest adventure of my seven years until finding I could not sleep on the makeshift cot and to my shame cried for mother. When we did get through the snow I was so delighted to be home and have an extended winter holiday as the school was closed for three whole weeks. Coal was in short supply that year, to the farm and the school and I remember mother making extra large stews on the fire in case we ran out of coal and she was unable to cook more.

Other childhood memories are blurred and indistinct but I was always happy and loved farm and village life. By the end of rationing in nineteen fifty four, I was fourteen and had never known the village shop to sell sweets without having to use a ration book. It seemed like heaven at the time, having been limited to twelve ounces of sweets every four weeks, now I could buy that much in a week or a day if I could afford it! Such were the priorities of my young life. You are probably wondering why I am telling you all this? Well Maggie, I want you to understand how life was, what I was in those days, a simple girl who, although born into a country at war, had been shielded from its horrors to a great extent. I was an innocent, life was straight forward for me and, I assumed, for everyone else too. By the age of seventeen I thought I was grown up, mature and ready to meet the wider world, but I was mistaken. Childhood dreams of handsome princes had turned into crushes on local village boys, to experimental flirting and even the odd kiss when no-one was around to chaperone. But I was still a child in many ways and unprepared for the kind of world into which I was about to be thrust.

George Armstrong was ten years older than I, a mature man in my romantic mind's eye, tall and handsome which was enough for an impressionable farm girl who believed wholeheartedly in love at first sight. At first he seemed to be from another world, one of glamour and wealth, a whole universe away from my own simple existence and therefore unreachable. I latched onto every scrap of information learned about him from whatever source, storing it, together with my daydreams until he was the personification of the perfect man, an image growing out of all proportion in my mind. Our paths rarely crossed which served only to add to the mystery and romance I had weaved around him so that by the time we did meet properly I thought I knew everything there was to know about him. But of course that was not so. With such a build up you would be justified in thinking that I was heading towards disappointment but you would be wrong. George Armstrong, third son of Lord and Lady Henry Armstrong was a true gentleman and I fell in love with him during our first tentative conversation. It was at a young farmer's dance, I had recently begun to join in the activities of the popular, thriving group and George was the president in nineteen fifty seven. He seemed like any other of the young men in the group, his manners perhaps a little more refined than most and clothes of a slightly better quality but he joined in the dancing and the laughter, favouring no one above any other. In fact he seemed determined that we should all have a good time and made a point of seeking out the wall flowers amongst the group to ask them to dance. And that is how we met. George took my hand to lead me to the dance floor and from that moment I belonged to him and was pleased to say that he felt exactly the same way about me.

The nineteen fifties heralded a new era in Britain. If the mid forties had brought elation with the end of the war, the fifties saw a tremendous sense of optimism and a determination throughout the country to live life to the full, to build on the victory we had won at such a dreadful cost and to make Britain truly great once more. Rationing had lingered on into the early fifties but as trade resumed with other countries and our factories could turn away from producing weapons and return to producing consumer goods, we could move on to prosper as individuals and as a nation. But it was not only tangible change that was happening. People's lives had been battered and bruised and those who were able put their efforts into moving on, helping themselves and their communities to build a brighter future. Gone too were many of the prejudices of pre-war times, not least of which was to be seen in the class system. If George and I had fallen in love before the war we would have faced certain and direct opposition from his family and possibly from mine too. But gone were the days of 'knowing one's place,' most significantly illustrated for me by the way George's family accepted me as an equal. I soon realised that this was due partly to the family's tragic loss during the war. George was actually the baby of the family with two older brothers who had both enlisted and been killed in the same year, nineteen forty four, an almost unbearable loss for Lord and Lady Armstrong. They had borne it stoically in public but I could not begin to imagine their private agony. However it was their grief which smoothed the path of my acceptance into the family. Lady Armstrong had lost her two eldest sons and was in no way going to risk estrangement from her youngest and now only son and heir.

Perhaps my words do them an injustice, who knows what their reaction might have been in different circumstances. All I do know is that when George and I declared our intention of getting engaged, any anxious fears were unfounded and indeed there is much to thank my parents-in-law for. They graciously prepared me for a life which I, or my own parents would never have dreamed possible and I owe them a debt of gratitude for those early days... even if they later betrayed my loyalty and took advantage of my youth and inexperience. Have I shocked you Maggie? No, for surely you have heard far worse but I want to tell you everything with the hope that in doing so I may see myself and the way ahead in a clearer perspective. There is no longer any reason to care about status and what people may think. When days are in short supply, hours and minutes are not to be wasted. However, I am rather tired now and would like to finish for today if that suits you?'

Lydia Armstrong did appear to be tired, emotionally as well as physically and concerned that the old lady may make herself ill, Maggie took her leave, promising to return in just three days time. These visits would normally be considered too close together but Lady Armstrong's time was rationed and her counsellor intended to be as flexible as possible.

Chapter 4

Sean made the all important phone call to 'The Bridge' and the wedding venue was provisionally booked, to be confirmed on receipt of a deposit. Putting the phone down he threw his arms around Rae, sweeping her off the ground and high into the air.

'Less than six months time and you will be Mrs Sean Russell, how does that suit you?' he grinned.

'Wonderful, I can't wait… shall I ring Mum and Dad now?' Her enthusiasm matched his and she could not wait to tell her parents.

'You better had, especially if we want them to pay half for this 'do'.' Sean laughed, ducking out of the way of her flying arm trying playfully to land a punch on his chest.

Rae's parents now lived in France having moved there after retirement eighteen months previously. Buying an ancient farmhouse as a 'project', they found it greedily occupied the first year of their retirement yet brought them enormous pleasure in witnessing the transformation from a virtual ruin into a comfortable home with modern conveniences cleverly integrated amongst the lovingly restored original features. The house was situated in a fairly remote location, a few miles south of Rouen and less than an hour's drive to Paris. Rae and Sean had spent several long weekends helping with the work and now looked forward to a relaxing holiday there in a few weeks time which would be the first opportunity for them to view the completed home.

'Well, what did they say?' Sean asked twenty minutes later when the conversation was finished.

'They're delighted for us of course and even surprised at how reasonable the cost is. In fact Dad has offered to pay the full amount.' She grinned at the astonished look on her fiancé's face.

'We can't let them do that, we agreed to go fifty-fifty, that is way too generous!'

'No it's not and Dad means it. I am their only child and they have planned this for a long time. I know when you asked me to marry you, you expected to pay for the wedding yourself but Dad is such a traditionalist. I always knew he would pay for it all.'

Sean relaxed, hands raised in mock surrender,

'Okay, I concede, after all I wouldn't want to offend your parents by refusing such a generous offer!'

For both of them this generosity came as a huge relief. It was going to be financially tight to pay for the wedding they really wanted and to do some much needed renovations to their own home. This good news ensured that they could go ahead with the new kitchen and bathroom their house so desperately needed and possibly have the work completed before the wedding. It was such an exciting time and Rae loved the traditional three bedroomed semi they had bought from her grandmother. The offer from her parents was a more than welcome gesture which would help the young couple enormously. Her father however, was not the only traditionalist in the family. Rae and Sean had taken the unusual decision not to live together until after their wedding. Friends had declared them mad as they had found their 'together home' but it was the way they both wanted it and Rae strongly believed that she should remain a virgin until married. Sean readily agreed, although he wanted her so much at times that it was not easy but the arrangement somehow made him feel special and important to her.

Their decision, although seen by many as old fashioned, seemed to bring them closer together and made the wedding preparations a magical time, enriching their relationship and making it truly romantic. For practical reasons Rae had moved into the house as soon as it had been bought. Having been renting a flat since her parents moved to France, it was obvious that the rent money could be better spent in paying the mortgage and Sean, who lived with his parents, would move in after the honeymoon. Furnishing the house was also coming together well. Rae's grandmother had moved into a retirement flat which necessitated a huge downsizing effort for the old lady, something they both helped with in the absence of her parents. The house had been sold to them for a very reasonable price and they had been offered whatever furniture they wanted. Much of it was dated, however it served their purpose until they could afford better. There were boxes of books and photograph albums stored in the little back bedroom which still needed sorting out, but they were at the bottom of the list of priorities. Rae didn't want to throw anything away until she'd had the opportunity to sort through it thoroughly, which by the time she got round to it could even be when they needed the room for a nursery.

****

'Great barbeque on Saturday Maggie, thanks again we had a fantastic time.' Arriving for work on Monday morning Sue greeted her friend warmly, expressing genuine gratitude for a time they had thoroughly enjoyed. Since Rose had been born, Sue had returned to work on a part time basis for three days a week having found her daughter a place in an excellent day nursery which the little girl seemed to really love. Maggie missed having her friend at the surgery every day but the arrangement seemed to suit the family well and offered the best of both worlds.

'I'm glad you enjoyed it, we certainly did and it was so good to see the three little ones having so much fun. I think Rose and Robbie might have a future together, what do you think?'

'Hmm, an arranged marriage could save a lot of hassle in years to come. I'll have to think about it! By the way, are you still free this afternoon to go to that new water aerobics class? It sounds as if it might be fun.'

'I'd rather hoped you had forgotten about that and here I am without a plausible excuse. Okay, I'll come. Is your Mum minding Rose?'

'No, Alan's off work but has a few things to catch up with so she's at nursery. He'll probably ring if he has time to pick her up otherwise we'll collect her on the way home if that's okay with you?'

'Well I had put Robbie's car seat in, just on the off chance.' Maggie was delighted at the thought of seeing Rose again. 'She loves nursery doesn't she?

'Absolutely, the excitement when I get her coat and tell her where we're going is a little disconcerting, as is how readily she leaves me when we get there without even a backwards glance.'

'A sure sign that she's a happy and secure little girl, don't you think?'

'Yeah, I know. Now look, if I don't see you later, we'll meet at the leisure club at three?'

'Fine' Maggie sighed resignedly.

****

Alan always enjoyed a mid week day off. It offered time to catch up with the gardening and any little chores in the house and he so loved to pick Rose up from nursery, her excited laughter and the way she bounced up and down as he approached never failed to delight him. He would go for her mid afternoon after calling at Maggie and Peter's house to return the drill Peter had lent him on Saturday. It was such a glorious day, the drive to the outskirts where they lived would be a pleasure, it was as close to a rural setting as you could get without going too far out of Fenbridge. Perhaps he and Sue should look at the houses which were nearly complete on the neighbouring plot. It would be a great place for Rose to grow up and they would be assured of good neighbours. After cutting the lawn and tidying the borders, a never ending job in high summer, Alan made a sandwich and coffee and sat in the garden to admire his morning's efforts. With the hum of a rather large honey bee the only sound and the weather at its brilliant August best, he couldn't help but feel so blessed with his life. Sue was the woman of his dreams and more and when Rose had been born it seemed as if life could get no better. Yes, they would love another child when the time was right but he couldn't imagine loving another baby like he did Rose, yet he knew he would. Becoming a father had in some strange way completed him and simply looking at his little daughter melted his heart. It was hard to equate this wonderful life with some of the terrible cases he came across at work. But today was a day off. A quick shower was in order then he would set off to see Peter who was working at home.

'You didn't have to bring it back so soon I'm in no hurry.' Peter greeted him, 'But come in for a coffee, I could do with a break.'

Alan followed him through to the lounge where the huge patio windows were open onto the courtyard. Maggie's crimson geraniums brightened the stone troughs, hugging the walls and the view over open countryside was stunning.

'It's a great spot here Pete, I wouldn't mind waking up to a view like this every morning.'

'Well, they are already getting enquiries for the new houses over the way, why don't you take a look at them?'

'Yeah I know. Sue wouldn't take any persuading to move out here, I think I might just do that.'

After a pleasant hour together, Alan decided he had taken up enough of his friend's time and left to head for home and pick Rose up from nursery on the way. There was a tiny post office cum newsagents not far from Peter's and he would call in to buy the local paper, a property supplement was in that day which he might just enjoy browsing through.

Alan pulled up behind a black Range Rover, the driver of which was sitting inside with the engine running. Turning off his own engine, he walked into the shop looking around to find the newspapers. Barely three strides inside the doorway he realised something was terribly wrong. At the back of the shop a female assistant was gulping back heavy sobs as a stocky man with a balaclava covering his head and holding some kind of handgun, leaned over the counter with the muzzle of the gun pointed directly at the frightened woman's face. There appeared to be no-one else in the shop and Alan realised that his presence had not yet been noticed. Instinctively he went to duck behind the shelves, intending to circle round and approach the gunman from the other side. Just as he began to move, a prolonged blast of a car horn sounded from outside the shop, alerting the gunman who swung round coming face to face with Alan. There was no more than six or seven yards between them and for an instant they eyed each other in silence.

'Don't try anything clever!' the gunman growled, 'It's loaded.' He then motioned with the gun to the side wall where he clearly wanted Alan to stand whilst completing his task. Alan moved slowly, arms held well away from his body and hands open with palms facing forward in a non threatening manner. Not being in any way a firearms expert, he couldn't be sure if the gun was real or some kind of replica but knew the sensible thing to do was to assume it was real and loaded as the man had said.

'Why don't you stop and think about this mate?' Alan kept an even and almost friendly tone in his voice. 'Is it really worth it for the paltry amount that will be in that till?'

'Keep your mouth shut you!' The gun was again swung in his direction then back at the frightened woman who was visibly trembling while fumbling with handfuls of notes, pushing them towards her assailant. It was quiet for a moment which dragged like an eternity.

'You could give me the gun now and we can sort it all out...'

'Who the hell are you then, a cop or something?' The gun swung back to Alan.

'Yes, I am a cop and you're not going to get away with this, but if you put the gun down now we can...'

The last thing Alan remembered was a piercing scream and a thundering, deafening explosion as the gun went off. A white hot heat penetrated his chest, then nothing more.

****

The changing rooms were rather grand for a swimming pool, unlike the ones Maggie remembered from childhood when she went to what they then called 'the baths' but things had come a long way since then. Making their way to the training pool where the aerobics class was to be held she felt a little self conscious in her costume, being at that time of life when everything seemed to be going south. Sue however didn't seem to care, until that is they saw two girls standing by the pool in tiny bikinis with flawless, slim bodies.

'Don't you just hate them?' Sue remarked. 'There ought to be a law against having bodies that good.'

Nodding in agreement Maggie was comforted to notice that most of the others in the class were older than the two 'stick insects' as her friend had labelled them. The instructor introduced herself as Yvonne and asked what their aims were in joining the group. Sue patted her stomach,

'The baby came out but the flab's still there,' she groaned. Yvonne smiled and turned questioningly to Maggie.

'Well, I know I don't get enough exercise other than walking the dog, so I thought I'd see if this suited me.'

'Good for you,' Yvonne remarked. 'Walking is great but you need a little more than that to get your heartbeat racing. Take it at your own pace today ladies and don't be too ambitious.'

They entered the water rather tentatively, getting a shock at how cold it felt.

'Ice-berg alert!' Sue gasped.

'Shh, don't be showing me up!' Maggie laughed.

The session proved to be good. Yvonne had been right about getting their heartbeats racing, they were both slightly breathless but exhilarated. The instructor gave a little pep talk about exercising a little each day as they cooled down with a few gentle stretches.

'Walk instead of taking the car everywhere, get off the bus a stop earlier or take the stairs instead of using the lift.'

'I've given up using the lift,' Sue whispered, 'It's much healthier to take the escalator!'

Giggling like schoolgirls they went back to the changing room, the general consensus being that it had been fun and they would come again the following week.

Rose was happily stacking graded plastic cups on top of each other but not necessarily in the right order. She beamed at the sight of her Mummy and Maggie, showing the two little teeth which had been the cause of so many sleepless nights of late. Sue picked up her daughter, kissing the little upturned face and hugging her close. Then it was 'Auntie Mags' turn and the little girl seemed as pleased to see her as she was her mother. The journey home was filled in with several verses of 'The Wheels on the Bus' followed by 'Row Row Row your Boat' in an effort to keep Rose awake.

'This is the worst time of day for her to sleep. If I can keep her going now she'll brighten up at bath time and be ready for a bottle before bed.' Sue explained.

Maggie couldn't help thinking how much motherhood had changed her friend. The quirky sense of humour was still evident but a different Sue had emerged, a responsible caring mother, a role to which she was well suited.

'Hey, what's going on?' Sue's voice held a slight quiver as they drew near home to the sight of a police car parked outside with two men inside.

'If Alan's having some kind of party...' the quip was forced from an already breaking voice. As they parked behind the car the two men got out, moving towards the women with solemn faces. Recognising the nearest man as the Chief Superintendant from Alan's station, Sue's legs almost buckled beneath her. Maggie had already unstrapped Rose and lifted her from the car so was pleased to see the second police officer grasp Sue's arm in a steadying gesture, keeping it there as the little procession moved towards the house. Her own heart was beating so fast she could hardly breathe and could barely imagine how her friend must be feeling. An anxious look at the Chief Superintendent prompted nothing more than a few words,

'Shall we go inside?' When Sue was seated and no longer in danger of falling down, the Super continued,

'There's been an incident Mrs Hurst and I'm afraid Alan has been hurt.'

'But he's off duty today, how is... where is he?' Tears were flowing freely now and Maggie, sitting next to her on the sofa holding Rose, moved closer to put an arm around her shoulders.

'He is in hospital, it seems he came across an armed robbery and tried to intervene...'

'Armed robbery? Shot? No, is he going to be alright?'

'We don't know very much at the moment, there's a bullet wound to his chest and they took him straight to theatre, we should know more later.'

'Take me to him, which hospital?' Sue began to get up then fell back as the emotion caught up with her. Turning towards Maggie and pulling Rose onto her knee, she hugged the child close, sobbing quietly. The Chief Superintendent, who had introduced himself as Jack Swanson and his colleague as DC Madison, spoke softly,

'Of course we will take you if you want to go, but he's likely to be in theatre for several hours. Is there anyone you would like us to call for you Mrs Hurst?'

Maggie stroked Sue's hair and asked,

'Shall I ring your Mum, or Alan's parents?'

'Yes but I still need to go to the hospital. Will you come with me?'

'Of course, your Mum will want to come straight over. I'll ask her to look after Rose shall I?'

A nod sent her swiftly to the phone to make the necessary calls. There was no answer from Sue's Mum so she left a message, worded in such a way as to indicate the urgency of the situation without giving rise to panic. Alan's parents lived in Devon. His mother answered the phone and again Maggie attempted to relay what had happened as calmly as possible. It was agreed that she would keep them informed of any news as soon as they received it themselves. Lastly she rang Peter who could barely take in the news, having been with Alan only a short while ago. Agreeing to come straight over it was decided that he would look after Rose until her grandmother could be found. When she returned to the room, the Chief Superintendent was on his mobile phone, his expression unreadable. Closing the phone he addressed his sergeant's wife,

'Nothing to report yet I'm afraid, Alan's still in surgery.'

Maggie again stepped in,

'There's no reply from your Mum but Peter's coming round to look after Rose and keep trying to reach her. Alan's parents send their love. They'll be praying for you all and asked to be kept in touch. How about we get Rose bathed and ready for bed while we wait?'

'And I'll make a pot of tea shall I?' asked the Detective Constable.

By the time they returned to the lounge with a newly bathed, sleepy Rose, Peter had arrived and was talking to the two officers who were both drinking tea. They again tried to reach Sue's Mum without any real hope of an answer, knowing that if she was home she would surely have rung them by now, so Rose was left in Peter's care as the two women went with the police officers to the hospital.

Chapter 5

The estimates for the new kitchen and bathroom were, as expected, expensive and both Rae and Sean realised that they would also need to allow for contingencies knowing that nothing was ever straightforward, especially with an older house. The money they had put by towards the wedding could now be invested in their home, thanks to her parent's generosity and Rae couldn't wait for the builders to begin, which would hopefully be in less than three weeks time. While things were on hold she decided to take the opportunity to sort through some of her grandmother's boxes, the unwanted books would mostly go to charity shops and once the room was cleared they could begin preparing for decorating the upstairs of the house as the builders worked downstairs. It was glorious weekend weather, clear blue skies with a whisper of a breeze, so tempting to go outside and enjoy it but Rae could procrastinate no longer, Sean was playing football with his mates so she would get on with the task in hand.

The little back room smelt faintly musty, most probably from the books and the heat, so the first job was to open the window as wide as possible in the hope that the breeze would freshen the atmosphere. A layer of dust had settled on the boxes which she blew off before opening the first to explore what treasures it might hold. Her grandmother had been a fan of Georgette Heyer and some of the books Rae remembered seeing on the old lady's many bookshelves were on top of the first box. All of them were hard backs with their original dust covers intact, depicting colourful pictures of the regency characters featured in their pages. Fingering a copy of 'Charity Girl' she took pleasure in the evocative smell of the yellowed pages. Next were 'Arabella' and 'Black Moth', all in relatively good condition for their age. A sudden urge to read them took hold of her, whether simply for the connection to her grandmother or out of plain curiosity she did not know, but it had become impossible to discard them. Carefully each one was dusted and placed beside the door to be re-packed in a box of items to keep. Not a great start but they were a matching set and she would prefer to see books displayed on shelves rather than ornaments, at least they were functional. Most of the others could go. They were mainly paperback copies of her grandfather's heroes, books she would never read and were probably of little interest to Sean either, who did his reading electronically these days on a tablet. Thankfully there were soon more boxes to discard than to keep but would the photographs change that? Rae had bought some brightly coloured storage boxes to replace the dog-eared albums which had been accumulated by her great-grandmother over the years, thinking that they would take less space than the bulky albums and keep the photographs much cleaner. Sadly, many of the older images, most probably ancestors, were un-named but hopefully her grandmother would be able to enlighten her as to who they were next time she visited. Rae, who possessed a strong sense of history and family, felt it was important to know who she was and where she had come from and really hoped these solemn looking people in their Sunday finery could be readily identified.

 With a stiff neck and aching knees, she took a much needed break to make a coffee and a sandwich before venturing into the garden to eat. The sun was at its hottest so pulling the bench into a patch of shade and kicking off her sandals, Rae relaxed. It was a small garden, which suited them both and was very well tended. Years ago it had been her grandfather's pride and joy but after his death, her parents had paid to have it landscaped, including more patio areas with less grass and borders to maintain. Even this had been too much for her grandmother who had latterly paid a man to come in every fortnight to keep it tidy. The young couple were now to benefit from this, although they wanted outdoor space neither were keen gardeners so the easy maintenance design suited them well. A few pots provided colour and a dwarf lilac tree, past its best now at the end of August, gave off a heady scent in spring. There was always something to look forward to in a garden, even one as tiny as this. Having finished lunch Rae again climbed the stairs to continue with the next box. At the bottom of the pile of photographs were images of recognisable family members, several of her mother as a child with both parents looking on, a tender record of a toddler turning into a little girl, a leggy twelve year old and eventually blossoming into a winsome teenager. The similarities between her mother and herself were more noticeable during the latter's teenage years, the same green eyes and red hair which Rae still wore long but mostly tied back in a thick plait or wound onto a knot on top of her head. Her mother's had been cut long ago and the red was no longer as vivid as it had once been. As the photo's continued to record the family history, Rae's father began to appear, tall and handsome and always laughing, as were those of her mother. This wasn't quite the image she carried of her parents, yes they were happy enough people, but she couldn't remember seeing those utterly carefree expressions and the unrestrained laughter portrayed in these images seemed to have been replaced today by more gentle smiles. Still, it was perhaps fitting, we all mellow to some degree with age. David and Barbara's wedding photographs came next, again with such happiness evident even in the rather formal poses. Both sets of her grandparents featured in these, middle aged people unlike the ones she knew. Sadly there was only her grandmother Edith left now the other three in the photos had all passed away and were little more than a distant memory.

Stacking the wedding photographs away, Rae turned to the last box which contained the more recent family pictures. She was surprised to find that there were none of herself as a baby and having expected christening photos and the usual proud parent poses, there was nothing before the age of about three. The earliest pictures were taken here in the home which was then her grandmother's and must have been when their own house was being rebuilt after the fire. In later images when, guessing from the missing teeth, she would be about six, they were back in the family home They were the usual silly pictures, with her tongue out, a tea-party in the garden, having a piggy-back from father, all of which made her smile and think of how Sean would find them amusing. As she was about to discard the last of the albums, a picture fell from the inside cover, a photograph which turned her flushed face suddenly pale. In her trembling hand, the unmistakable reflection of her three year old self smiled up from the picture, red hair tied in bunches and nose covered with summer freckles. Close beside her, holding hands and with an equally big smile was another little girl, a mirror image of Rae herself. Staring in disbelief and trying to make sense of what she was seeing, several minutes passed and her brain felt numb. The room was suddenly cold and there was an inexplicable ache in her chest. Studying first one child and then the other, it was impossible to tell which one was her. Trying to rationalise the photograph, various thoughts swam through her mind, but in all honesty she had known at first glance what it meant. The photograph was of herself and her identical twin sister.

****

Maggie and Sue had been waiting for two hours. Alan was still in theatre and the last report they had been given was that the operation was going as well as could be expected, whatever that meant. The sister who imparted this information said it did no good to speculate and they really would tell them when there was anything new to report. Sue had vacillated from sobbing to anger, from being terribly afraid to chiding herself for being pessimistic. Maggie had simply been there for her friend. Hospitals were most certainly not her favourite place, memories of Chris, her first husband were re-lived in these corridors but today those thoughts were kept in check knowing that Sue needed comfort and strength and that her focus must be on the present and not the past. The sister allowed them to keep their mobile phones switched on and they had heard from Peter to say that Sue's mother, Ruby had arrived and taken over looking after Rose who by that time was soundly asleep. DC Paul Madison waited with them at the hospital, bringing cups of unwanted vending machine coffee and leaving occasionally to ring the station with uninformative updates. The Chief Superintendent had left them with the DC, informing them that he was to be their family liaison officer, a title Sue immediately associated with murder investigations, a train of thought which seemed to knock any thread of hope she had been clinging to right out of her mind.

At last the surgeon appeared, still attired in a green theatre gown and both women jumped up, turning towards him, eager for news.

'The operation seems to have gone well,' he spoke with only a hint of a smile, very practiced and professional, 'and your husband is in recovery.'

'Is he awake?' Sue was anxious.

'Not at the moment, it's too soon but when he does begin to regain consciousness I'm afraid we will be sedating him. His body has suffered an enormous trauma and it is important that he remains still and quiet, so sedation is in his best interests for the moment.'

'He is going to be alright though?'

'I can't give a definitive answer to that yet, he is certainly very lucky to be alive and the next forty eight hours will be critical. All I can say is that we have managed to repair most of the damage caused by the bullet, which was a considerable amount, but your husband is young, fit and hopefully a fighter. Naturally we need to monitor progress carefully and hope that complications don't set in. You will be able to see him shortly but then I suggest you go home to get some sleep. As I said, when he does show signs of coming round we will be administering a sedative so there is really nothing you can do here.'

Half an hour later Sue was allowed into the intensive care unit to see a still unconscious Alan. He looked pale as she gently kissed him and whispered,

'I can't trust you to do anything right can I my love? I have to go soon to see to Rose, she'll be missing her Daddy so you just hurry up and get well again.' She sat for a little while holding his hand, trying to be brave but with silent tears falling onto the sheets. Seeing the monitors and drips was frightening, would he really pull through? She loved him so much and didn't know what she would do without him. They needed him and life without Alan would be unbearable. A nurse had moved silently into the room startling her by placing a gentle hand on her arm, disturbing those dark thoughts and suggesting that the patient should be left alone to rest, there was nothing more to be done that night.

Maggie rang for Peter to come to the hospital and take them home and while they waited she rang Alan's parents, passing the phone to Sue who could only manage a few words before again breaking down. Taking the phone back she attempted to reassure Alan's father, telling him everything they knew and that they were leaving the hospital to go home. When Peter arrived they half carried Sue to the car where Maggie sat in the back with her whilst Peter drove.

'Do you want me to stay with you tonight? She offered.

'I think Mum will insist on staying but will you come back in the morning?'

'Of course, I'll be round first thing to take you to the hospital but if you need anything before then, please ring, whatever the time.'

Peter endorsed the offer and the two went in with her to find out if Rose was okay.

'She's been fast asleep the whole time bless her, now I'll put the kettle on and you can bring me up to date.' Ruby was making a tremendous effort to be strong for her daughter. Maggie followed her into the kitchen to help, giving her a comforting hug. They stayed for a cup of tea, only leaving when Sue finally admitted to being exhausted and wanting to go to bed.

There were no appointments the next morning needing to be changed but Maggie rang the surgery to inform them of recent events, letting them know that Sue would be off work for an indefinite time and then, as promised she set off to pick her up and take her to the hospital. On arriving at her friends, Rose became the centre of attention, thankfully oblivious to the drama playing out around her and of the danger that her Daddy was in. The child unwittingly gave the adults a focus and Sue was busy feeding her when Maggie went in.

'I rang the hospital and it's exactly as they said last night, they are keeping Alan sedated but said he'd had a comfortable night. I never asked if you were working this morning Mags, I sort of assumed that you were available, are you?'

'Yes, I'm free this morning and I can cancel this afternoon's client if you want me to, it's no problem.'

'You can't cancel clients!'

'Of course I can, you and Alan are my priority now.'
After kissing her mother and daughter, they left for the hospital.

There was no change in Alan's condition, a fact which they were unsure whether to interpret as bad news or good. It was only nine o'clock and the surgeon would not be round for another hour but they were allowed to wait in Alan's room, a concession which his wife badly needed. Pulling a chair up closer to the bed and kissing her husband, she held his hand determinedly as if having no intention of moving from his side ever again. During the next hour, Maggie tactfully left the room on a couple of occasions to allow her friends to be alone for a few minutes. Eventually the doctor arrived but with nothing new to add to the sister's update. Apparently Alan was still classed as 'critical' and there was little to be done except monitor his condition and wait. When the surgeon left Sue insisted that her friend should take her afternoon appointment and as it was obvious that there was little to be done other than wait, Maggie agreed on condition that she was allowed to come straight back afterwards.

Leaving the hospital was made slightly easier after lunch when the family liaison officer Paul Madison arrived, bringing coffee and obviously intending to stay for some time. Maggie left with a lighter heart. The client that afternoon was Lydia Armstrong and the twenty minute drive proved invaluable for collecting her thoughts and preparing to focus on Lydia instead of Sue and Alan.

Chapter 6

If approaching Lydia's beautiful home usually seemed like entering a different world, the feeling was accentuated that afternoon in having come straight from the clinical atmosphere of the hospital. But there was sadness here too. Something in Lydia's past was stealing her peace in the present and in her very limited future. Perhaps today Maggie might learn more of the historical events which were the catalyst of such a troubled mind. Lydia had expressed a desire to move quickly in their sessions but in reality seemed to have a greater desire to verbalise all those haunting memories. Never before had she had a client who needed to relate their past in such minute detail but this was Lydia's time and Maggie would, today especially, have to concentrate hard to understand these unusual issues.

What had become a routine of tea on arrival was no different that day and Maggie, who had eaten only a biscuit with her coffee at the hospital, was glad of the ritual. Lydia appeared frail, more so on each occasion now, possibly from the increasing dosage of medication or simply the pressure of knowing that time was running out, yet she greeted Maggie warmly and appeared eager to continue her story.

We married in the summer of nineteen fifty-nine, two weeks before my nineteenth birthday. It was an extravagant affair, those were days when any occasion was to be celebrated, the depravations of the war years were still uppermost in people's minds and a wedding, particularly in a titled family, brought certain expectations. My own parents were out of their depth. We were a small family, simple country folk, so George's mother undertook all the arrangements, graciously asking my mother's opinions in a polite effort to involve her.

I was ecstatic, living in a fairytale world, in love with my intended and life itself. Simply breathing in the air around me brought a rush of pleasure, of anticipation of the perfect life stretching out before me in never ending wonder. And ah, the wedding dress! It was every girl's dream, yards of exquisitely flowing raw silk and tulle with the longest train I had ever seen. I felt like royalty. My bouquet was yet another extravagance, lilies and roses tumbling almost to the floor, as was the fashion. I can almost smell them now. The Church too was decked in white flowers and here, this house of which I was to become mistress, was the venue for the wedding breakfast. Everything was perfect, wedding, husband, new home, I had it all and it was probably the happiest time of my life. We honeymooned in Paris, a farmer's daughter who had never travelled beyond fifty miles of home and I was in glorious Paris with my dashing husband, attired in expensive clothes befitting my new station. The first year of marriage was like one long honeymoon after which to everyone's delight, I became pregnant. Naturally George and I were thrilled and telling the family made everyone so happy, you would think I had presented them with the crown jewels. Of course I knew how much this baby meant to George's family. Hopefully I would bear a son to inherit the title and carry on the family name and for their sakes I prayed for a boy, although for myself I didn't care, if we had a girl we could always try again, I wanted a large family, we both did.

An idyllic life you might think, I certainly did. The pregnancy though was not an easy one but I was well cared for and eventually my time came. I don't actually remember much about the birth. The pains took me by surprise, I had a charmed life and expected to sail through childbirth without problem but it was not to be. A bed in a private hospital had been booked to ensure the very best care. My labour seemed endless having started in the early morning, by evening

I was exhausted. The doctor talked about a forceps delivery but the midwife was concerned that the baby's head was not sufficiently engaged. The day is all a blur and whatever factor decided them to deliver by caesarean escapes me now but it was such a relief at not having to push any more. I was sedated and taken to theatre. My next recollection is of waking to find George beside me, his face pained with such a look of agony that I wanted to drift back to sleep again. I remember asking if the baby was a boy, thinking in my confused state that his expression might be because we had produced a daughter.

'It's a boy' he said and I smiled, drifting back into oblivion. James, we had decided a boy would be named James. When I next woke George had been joined by his parents. My mother-in-law's ice cold hand took mine and patted it.

'You have been a brave girl Lydia.'
I thought she was congratulating me, yet the words and her expression were incongruous.

'But you are going to have to be even braver my dear.'
Whatever could she mean, was my baby dead, why was he not here beside me? I began to panic and she gripped my hand even tighter speaking firmly, as if to a naughty child.

'You have given birth to a Mongol, and there were other complications too. The cord obstructed his breathing and he is severely brain damaged.'
Those words hit me harder than if she had slapped my face yet not only the words, the vehemence with which they were spoken was like an accusation, as if it was entirely my fault. I could barely take it in and I asked to see James.

'I have given instructions that you are not to see the boy, it will only distress you, and therefore it is in your own best interests.'

Oh Maggie, you are so good at keeping your professional air about you. No, I am not complaining, I so admire that in you. I was told that you never judge people and I believe that is true and am grateful for your impartiality. But this must be a strange story for you to comprehend. That very word 'Mongol' I know how you must feel, it is not a politically correct term today but it was then and expressed how most of society viewed such children. Perhaps you can imagine how I felt, I longed to see my baby but was already beginning to absorb the feeling of shame that I had given birth to such a child. I had never seen my mother-in-law like this before, cold and hard. She had made the decisions and I was not to have any say in the matter. I longed for her to leave so that George and I could be alone. He and his father stood behind Evelyn Armstrong like dutiful sentinels letting her do all the talking. I could not understand why I was not allowed to see the baby. I was his mother and would have to see him sometime. What did she think would happen when we took James home and had to care for him? George remained silent, his face expressionless. Evelyn stood and turned away from me,

'We will wait in the car George, do not be long, Lydia needs to rest.' Then she and Lord Armstrong left. I reached out to my husband who came and held me as I cried, silently smoothing my hair but unable to offer me the words I longed to hear. I wanted my own mother but had she too been issued 'instructions' about what to do? Eventually managing to compose myself I looked into his face to see those brown eyes, moist and filled with a sadness which nearly broke my heart. I began to feel as if I had done something terribly wrong, had let the whole family down, generations past and those to come. I asked George when I could see our son.

'You can't, did you not hear Mother? Try not to think about him, it will only upset you,' he said.

It seems so strange now but I still did not understand what they were telling me. At only twenty, I was hardly more than a child myself and my life had been so simple, so easy. I was ill equipped to cope with such devastating circumstances. George went on.

'Mother has made all the arrangements. The boy will be taken from here to a special place where such children are cared for. We will have other children Lydia, put this behind you and we can try again.'

It was staggering, unbelievable. This man hardly seemed like my husband. What happened next is again unclear, I think I became hysterical and George called for a nurse who gave me a sedative. That was most probably the worst day of my life.

When I awoke it was night, all was quiet and I felt very much alone. As reality again began to flood my mind, it was accompanied by a feeling of utter desperation. I was no longer in control of my life or my son's life but hadn't that always been the case? Had my previous happiness been so shallow, nothing more than a sham? Unable to bear such thoughts, I was overcome by such a powerful urge to see my baby and struggled to get out of bed. In those days it was not the 'done' thing to get up for at least a week after giving birth, longer if it had been a caesarean section but I was driven on by my desire to see this baby who unwittingly had caused so much grief. The door to my room was ajar and in the distance I could hear female voices talking in hushed tones but looking out into the corridor could see no one. From the hazy memories of my arrival, I knew that the nursery was, fortunately, in the opposite direction from the sound of those voices and I turned that way to find my son, bare feet soundless on the linoleum floor. Opening the door as silently as possible I moved towards the six cots in the nursery. Only two were occupied, the first held a little girl, or so the pink blanket led me to believe. She was sleeping peacefully with tiny bubbles resting on rosebud lips. I turned to the other cot, steeling myself for meeting some kind of monster but when I looked at my baby, my heart melted. James was awake, laid on his back with his little head turned towards the light. His face appeared to be flat, larger than a newborn's should have been and his eyes had that unmistakable almond shape. But the overwhelming first impression of my son was that he was helpless, he needed his mother, he needed me. I reached into the cot putting my finger into his tiny palm expecting that instinctive grip that babies always have but no, he did not grasp my finger. It was as if James was unaware of the physical contact and of my very presence. Bending carefully, I lifted him out and held him close to my body but again there was no reaction. His little form was limp and floppy as I supported him in my arms, rocking to and fro in an effort to comfort us both. My tears dripped onto his blanket as

I stood for what seemed an age, disturbed only by the sharp voice of a nurse who had discovered my transgression.

'Mrs Armstrong, you know you should not be in here!' she scolded and I was too exhausted to argue as she took my son from me, placing him back in the cot and I dutifully returned to my bed.

That was the only time I saw my baby son, the only time I held him in my arms. The next few days were a blur, I think I was being kept sedated and by the time I was ready to leave the hospital the nurses informed me that James had already been moved to a special home where he would live among others with the same disabilities, spending the rest of his days there, with strangers. When I came home, here to this house which George and I shared with his parents, there was an air of mourning. Evelyn, my mother-in-law came to see me to instruct me on what I was to say to the servants and any visitors who might call.

'The child died at birth. There was nothing the doctors could do and we are striving to put the whole affair behind us.'

I tried to remonstrate, to stand up for my son, but to the Armstrong family he was already 'dead' never to be mentioned again and the lie had already begun to circulate. People treated me like a bereaved mother offering useless platitudes. Even my own mother spoke in hushed tones, saying that it was all for the best and least said soonest mended. George too was unwilling to discuss the matter, if I tried to talk about our son, he found an excuse to leave the house and I spent many hours alone grieving for James who to me may as well be dead.

I thought I would never recover, never want to recover, but time moved on and, I am ashamed to say that I began to join in the pretence, outwardly at least, believing that I was defeated and would never see my son again.

I lived that shameful lie for ten years during which time James's name was never mentioned but there was not a single day went by when I did not think about him. It was three years before George and I began to talk about having another child and when Patrick was conceived the event brought mixed blessings, even though the doctors had assured me that there was no reason why I should not produce a healthy child. Elizabeth was born two years after Patrick and our family was complete, the children never knew they had an older brother. It was as if James simply did not exist.

****

Linda Johnson scanned the waiting area of the surgery wondering what on earth she was going to say to a counsellor. The glaring magnolia room with the sun almost bouncing off the walls provided no inspiration whatsoever. Patients were coming and going each wrapped up in their own little issues, good or bad, but no one could help her. If only Dr. Parker had prescribed a repeat prescription there would be no reason to go through this charade. All she needed was a little boost from the pills, just until things were sorted out at home. Now this counsellor would be prying into matters which didn't concern her when Linda knew all she really needed was the pills.

'Linda Johnson?' a quiet voice interrupted her thoughts and turning in the direction they had come from, she saw a woman of about her own age only a few feet away, smiling cheerfully. Standing abruptly there was no option but to follow the lady down the corridor and into another magnolia room.

'Sit down Linda, please' the counsellor asked and she obediently sat, eyeing up this person before her, wondering at the same time how to appear co-operative yet get out of there as soon as possible. Maggie introduced herself and began to give some sort of verbal contract, something about confidentiality, Linda wasn't really listening. Her mind was still trying to form some sort of plan.

'Is that okay with you?' the pleasant woman asked.

'What? Oh yes, fine, whatever.' She mentally shook herself back into concentration mode, needing to get this woman on her side without having to disclose any personal details.

'You can ask questions if you need to clarify anything.' Maggie offered and Linda felt suddenly embarrassed. She was not normally a rude person but must appear so to this counsellor.

'I'm sorry Ms Sayer, I didn't catch what you said, perhaps you could repeat it?'

'Of course and please, call me Maggie. Is it all right to call you Linda?'

'Yes, fine.'

'I was just outlining a verbal contract as I do with all my clients. I'd like you to know that whatever you tell me in this room is confidential and will go no further, with only a few exceptions. They are, if you tell me something which indicates that you might harm yourself, or someone else, or if you give details of a child who might be at risk. In those cases I would have to discuss the matter with another professional.'

'Right I see, there's no problem there for me.' No, Linda thought, it wouldn't be an issue because she had no intention of telling this woman anything at all about her situation.

'We have about an hour this morning and then we can think about when you would like to come again and perhaps plan how we can use this time for your benefit. The only notes I have from Dr. Parker say very little, which is generally how I like to work, then there are no expectations on either side. We can build a relationship of trust purely on the time we spend together.' Maggie sat forward slightly in the chair, picking up that this client was avoiding eye contact and seemed totally distracted from the present. Allowing a few moments of silence, she then addressed Linda more directly.

'What is it you would like to get out of these sessions? Is there a particular goal you have in mind or perhaps simply the need for some space to sort an issue out?'
This caught Linda's attention and she looked directly at Maggie before replying,

'Actually, it wasn't my idea to come. Dr. Parker has been prescribing Prozac for me for two years now but has suddenly decided not to give me anymore! She said it was time to get to the underlying root of the problem, but there isn't one! The pills sort of help me cope with day to day things. It's not too much to ask for surely? I wouldn't be here wasting your time if she would give me another prescription, could you talk to her for me?'

'That probably would do no good. The doctor must have a good reason for wanting to take you off the medication. How has your general health been, do you have high blood pressure or any cardiac problems?'

'Well, yes my blood pressure's a bit high but surely the pills will help to calm me and it'll go down again?'

'It doesn't always work that way. It would be far better if you could manage without the Prozac and if your blood pressure remains high, Dr. Parker will look at ways of controlling it then. Has she tried to cut the dosage down at all?'

'Yes, a few months ago she said to cut the number down each day but I didn't manage to do that, I couldn't and now there are nearly none left but she won't prescribe anymore.'

'Well I will try to talk to Dr. Parker later today but I know the reason for referring you to me was as an alternative remedy to medication. Sometimes taking pills simply masks our real problems instead of dealing with the actual cause. Counselling is a way of talking things through, occasionally using simple techniques to gain a better understanding of why we feel a certain way. It's often an education of sorts where we learn about ourselves and what makes us act in certain ways, what makes us tick if you like. Perhaps if you tried to remember why it was you first went to see the doctor and why you began taking the Prozac, it could be a starting point?'

'It was for depression. My husband had left me and it was a bad time, that's all, nothing more than what happens to hundreds of other people every day. The pills helped me get through it and that's what I need now. Talking won't bring him back, not that I want him back mind you! You could save yourself a lot of time if you just had a word with the doctor and told her I need another prescription.'

'This isn't about my time Linda, it's about you. Of course you don't have to tell me anything you don't want to but you have made a good start by telling me about your husband leaving. It must have been a very difficult time?'

Linda had not meant to tell the counsellor anything but hoped that mentioning her husband leaving would have been enough to get her on-side and hopefully ask the doctor for another prescription. Strangely though, in spite of her determination not to talk, the thought of sharing some of the bad things really appealed. To have someone focussed entirely on you, someone who wouldn't judge or throw your mistakes back at you, it would be good, but no, it would be selfish and it wasn't all about her really, there was Danny to consider. Yes, there was always Danny to consider.

Chapter 7

'You're becoming a proper suburban curtain twitcher!' Sean let himself into the house wondering what had caused Rae to once again be so upset. If it was another nightmare why had she left it until so late to ring? She was watching from the window but the joke fell flat as soon as he saw her expression, and regretting the flippancy he opened his arms in a much needed gesture of comfort. He had been concerned at his fiancée's enigmatic behaviour during the last few days, floundering as to whether he was able to help and feeling somewhat useless. After a prolonged hug, Rae pulled away holding out an old photograph for him to see. Two little girls smiled at the camera, as alike as two peas in a pod and at first the relevance was unclear.

'One of them is me.' She watched the reality dawning on his face.

'But they are twins, it's so obvious. I didn't know you were a twin!'

'Nor did I, I don't think I have ever seen photographs of myself at this age, only older and now I know why. I have, or had, a twin sister but I simply can't remember her!'

'So, your parents have never talked about her?'
She shook her head,
'Then where is she, what happened to her?'

'I've just told you I don't know, but I certainly intend to find out!'

Grabbing the car keys, Rae announced that they were going to visit her grandmother, no surprise there, but Sean quickly snatched the keys from her hand, knowing that she was in no fit state to drive. During the short journey he asked if she could think of any possible explanation for this remarkable discovery and receiving only a grunt assumed that the answer was probably yes, but she was apparently unable to verbalise any thoughts or feelings whilst in such a distressed state.

It took only fifteen minutes to reach her grandmother's home. The little complex of bungalows was arranged in a square around a well tended central garden with designated parking spots outside each residence. If Edith Chapman was surprised at her unexpected visitors, it didn't show, a warm smile greeted them and she moved automatically to put the kettle on.

'No Gran, please sit down we don't need any tea.'
It was then apparent to Edith that something was wrong and she sat opposite her visitors on the tiny chintzy sofa recently purchased for her new home. Without any preamble or warning of what was coming, her granddaughter reached into her bag and withdrew the old photograph. She passed it to Edith who, keeping her eyes on Rae, took it and without looking at it began to nod.

'I knew this day would come,' her voice was low and filled with compassion, 'I am so sorry you had to find out this way, it must have been a terrible shock.'

'Of course it was a shock! I have a twin sister of whom I know absolutely nothing, don't you think I deserve to know the truth!'

'Yes my dear, you do. Perhaps it should be your parents telling you this but in their absence I'll try to explain. You did have a twin sister who died shortly after this photograph was taken. Her name was Patricia and as you can see, you were identical.'

It was Rae's turn to nod as the name struck a chord somewhere inside, hovering on the borders of her subconscious mind.

'Pattie!' she cried, 'My Pattie.'

'Yes... that was your special name for her. You were inseparable, as if joined at the hip, where one went the other followed. Patricia died in the fire but I'm sure you must have already worked that one out.'

Rae moaned as if in terrible pain. Yes, she had guessed as much on discovering the photograph, if her twin was still living she would somehow instinctively know but it had taken someone to actually speak the words that Pattie was dead to make this knowledge a reality. Sean did his best to comfort her, hardly able to comprehend what she must be feeling and at the same time acutely aware of the pain the old lady was also suffering. After a few moments of attempting to compose herself, she asked her grandmother the obvious question,

'But why? Why did Mum and Dad, and even you, not tell me?'

Edith drew in a deep breath, recalling so many painful memories.

'It was a harrowing night, the fire swept so swiftly and ferociously through the house that your parents were helpless. Your father had managed to pick you up and drag you and your mother down the stairs but it was impossible to get back in again for Patricia, although he tried desperately. The staircase had collapsed and he was severely burned yet made several attempts to reach her. When the fire crew arrived it was obvious that no-one could have survived such an inferno. The bedroom window had blown out with the heat and although the firemen attempted to get in that way it was too late. Patricia was curled up in her bed; they said it would have been the smoke that killed her.' Edith's voice was breaking as she finished summarising that dreadful night but Rae was still not satisfied.

'But why have I never been told, surely I must have missed her? If we were that close I would have asked for her. I just don't understand why you never told me about Pattie?'

'Of course you asked for her, right from that very night. At first we were too upset to explain and you were only three, hardly able to understand. Your parents were devastated, we all were, and you were the only bit of joy left in our lives. We never meant to dismiss Patricia as if she had never existed but at first it was the easiest thing to do. When you asked for her we diverted your attention. I know it was selfish of us but your mother could barely cope with having to go on living and after a while it seemed as if not talking about your sister was best for everyone. We concentrated on you and your future and eventually you stopped asking for Pattie. By the time you were old enough to have any kind of understanding, it had become the only way of coping, particularly for your mother, so we continued the pretence... that you were an only child.'

'You let me forget my own sister, my twin!' Rae was almost hysterical and Sean wrapped his arms around her to stop her flailing about and hurting herself.

'It wasn't like that, rightly or wrongly it was our way of coping, and your mother's way to get over it all. There were times in later years when your father and I discussed it but any mention of the fire sent your mother spiralling back into a deep depression, so we left things as they were. Our intentions were for the best, for you and for Barbara.' Edith was exhausted and consumed with shame and guilt at having kept this secret from her granddaughter, but she had always believed it was not her secret to share and her son and his wife should have been the ones to tell her.

When she had calmed down sufficiently, Sean made the decision to take Rae home. The encounter had been emotional for both women and neither was in a fit state to discuss the matter rationally. Promising to ring Edith later, he led his fiancée out to the car. Although still a hot afternoon, Rae was shivering as they went inside and he settled her on the old sofa, wrapping a throw around her and sitting close enough to hold her tightly. They sat in silence for several minutes, as close together as possible, trying to draw strength and comfort from each other as they wrestled with the shocking facts that they had just learned. Eventually Rae spoke,

'You must think I'm a neurotic imbecile or something, first all that fuss with the candles and now this, I'm so sorry.'

'Hey, no need to apologise! This has been quite some revelation and the two issues are obviously connected. How strange that you should begin to have the nightmares again and the fear of fire should crop up, right before you find out about your sister.'

'I do remember now, I called her Pattie and 'Twinnie' keeps spinning round my head, I think I called her 'Twinnie'.'

'Listen love, I'd been thinking, before today, about your fear of fire and wondered if some kind of therapy might help. You know Mum works at the hospital? Well she's a firm believer in counselling and I thought that now, with finding out about Pattie, it might help if you go to see someone?'

'A counsellor, don't you have to pay for that? We can't afford it Sean and who's to say it will help?'

'If you see your GP you won't have to pay, sometimes doctors have counsellors working with them at their surgeries. What do you think, it might be worth asking?'

'I'll think about it, right now I'm just so tired, perhaps I'll lie down for a while. Will you stay?'

'Of course, you have a good rest while I mow the lawn and then cook us something tasty for tea, how's that?'

'Wonderful, I do love you, I'm so lucky to have you.'

'Yes I know, superman that's me, now off you go to bed.'

****

It was two full days since Alan had been shot and there was very little change in his condition. Sue spent most of her time at the hospital only leaving to keep some sense of normality and routine for Rose and making the nurses promise to ring at the slightest change in her husband's condition. The surgeon still felt it prudent to keep Alan sedated, something Sue was becoming increasingly uncomfortable about but was persuaded that the doctors knew what was for the best. Maggie spent as much time with them as possible, as did Ruby, with the consequence that Rose received plenty of attention and seemed almost blissfully oblivious to the events surrounding her. Before Sue left for the hospital that third morning, Chief Superintendent Jack Swanson had made an appointment to update her on the investigation into the shooting. The family liaison officer, Paul Madison, was spending much of his time with Sue, either at home or at the hospital and had proved to be an invaluable source of strength and support, even leaving a mobile phone number on which he could be contacted at any time. Paul arrived with Jack Swanson promptly at nine am, as arranged just as Ruby had taken Rose to the park to give her mother some time alone with the officers without distraction.

'Shall I put the kettle on?' Paul asked as usual, setting an informal tone to the meeting. Sue smiled, thinking how Paul knew his way around the kitchen almost better than

Alan did. Jack enquired about the latest news from the hospital which she informed him was the same as it had been since the operation. The formalities over, he proceeded to tell his detective sergeant's wife how the police enquiries were progressing.

'The whole major incident crime team is working flat out on this case,' he said, endeavouring to put across the importance of their investigation. 'We're working closely with our intelligence cell, using all information on those known to us who have firearms and we have tasked our regular informers to seek out any information. In short Mrs Hurst we are doing everything possible to find this man.'

'And what will happen when you do catch him?' Her tone was perhaps a little sarcastic, fearing that the justice system might not punish the perpetrator enough. Jack nodded understandingly and explained,

'We are actually looking for at least two men, possibly more and there are several charges we can, and will, bring against them. Obviously with regard to Alan, we will be looking at attempted murder, discharge of a weapon, grievous bodily harm and possibly illegal possession of a firearm. With regard to the robbery itself, there is intent to commit an indictable offence, conspiracy to commit armed robbery and taking a vehicle without consent. Anyone who had anything to do with the planning and execution of this crime will be considered culpable and will face charges.'

She had to concede that it seemed as if the police were indeed doing everything possible to catch the culprits and some of the animosity of feeling towards the Chief Superintendent was melting away. Naturally her one big fear was that this could turn into a murder inquiry, a thought which was never far away, but one she tried desperately not to dwell on. Paul had already told her that they had found the Range Rover used in the robbery, abandoned about two miles from the scene. This also suggested a planned crime with possibly more than two men involved.

'Have you found anything of help in the vehicle?' Sue asked.

'Yes, there are traces of DNA from several people and we are now trying to obtain samples from the legal owner and his family for elimination purposes and that's ongoing as we speak.'

Sue nodded then accepted the tea which Paul was offering as she thought about how to phrase another question which had been troubling her.

'Will Alan's intervention in this crime go against him in any way, being off duty I mean?'

'Certainly not; the minute he took that decision to get involved he placed himself on duty again and according to the lady attending the shop, a reliable eye witness, Alan identified himself as a police officer. He will have the full support of the division Mrs Hurst. His actions were extremely brave and nothing short of commendable.'

It was a relief to hear these words. Although her primary concern was naturally for her husband's recovery, a niggling fear had been dancing at the back of her mind, a concern that Alan might be in some kind of trouble for his actions but the superintendent's emphatic answer had alleviated that fear.

Arriving at the hospital only an hour later than usual, Sue went straight to the intensive care ward. The doctor was still on the ward with another patient and she was pleased not to have missed him.

'Good morning Mrs Hurst.' He smiled on entering the room, picking up the chart from the bottom of the bed and studying it in silence for a few moments.

'Your husband seems to be stable at present. Last night we discontinued the medication which was keeping him sedated, so we can expect that sometime today, sooner rather than later, he will come round. Generally his body seems to have coped well with the trauma of the shooting and the state of unconsciousness appears to have worked in that it has afforded the time to heal, so hopefully we are now past the danger of internal bleeding from the lung and shoulder damage.'

Sue could have kissed the man but settled instead for a huge grin.

'It is a serious injury, however and although I am more confident now of a good recovery we still have to take things slowly. Mr Hurst will need plenty of rest and as yet we don't know to what extent the shoulder injury will affect the movement in his arm. We can of course be grateful that it was the right side of the chest which took the full force of the bullet otherwise I don't think he would be here today. When he's conscious we should be able to tell you more about the treatment over the next few weeks. There will of course be physiotherapy but the damage to his lung needs to heal before we can go down that road and with plenty of rest and care, your husband may be well enough to leave us in another three weeks.'

Three weeks! The thought instantly deflated her buoyant mood, hospitals don't keep patients any longer than necessary. She had been discharged within six hours of giving birth to Rose! And damage to his lung, that sounded serious, poor Alan, he wasn't one to cope well with inactivity. Sue thanked the doctor before taking up her usual position at Alan's side, accompanied today by a frisson of excitement knowing that he might wake up at any time.

Chapter 8

It was a phone call she was dreading, but the need to speak to her parents was overwhelming, to learn some answers and to ask them a hundred whys. Incredibly she had slept well despite the events of the previous day. Having anticipated the return of the nightmare, the welcome seven hours sleep had been surprisingly dreamless and on waking Rae felt unexpectedly refreshed. Perhaps it was the knowledge that her fiancé was downstairs. Good, reliable Sean who as promised had cooked a meal for them both before going back to his parents, grabbing an overnight bag and then returning to spend the night on the sofa. He was still sleeping when Rae crept downstairs, with the sleeping bag twisted around his lanky frame looking most uncomfortable. She kissed his mussed-up hair and padded into the kitchen to make coffee while he pulled himself together. They had discussed the phone call the evening before. Sean having suggested they sleep on this new found knowledge before confronting her parents, a sensible idea to which she acquiesced yet now was keen to get over with before facing the rest of the day. It was Sunday but knowing her parents were early risers and after a much needed caffeine boost, Rae dialled their number.

David and Barbara Chapman were expecting the call. Edith had rung the evening before to tell them of her visitors and to relate what she had revealed about Patricia. Unlike her daughter, Barbara had had a terrible night, hardly sleeping at all with troubling memories of the fire and the way they had handled things since skipping through her mind and making any kind of rest impossible. She usually possessed an ability to compartmentalize her thoughts, anything unpleasant or difficult being stored away to be dealt with at a later date or completely ignored in the hope that it would go away. This aptitude for avoidance had, she always thought, served her well, but now the past, the most horrific time ever, was revisiting her and she was completely at a loss to know what to do. David did his best to comfort his wife throughout the night with the result of being incredibly tired himself yet knowing he was soon to encounter a difficult phone conversation with his daughter. This day was one which had always hovered over them, a day when their secret would come to light and explanations would have to be given. Over the years he had done his utmost to shield his wife from heartache and pain, continuing the 'pretence' in an effort to maintain some degree of normality and happiness in their life. But had this been the right thing to do? Deciding that he would take the call, another attempt to protect Barbara, they both knew that the time had arrived to bring things out into the open, no more secrets, no more pretending. David could barely imagine how Rae must be feeling having been so suddenly confronted with the knowledge of her lost twin sister.

His voice on answering the telephone sounded weary, which had the effect of softening Rae's attitude. Having felt such anger towards her parents the previous day it was now virtually impossible to find the right words to say. It was also no surprise that Edith had been in touch with them, she had expected nothing less and therefore there was no skirting about the issue.

'Why Dad, why on earth did you never tell me about Pattie?'

Listening to her speaking her twin's name the way she had always spoken it, nearly broke his heart and the knowledge of their misguided actions struck him like a physical blow. His daughter continued.

'It's as if she had never existed! How could you do that to Pattie... to me?'

There was no reasonable answer. Feeling her grief every bit as keenly as she, David listened as she vented anger and frustration and he could offer no plausible reason which did not sound like an excuse. The conversation was short and they finally agreed to leave the matter for a day or two knowing this was not a subject which would be easily resolved, especially over the telephone. David, hands trembling, put down the receiver then went to find Barbara to give an edited report of the conversation. Rae too was shaking. Sean was making more coffee in the kitchen when she found him and she sobbed bitterly on his shoulder.

The following morning Rae was seated in the doctor's surgery, a place she rarely had cause to visit. Ten minutes had passed and her name had still not flashed up on the annoying screen which beeped every time a new message appeared. Concentrating on a magazine was impossible as she was edgy and unusually anxious about seeing her GP. Sean would have come too but had very little holiday left at work having booked two weeks for their forthcoming visit to France but she assured him everything would be fine. What exactly to say to the doctor had been puzzling her since she made the appointment, Dr Williams probably wouldn't even remember her, the last time she was there was with a nasty case of chicken pox at fourteen years old, a very uncomfortable embarrassment for a teenager.

The dream had recurred the night before. The nightmare seeming more potent than ever with the knowledge that it was not simply her material world which had been destroyed but her beloved Pattie, her twin and other half. Rae had not only been herself standing in the garden, she had been Pattie, afraid and alone, trapped in their bedroom. She had woken up coughing, eyes streaming and the name Pattie on her lips. For one terrifying moment she believed her new home to be on fire, so vivid was the dream that even the realisation that it was not real could not take away the pain. Her twin was gone, she would never see her again and the grief was almost too much to bear.

Just as she was tempted to leave the surgery and forget the whole idea of counselling, her name flashed onto the screen and it was too late to escape. Knocking softly on the doctor's door, the soft Scottish accent invited her to 'come in' and on seeing the elderly man, formally dressed and with a beaming smile, those childhood visits were remembered in detail.

'Hello my dear, it's been a long time since we've seen you in surgery. You're all grown up now, which really makes me feel my age. I seem to recall a little girl with pigtails and chicken pox!'

Amazed at his astute memory, even with the advantage of notes to refer to, it suddenly occurred to her that he might have known Pattie. She could not remember how long he had been their family doctor but perhaps this was an opportunity to find out more about her sister. Dr Williams was trying to make her feel comfortable; could he possibly know what was troubling her? No of course not, it was just his usual practiced way. Doctors must encounter every kind of problem imaginable and not simply physical ones. She may as well get straight to the point,

'I have been wondering about the possibility of some form of counselling,' she began. 'I'm getting married at Christmas... which isn't the issue, it's the dreams I've been having lately, nightmares really and an irrational fear of fire, naked flames and such like. Sorry, this must sound confusing but I'm really low at the moment even though this should be the happiest time of my life. I've also found out things about my past recently which have come as a shock. Counselling might not even be appropriate but my boyfriend suggested it might help, so basically that's why I'm here.'

'It's not confusing Rae and our fears are rarely irrational so counselling is a good way to explore our feelings. You are on the point of a major life change too with getting married. People often pressurise themselves when they don't feel as happy as they expect to. I'd like to ask a few questions now which are designed to help me know if counselling is appropriate in your case. Please try to answer as honestly as possible, and then we can take it from there.'

'Can I ask you a question first?' she decided on the direct approach as the doctor smiled and nodded. 'Did you know that I had a twin sister who died in a house fire when we were three?'

Dr. Williams sat up and leaning forward answered,

'No, I didn't.' Scrolling down the computer screen he explained, 'You must have been about eight or nine when I first came to this practice and quite honestly these computerized notes don't even go that far back. There will probably be paper records in the archives somewhere but I have never had cause to refer to them. Is this what you found out recently which has been so upsetting?'

'Yes it is. I only found out by accident, my parents live in France now so I was helping to clear my grandmother's house when she moved and found an old photograph. No one had ever told me about my sister but when I saw the photo, memories came flooding back. My grandmother has told me some of what happened but it's so hard to understand why they would keep this a secret.' She stopped talking, biting her bottom lip in an attempt to maintain composure.

'This is obviously a difficult situation for you. You described your fear of fire as irrational but it would seem to me that it's all linked with the house fire. A trauma such as the one you suffered would be treated so differently back then to how it would be today. People assumed it was a sign of weakness if they admitted to being unable to cope but fortunately today it is more acceptable to ask for a little help at times like these. I think you are very sensible and brave in asking for counselling and I'm quite happy to refer you straight away. We're blessed with two really good counsellors working here in the practice and I think you'll get on well with Maggie, Mrs Sayer, a very approachable and compassionate lady who I feel sure will be able to help you. I'll have a chat with her and see how soon she can fit you in and then with your permission I'll pass on your phone number so Maggie can get in touch with you directly, is that okay?'

'That's fine, thank you so much. I feel better already knowing there'll be someone to talk to openly about this.'

'Have you spoken to your parents since you found out about your sister?'

'Yes, I had a brief conversation with my father yesterday morning but I can't say I feel any better for it. I'm struggling to understand why they have kept such a secret for so long.'

Dr Williams nodded; the shock this young woman had experienced raised so many issues to process. It would be a good thing for her to see a counsellor and he knew that Maggie would be the perfect candidate to help his patient through this difficult time.

****

The walk home from the surgery left Linda feeling hot and sticky and no longer a fan of sunshine. It was too bright for her these days, showing up dirty marks on the windows and making people smile, acting as if they were your friends when they barely knew you. Turning the key in the lock, she hoped Danny would not be at home and when empty silence greeted her she breathed a sigh of relief. A quick glance in the hall mirror brought her to a sudden stop. The reflection was salutary, making her ponder what she had become over the last two years. A face stared back which held too many wrinkles; the gray skin of a heavy smoker and the dark rimmed eyes of someone who rarely enjoyed a good night's sleep. The counsellor, Maggie, was about the same age but looked so vital and alive, not a classic beauty but an attractive, confident woman. Linda couldn't remember the last time she had felt confident or attractive, it must have been nearly twenty years ago, before her marriage. On the day her husband finally walked out there was nothing left but relief. Fred had been a selfish bully, treating his wife no better than a slave and far worse than a dog. She dared to hope that life would improve without him, that still in her forties, there could be better things ahead but she hadn't reckoned on how her son would emulate his father in so very many ways, stepping right into Fred's shoes! Dan was thirteen when Fred left, a difficult age at the best of times and she tried desperately to be both mother and father. Not an easy task while having to work every possible hour simply to make ends meet. He very quickly began to behave exactly like his Dad; barking orders, shouting if meals were not ready on time, a real chip off the old block! Tall for his age even then and already taller than his mother, for the next two years she watched him fill out, add another three inches in height and become so much like Fred that she felt intimidated simply looking at him. At fifteen, he was undisciplined, selfish, rude and arrogant, rarely attending school which was frightening knowing that she could get into serious trouble for this. But Danny seemed to have it all worked out and knew exactly how long he could get away with non-attendance before needing to put in an appearance. Money regularly went missing from her purse too until she took to hiding any spare cash, leaving only sufficient in the purse to keep him happy but that wasn't enough. It soon became obvious that her son had another source of income which he did not come by from honest hard work. Things began appearing in his bedroom, a laptop, several mobile phones and other gadgets, some of which she didn't even recognise. At times there were new goods, still boxed and in large quantities, which appeared for a few days then vanished. Linda was too scared to ask questions and the truth of the matter was that she was becoming almost as afraid of him as she had been of Fred. This wasn't to say that she didn't love the boy, he was her son and always would be but unfortunately he was even more his father's son and living with Dan was every bit as unpredictable as living with Fred had been. There was no one who could help either, friends had turned their backs years ago when she chose to remain loyal to Fred and there was no family to speak of. When things had become really bad she had even considered asking social services to step in but Dan was her responsibility and there was always hope that he would change wasn't there?

The door banged, making her jump, the tea wasn't ready and there would inevitably be repercussions, yet instead of coming into the kitchen to seek food, Danny went straight upstairs. Linda was perplexed, during the last few days he had been uncharacteristically quiet, less aggressive even, which should have been a welcome change but was actually more worrying. When tea was ready, poached eggs with beans on toast, she went upstairs and knocked on the bedroom door. It was slightly ajar and swung open to reveal the sight of her son, curled in a foetal position on the bed, actually sobbing! Instinctively moving to comfort him and wrapping her arms around those wide strong shoulders, her son turned into the warmth of his mother's arms and wept like a little boy.

Chapter 9

There had been four visits to Lydia Armstrong in the space of two weeks and approaching the old lady's home for the fifth time, Maggie pondered if today would be the day her client would finally confide what was at the root of her troubles. It was obvious that there was a deep regret at the way Lydia had allowed her husband's family to take over and decide their firstborn son's fate, and she knew that this was the source of her client's feelings now. The enigma lay in knowing what the old lady wished to accomplish from their meetings. She had been honest in the revelations of her past life but what, if anything, was this leading to? Whatever it was, Maggie would not hurry her, their sessions were for the client's benefit alone and if it turned out that all she needed was to get everything out in the open then she would be satisfied with that. The past stretched behind in a long trail of yesterdays but Lydia's future was measured, in her own way she was preparing for the end of her life.

'My mother-in-law died ten years to the day after James was born. I was busy with my young family and the duties of my position as George's wife but I had never forgotten my first son. It seemed a bitter irony that Evelyn died on the same date that he had come into the world. She had not been ill and was taken suddenly with a heart attack. It was a shock to George and Stanley, his father, but I am afraid to say I could shed no tears at her passing. We had maintained a cordial relationship but both of us knew deep down that it was a sham. Evelyn had ruled the family with out-

dated ideas and standards and I grew to see her as a very shallow woman whose affections proved to be superficial. This was confirmed to me with the fact that neither Patrick nor Elizabeth experienced any real sense of grief at their grandmother's passing. I often think children are a great judge of character and had her affections for them been genuine, their reaction to her loss would have equalled it. Still, that is not pertinent now; it was a long time ago. It was however the day I decided to make contact with James. At first I vacillated over telling George, so decided to wait until after the event and see what happened before I confided in him. It was fairly easy to arrange, I often had a weekend in London to do some shopping and we had a nanny for the children so I was quite a free agent. I arranged my 'shopping trip' and left for the station as usual but before catching the train made my way to the home where James lived, having telephoned earlier to confirm it would be a convenient time to visit. My thoughts were in turmoil, not even knowing what my son looked like, whether he could communicate, or what his level of understanding would be. My legs trembled as I arrived and the outward composure which I usually possessed deserted me. It seemed appropriate to seek out the manager first, in some ways to attempt an explanation of my sudden interest but also to ask about my son before we met.

The manager, a small framed man who seemed rather suspicious of me, was outwardly courteous and gave me a breakdown of James's problems. It seemed that his mobility and speech were impaired but his understanding of his confined world was comparatively good. They believed him to be happy and although the manager did not ask the questions which were so obviously hovering behind his eyes, he finished the brief report then stared at me expectantly. I felt so small Maggie, but could find no words to justify myself so remained silent. Perhaps I did owe him an explanation, I don't know, but I could think of none so simply asked to be allowed to see my son. There are no words to describe how I felt finally seeing James. My heart was pounding and my legs were weak. Before he saw me I had chance to study him. He was sprawled in a wheelchair and holding some kind of conversation with a boy of a similar age who was sitting at a table next to him. It was an effort to keep from breaking down. Love, shame and a whole host of other emotions almost overwhelmed me as I moved closer and stood in his sight-line. The first thing I noticed was that he had his father's eyes, the same powder blue in colour yet the unmistakable almond shape of a child with Down's Syndrome. James smiled up at me and I was very nearly undone.

'Who are you?' His companion asked a question I did not know how to answer.

'I've come to visit James,' was my pathetic attempt at a response. James then took me by surprise when he reached out an unsteady hand to grasp mine. It was electric, like falling in love at first sight for want of a better way to describe it. I hugged him then and whispered,

'I'm your Mummy James.'

For ten years I had been denied these feelings of love for my child, but was it a self denial? Should I have stood up to George's mother, could I have stood up to her? We spent two hours together. I pushed him around the grounds then took him to the dining room where lunch was served and helped to feed him. James spoke in an indistinguishable language but by the tone of his voice, I could understand some of what he was saying. In a nutshell, we bonded. This was something I did not expect, had not dared to hope for and was unsure that I deserved, but I knew then that I wanted my first born son to be part of my life and no one would stop me now.

I did not go to London as intended, feeling the desire instead to go straight home and talk to George. At first he was appalled that I had been to see James when, as he declared, his mother was barely cold in her grave. We actually had an argument, a rare happening between us. With hindsight it was too soon for George after his mother's passing. He was still grieving and took my actions as a personal affront to Evelyn's memory but he could tell that my mind was made up and we left the topic to discuss later after we had both had chance to think things through. I promised not to say anything to the children until we had talked further and of course it was unthinkable that I would dare to broach the subject with Sir

Stanley Armstrong. I visited James again two weeks later, this time telling George beforehand where I was going. We had not had the rest of the 'James' conversation and I hoped that when he saw my determination to continue this newly established contact that he would mellow and possibly even accompany me on future visits. How wrong I was. When we did finally sit down to discuss the issue I saw a different facet to my husband's personality, one which I had not seen before. He was most certainly his mother's son. I had thought him weak and at times assumed that he had not wanted our son to be packed off to a home, just as I hadn't. But I was terribly mistaken Maggie and we re-lived the same arguments and reasoning from a decade earlier, except now it was my husband who was the one to insist on maintaining the secrecy, arguing that it was too late to suddenly announce that we had a son and reminded me that we had told friends that James had died. I could see his point, but to my mind making that decision all over again was untenable. I could perhaps live with myself having denied the child once but to do it again would be unforgivable. And so, as in all civilized families we came to a compromise, albeit an uneasy one. George forbade me to tell Patrick and Elizabeth or to mention James to his father. In return for my acquiescence in this, I could visit our son as often as I wished. In short we were continuing the pretence, but I at least could see James and I always had hope that George would one day change his mind and meet his son, sadly a day which never came.

I still see James, at least once a fortnight but usually each week. George refused to acknowledge him for the rest of his life and now I will soon have to leave him too. So you see Maggie, I have kept my boy a secret and it has brought such pain. My dilemma now is whether to tell Patrick and Elizabeth about their older brother. When George died, I felt that at last I had the freedom to own my son publicly. It seemed easy, I would tell the children, they were independent adults by then and we would all live happily ever after. But I hesitated to think about what I would be telling them. I would be painting their grandmother as some kind of wicked witch and their father as a liar. Suddenly it was not so simple after all. Had I the right to stain their memory of the father they loved or the *grandmother they at the very least respected? And what would they think of me? I too had lied by participating with the whole pretence, what kind of mother would they judge me to be if they knew I had allowed my firstborn child to be packed off to a home because he was an embarrassment? I was a coward Maggie and yet again I perpetuated the lie and justified it to myself by pretending it was for their good, and George and Evelyn's memory. But the reality was that I didn't want them to see how weak I had been and what a shameful mother I really was. Do you know the story in the Bible about Peter denying Jesus three times? Well that is what I have done. I denied my son three times, at birth, when his grandmother died and again when his father died. Jesus forgave Peter and I only hope that when my time comes, I too will receive forgiveness, even though I do not deserve it.*

****

Alan was showing signs of restlessness and his head was rolling from side to side. His waiting wife pulled the chair closer and squeezed his hand.

'Alan, you're dreaming and it's time to wake up now!' She felt sure that he could hear her, a faith which was rewarded with the slow opening of an eye as he turned in her direction. This would be the point in a film when she would ring for a nurse before covering his face with kisses mingled with tears, but Sue's overwhelming emotion was the sudden release of days of bottled up anger and although she did hug her husband, she began to chastise him for all the worry he had caused.

'Do you know what you've put us through these last few days? Why on earth did you go and get yourself shot, you oaf. It's driven me nearly out of my mind!'

A flicker of a smile crossed his face as he mouthed the word 'sorry', with a weak, barely audible voice. Sue smiled deciding maybe she should ring for the nurse after all and then after pressing the bell asked,

'How do you feel love, are you in a lot of pain?'
He nodded and she realised what a silly question it had been, of course he would be in pain. The staff nurse came almost immediately only to ask him the same question, prompting another nod which was obviously an effort. The nurse left, returning after a few moments with a syringe of pain killers and after attaching it to the cannula in his arm, promised it would be effective quickly. After taking both pulse and blood pressure, she left them alone as already Alan's pain was subsiding.

'How long have I been here?'

'Too bloody long! This is day three but it seems like a lifetime, you gave me such a fright, why didn't you just turn and run when you saw that gun?'

'I'm a policeman, it's what I do love, you know that.' Alan's voice was hoarse and his eyes looked heavy as if it was an effort to keep them open.

'How's Rose?' he asked.

'Missing her Daddy, she's with Mum today, maybe if you are up to it this afternoon I'll bring her in for a while?'

'Hmm, please.'

The nurse came back, closely followed by the doctor.

'Good morning Mr. Hurst, nice to finally meet you. My name is Ian Grey and I was the one who had the pleasure of patching you up. I'd like to take a look at your chest now and then nurse will change your dressing, are you okay with that?'

Alan nodded, giving his consent. Sue took this as her cue to leave the room as the doctor and nurse moved closer, not liking the look of the tube running from his chest and certainly not wanting a closer view. A few minutes later when the doctor came out, she looked expectantly at him.

'Your husband is doing okay for now. Still not out of the woods but I think we can take him off the critical list. It's going to take time to regain his strength and the injury will be painful for some time to come, which of course we can help to control with medication. The Physiotherapist will be paying a visit this afternoon and will work out a plan for the coming weeks. I'm sure I don't need to ask you not to tire him?' The doctor looked at her as if she was a child.

'Of course not, I'll stay a little while then go home to bring our daughter in, he can rest then but I know he's keen to see Rose.'

'Yes,' the doctor had to agree, 'it will be good for him to see his little girl, but no other visitors for today and just yourself tomorrow until we feel he is well enough to move onto the ward.'

Returning to Alan she found him on the point of drifting back to sleep. He smiled apologetically but Sue told him to rest, content simply to sit with the precious and comforting knowledge that he was on the mend. As he dozed, she sent messages to her mother, Alan's parents and Maggie to update them on the day's progress, then firmly grasped his hand as if she would never let go again.

****

Maggie had thought about Lydia Armstrong many times during the last few days. Here was a lady who had apparently led a privileged life with wealth, position and the respect of her children and community. But Lydia had little respect for herself and to Maggie's mind that was sad. Everyone makes mistakes and most of us have a past littered with bad decisions and actions which bring shame when remembered. And now Lydia was coming to the end of her life and was again torn by this recurring problem, a decision made three times at various points throughout her life, yet about which she still had no peace. Lady Armstrong, failing fast, had talked about going to a hospice in the near future and she desperately wanted this lady to find peace before then. Approaching the beautiful home and immaculate grounds once again, she couldn't help but think that no one ever knows what sorrows their fellow human beings carry. Even Lydia's children did not know the anguish their mother had suffered. Was there still time for her to find peace and regain some measure of self-respect?

The elderly lady did not stand to greet her visitor. Her pallor was gray and translucent with the look of someone approaching death. It was a shock to witness such sudden deterioration. As Lydia held out a bony hand to her counsellor, Maggie knew she would grieve over this lady's passing as the women had formed an attachment even in such a short time. Lydia managed a smile and Maggie sat close to hear her words.

'Tell me what to do,' she asked.
Sadly the counsellor shook her head.
'You know I can't do that. Only you can make these decisions.' Sensing her client was too tired to talk she suggested leaving and returning another day but the old lady gripped her hand fiercely, shaking her head.

'Okay, I'll stay for a while but don't try to talk too much, save your strength.'
It was difficult, knowing that Lydia was frail yet so obviously desiring company; the compromise would be simply to stay and be there for her.

'How do you see me Maggie?' This was not normally the type of question she would answer but Lydia didn't have long and was in need of some degree of comfort. It was perhaps possible to answer honestly and in a way which would hopefully bring that comfort without giving empty platitudes.

'I see a very principled lady, someone who has strived to do her best throughout life. I only wish we had met years ago and in different circumstances, you are an interesting person Lydia. You are also very strong and have carried your burdens with dignity but I think you forget at times that you are human. When separated from James you were hardly more than a child yourself and things were taken out of your hands by people you trusted and respected. I cannot begin to imagine how terrible that must have been. Ten years later you were obviously an older and much stronger woman. The decision to seek out your son was a very brave thing to do and I admire you for that and for being faithful to him during the years since then. You gave him back his mother and the love he deserves, even though it brought the displeasure of your husband. From what you have told me about James' condition and environment it appears that your son has a happy home and one which has provided the comfort and security he needed. James may not understand why you will be leaving him soon which I'm sure is hard for you to bear. As for what to do, that must be your decision alone and I hope these times together have helped you to make the decision which is right for yourself. Your provision for James ensures that his life will continue to be comfortable and he'll be able to stay in his home, well cared for and with those who have become his family, for the rest of his life. Lydia, you have done your utmost to make it up to your son for what you believed to be a betrayal. What concerns me now is that you will forgive yourself and make the right decisions for your own peace of mind. I really do not know that anything else I can say that will be of help to you.'

'You have such a wonderful view of life, always looking for the silver lining. Bless you dear, you have helped me more than you will ever know.'

Maggie left shortly after this brief conversation, her heaviness of heart lifted only by the text message from Sue to say that Alan was awake and talking.

Chapter 10

Arriving at the surgery the following morning, Maggie cheerfully shared the good news that Sue's husband appeared to have turned a corner in his recovery and was no longer viewed as critical. Their colleagues were delighted, asking her to pass on their good wishes when she next saw Sue. Tom Williams was in the reception area and heard the news before following Maggie into her room, asking for a brief word. After expressing his own delight at Alan's progress he went on to share what was on his mind.

'It's one of my patients, a young woman whom I rarely see in the surgery. She's on the point of getting married and has recently learned some rather disturbing information from the past. As if that isn't enough, she's also in need of phobia therapy for a fear of fire, two issues which are almost certainly related.'

'Do you want me to see her immediately?' Dr. William's referrals usually came written up with copious notes, he rarely asked personally about a client unless the case merited priority.

'If you have an opening and could see her quite soon I'd really appreciate it. The wedding is not until Christmas but I think the poor wee girl is in need of working these issues out well before then if that's possible?'

Reluctantly acknowledging to herself that the regular visits to Lydia may soon be coming to an end her answer was positive.

'I think I could see her straight away if you think it's urgent, shall I get in touch or would you like to do that?'

'If you could ring I think that would be the better option. Rae will be expecting your call and I'm sure she'll be grateful to hear from you.'

She made it the first call of the day, wondering if the girl herself would answer or perhaps be at work. The call was answered almost immediately. After introducing herself she asked about the possibility of day-time appointments and was pleased to hear that Rae could be quite flexible and there was no problem in finding mutually convenient times. The young woman seemed eager to start so was offered an appointment for the following day, an offer which was readily accepted.

Maggie felt an inexplicable heaviness of heart during the rest of the day, almost as if on the cusp of a new phase in life. Counselling brought continual changes by the very nature of the work and sadly Lydia's sessions would soon be ended by death, perhaps this was the cause of her almost melancholy mood. She had lost patients to death before and it was never easy but Maggie had become particularly fond of the older lady whom at first had appeared rather aloof. These times of change and loss were when the support and ministrations of her supervisor, Joyce Patterson were particularly valued. All counsellors need regular supervision sessions during which they can offload any personal problems or discuss, in confidence, issues presented by clients which for one reason or another may be affecting them personally. Joyce had been a rock on numerous occasions and it was time to seek her out again very soon. It was feasible that the strain of Alan's condition was also taking its toll but now, having done her best to be supportive and available for her friends, she could relax in the knowledge that Alan was on the mend. Yet as always time moved along and the following day would bring a new client to her door and if

Maggie had learned one thing at all over her years as a counsellor it was that it was impossible to predict what issues a client might bring.

****

Rae was both surprised and delighted to hear from Maggie Sayer so soon. Dr Williams said he would make the referral and try to secure an early appointment, but this was wonderful, or was it? Sitting in the surgery ten minutes early, an old habit, she felt somewhat nervous, unsure what to expect and uncertain if counselling was the way forward at this point in time. But having never been one to run away from things she would give it a try and if it didn't feel right the sessions could always be terminated. Ms Sayer had sounded friendly enough on the phone and Rae was somewhat relieved to be seeing a female counsellor, always finding it easier to talk to another woman than to a man. Not very politically correct perhaps, but a fact. After only a five minute wait, a lady appeared from one of the rooms, scanning the waiting area until her eyes rested on Rae and she moved towards her.

'Miss Chapman?' a warm smile lit the woman's face and Rae stood and followed into the room from where she had appeared.

'How did you know who I was?'
The counsellor laughed softly.

'Nothing sinister there, you are about the age of the client I was expecting and you were looking at me with the same enquiring expression that I probably had, an informed guess you could say.' Directing Rae to a seat and taking the adjacent one for herself she smiled at the young woman.

'So, as you already know I'm Maggie Sayer and I hope we will be able to work together on whatever issues are troubling you. Our sessions are confidential with only a few exceptions, which are, if you tell me you intend to harm yourself, someone else, or a child. These would be the only times I would have to share information with another professional. Are you happy with this?'

'Yes, that seems reasonable enough but I have to say that the concept of counselling is completely new to me. I know I am at the point of needing some sort of help and my fiancé suggested this but I'm really not sure if this is what I want, or even need.'

'That's absolutely fine. It's good that you can be so open about it and if at any point you feel that our meetings are not helping please say so. Dr Williams must have thought that counselling was the best option for you at this point in time or he wouldn't have referred you. I was told only that part of the problem is a fear of fire but that you have also learned some disturbing facts about your childhood which prompted you to visit him. Would you like to tell me about that, or perhaps we could start with the phobia and I can explain the kind of therapy we use with this type of problem?'

Rae thought for a moment before answering.

'Maybe I should tell you the full story. Dr. Williams said the issues were connected and it seems likely that they are, so can I tell you what it is I've learned about my past?'

'Certainly, but please take your time and don't feel pressured, if there's anything which is too difficult just stop and we can leave it for another time.'

'No, I'll be okay, I have gone over and over this since finding out and I really think telling you the full story is the best way to start.'

Maggie nodded and her client began to describe the recent events which had brought her to this emotional state and which she had found so distressing and difficult to understand.

'It began with the nightmare, the same one that disturbed my sleep as a little girl and one which obviously has its origins from the fire at our home. I couldn't understand why the dream had returned again recently but put it down to being over tired, I'm engaged to be married and the wedding is at Christmas so we've been really busy with all the arrangements. We also have a new house which needs stacks of work doing. Anyway, the dream is always upsetting. At the beginning I'm standing in the garden with my mother watching our home burn down, yet at the same time I'm inside the house, upstairs in the bedroom and crying to get out. It's always been so vivid and I guessed it must have its origins from the actual fire but I've learned more about that time, which has added another rather disturbing dimension.'

'How old were you when this occurred?' Maggie was unsure of the timeline for these events and wanted to get everything clear before they moved on.

'I was three, only just I think. The fire gutted our home and we moved in with my grandmother while it was rebuilt. There's very little I remember of that time but I know I became very close to Gran, my mother always seemed unwell and my father was busy looking after her. Over this last weekend, sorry Maggie I should have told you that the house we bought was my Grandmothers and there are still boxes of her things left to sort out. Anyway, I found a photograph belonging to my grandmother which was taken before the fire. It's here, I take it everywhere with me now.' Rummaging in her bag for the photograph, she passed it to Maggie. It was such a beautiful, happy picture, identical twins with laughing faces, their red hair tied in bunches, glossy red hair which Rae still had today. Instinctively Maggie knew what was coming next.

'That's me with my twin sister, Pattie, but this weekend is the first time I had heard of her existence. She died in the fire, Patricia was the girl in the bedroom crying to get out, not me, but they got there too late... she was dead.' Rae bowed her head, studying the photograph which had been given back. There was silence for a few moments, then looking up she continued,

'Seeing this, I actually remembered her. My grandmother called her Patricia but I knew that she had been Pattie to me, or 'Twinnie', I distinctly remember calling her 'Twinnie'. My parents and grandmother apparently took the decision to cut Pattie out of our lives, to ignore the fact that my sister had even lived! How could they do that?' The words having been spoken gave release to the tears she had been holding back. Maggie passed the box of tissues along the coffee table and waited for the younger woman to compose herself.

'I'm sorry...' Rae began.

'No, please don't be, tears are cathartic, a release for our bodies and minds, don't worry about it.' Maggie's own eyes too were brimming with tears, threatening to spill over. It was such a sad and emotive story and one which was bringing the same kind of distress to Rae now as it must have brought to her family at the time.

'I feel so confused. I spoke to my father on the phone, they live in France now, and he didn't know what to say. I expected an explanation of sorts, to make some sense of why I was never told about Pattie but he couldn't give me one!'

'Do you think a face to face meeting with your parents would help?'

'That's another thing which I'm unsure about. Sean, my fiancé, and I are due to visit them in a couple of weeks but I really don't think I can go now, what would I say to them?'

'From what you are telling me it seems as if you are putting some degree of blame on your parents for what they decided, is that the case?'

'Well surely it is their fault don't you think?'

'It's what you think that matters. You are the one who has been affected by this. What sort of relationship have you had with your parents before you found out about Pattie, do you think it would help to go back a little and explore this?'

'I love my parents and always have. We have always been close and apart from a few of the usual adolescent arguments, pushing boundaries and the like, there have never been any significant problems between us. Of course I had thought that our close relationship was due in part to my being an only child but now that illusion has been shattered and it's as if I don't even know who my parents are any more. Finding out about my sister has suddenly made them strangers.' Turning to look away as she spoke these last words it was obvious how much of a painful revelation this had been.

'How do you feel about your parents at this moment, what's your primary emotion right now?' Maggie asked gently.

'Angry... and really annoyed with them for lying to me for all these years. I'm angry for Pattie's sake too. It's as if she hadn't existed. They seem to have drawn a line under the day of the fire, pretending that it didn't happen, that Pattie had never lived! How could they do that, surely they loved her too?'

'Perhaps it's because they loved her that they behaved in such a way. People react to grief in very different ways, we all develop a coping mechanism which helps us deal with traumatic events. For some it's to talk incessantly about the event or the person while for others it is quite the opposite. Could this have been the way for your parents?'

'I don't know, I suppose it might have been at the time but surely to keep it up for over twenty years. No, I think there must be more to it than that, I simply cannot understand all those years of pretending.'

'Do you feel anything else other than anger?' Another thoughtful pause hung heavily in the air as the younger woman considered the question before answering.

'Yes, sadness, it sounds stupid but I'm somehow missing Pattie yet how can that be when I didn't even know about her before this week?'

'It's far from stupid Rae, it's a natural emotion. You did know her for the first three years of your life. I'm no expert on twins but I do know that they have an extraordinarily strong bond, one which is difficult for someone who isn't a twin to understand. As a little girl your identity would have been closely wrapped up with your sisters, it's often described as not knowing where one twin ends and the other begins. Does this make any sense to you?'

As her client nodded silently, Maggie continued, feeling it necessary to help her comprehend the emotions she was experiencing.

'I believe that what you are going through now is bereavement, you are grieving for your twin sister which is perfectly natural. At the time you were too young to understand that Pattie had gone, let alone why, but the memories you have in your subconscious, and it sounds as if some of these are coming to your conscious mind now, are of pain and separation which you were unable to express or understand then. The anger you feel is a classic example of one of the stages of grief and something you may feel at various times for some while yet. Have you experienced any type of numbness and shock?'

'Yes, that's exactly how I felt when my grandmother told me about her. Stunned, unable to take it in and I didn't want to take it in because then it would be real and I couldn't cope with such a terrible reality.'

'Again, this is all part of the grieving process. You have an excellent understanding of your own emotions, which will certainly help you in the longer term. Grieving is a process which has no timescales. Each person processes issues differently so although I can't say how long you will feel like this, it will get easier to bear and hopefully coming here will help you reach that goal.'

'Do you know, even as I talk about Pattie now memories keep flashing into my mind; summer tea parties in the garden with water in a tiny plastic teapot and those little iced gems for food. I remember her climbing into my bed at night when she couldn't get to sleep. It seems so strange that I've never remembered any of this before.'

Rae continued to talk about her sister, wanting to grasp why it was that her family had never spoken of their other child but finding no logical explanation. Maggie was aware that their time together was coming to an end so when Rae paused to reflect, looking completely washed out by the emotion of the past hour, she took the opportunity to wind up their meeting.

'Would the same time next week be convenient for you, or would you like to think about today's session before you decide whether to come again?'

'No, I've already decided I want to come back and next week will be fine. I work in local government, on flexi-time, so this time of day is good, and thank you, you've given me plenty to think about. It seems so obvious now that I am grieving for my sister but that hadn't even occurred to me before, I really would like to come again next week.'

For the rest of the day Maggie's thoughts frequently strayed to Rae and then Lydia and the remarkable similarities in their stories. Rae's family had, for whatever reason, denied the existence of their dead daughter whilst Lydia's family had denied a living child's existence. In both cases these decisions had returned later in life to stir old wounds and memories. Maggie only hoped that she would be able to help them both find a measure of peace in the present which had been denied to them in the past.

Chapter 11

Later that evening at home and checking her emails, Maggie was delighted to find one from an old friend and former client, Julie, asking if they could get together sometime soon. A rather cryptic remark, 'News to tell you!' piqued her interest and judging by the exclamation mark she assumed it was good news. Julie Chambers had been a client two years previously when her life had been crushed by the actions of a violent husband who had eventually put her and their son in hospital. The boy, Simon, was seriously injured by his father yet went on to make a remarkable recovery to everyone's delight. The relationship between the two women gradually crossed from professional to a personal one during the time Julie and Simon were in hospital and Maggie became instrumental in reuniting her with her estranged family and offered continued support after her husband was killed in a freak accident during those same horrendously fraught two weeks. After a lengthy recovery, particularly for Simon, the family moved into a house at her sister's property to begin a new phase of life, Julie readily devoting time and energy into caring for her children and her sister's new baby. Despite being several years younger than her counsellor, the women had bonded and become firm friends though recently their contact had slipped somewhat, it was one of those situations where the busyness of life seemed to get in the way. The email therefore was more than welcome as was the chance to catch up with her friend and discover what the exciting news could be. She would ring later to arrange a meeting.

Peter had prepared their evening meal and as they ate, their conversation naturally drifted to the subject currently at the forefront of their minds, the Hurst family.

'Sue rang this afternoon. There's no change, which I think she finds frustrating but it was only yesterday that he came round, it's going to take a long time yet before there'll be a noticeable difference.' Peter told his wife.

'Well, you know what she's like, wants everything yesterday. This will have to be a lesson in patience as he's bound to be in hospital for a good while longer. I'll ring tonight after visiting time's over. That's two calls to make, I hope Julie's news is good, if anyone deserves some happiness in life it's her and the children.'

'Why not invite them round on Sunday? I know you haven't seen as much of them as you would like to lately and a catch-up's long overdue. Simon might like to watch the match with me; he's still keen on football isn't he?'

'I'm sure he will be, that's a great idea Peter, I'll ask when I ring.'

Julie was delighted to hear her friend's voice and readily accepted the invitation to tea. Playfully avoiding the questions about her 'news' only served to strengthen the case for it being something good. She would be drawn into saying nothing except that it concerned a relationship which she would like some advice about. After exchanging snippets about the children and Maggie telling her briefly about Alan and Sue, they fixed a time for Sunday and ended the call happily anticipating meeting up again.

****

Chief Superintendent Jack Swanson and DC Paul Madison were sitting at the hospital bedside as Sue arrived at 9.30 am to visit her husband. Both stood as she entered the room, noting the not too happy expression she wore.

'What's going on here then?' she asked.

Alan managed a weak smile,

'I'm just trying to remember more details about the shooting but it's still a bit hazy.'

'Too right it's hazy!' She turned to address the Superintendent, 'He only came round yesterday and hasn't even been out of bed yet, don't you think it's a bit early to be grilling him?'

'I didn't intend to 'grill' him Mrs Hurst. We simply wanted to see if he remembered anything which could help us apprehend the perpetrator.' Jack Swanson sounded defensive.

'I'm okay love,' Alan tried to calm his wife and his concerned expression had the desired effect.

'I'm sorry,' her attitude was softer, 'That was rather rude of me but he's still very weak. I thought you would give him a few days rest before involving him in the investigation.'

Paul Madison spoke next.

'We don't want to tire him but anything at all he can tell us will be of help. It's so important to move quickly before any trails go cold.'

'Well I haven't been much help.' Alan interrupted, 'You found the car so my description of that isn't necessary and the gunman was wearing a balaclava so I can't add any more than the shop assistant could.'

'You have done okay, now just concentrate on getting well. We'll leave you now Mrs Hurst, you are quite right, we don't want to tire him, goodbye and take care.' The police officers left the room and Sue dragged the chair closer to the bed in order to hold Alan's hand.

'How are you?'

'I'm okay, the painkillers work well and contrary to what you might think I am getting plenty of rest, so stop worrying.'

'Sorry, was I out of order then?'

'Well I wouldn't speak to the Chief Super like that and be able to get away with it.'

'The doctor had asked for no visitors except me today so I was surprised the staff had let them in, that's all.'

'I know, but they are right about moving quickly, too much time has elapsed already since the robbery.'

'Okay, I feel bad enough now, let's change the subject shall we?'

'How's Rose?'

'Fine, she was so pleased to see you yesterday but I think it was perhaps too early for you. I'll not bring her again until the weekend when hopefully you might be on the general ward.'

'Yes, they're talking about moving me tomorrow which will be great although the staff here are brilliant and can't do enough for you. So, tell me how things are going with your Mum staying, are you enjoying the experience?' There was a mischievous twinkle in his eyes.

'While you were on the critical list I have to say Mum was brilliant but now there is a little tension creeping in. I needed her to take over with Rose at first but she seems reluctant to give up that role. She's so strict too, meals at a certain time, eat everything on the plate, regimented nap, bath, bed time, it's taken me back to my own childhood, it's stifling!'

'Well it never worked with you, you turned out to be your own sweet self whatever your mother did and I have no doubt Rose will do exactly the same too.'

'I know, and it's only for a little while longer. When you're up and about I'll be able to bring Rose in more often and hopefully you will be home before we know it. Did you see the physiotherapist yesterday?'

'More like the physioterrorist! She has a regime planned which makes my eyes water, I think I'll play poorly for as long as I can get away with it!'

'You don't have to 'play' poorly, you really are. This is going to take quite a while to get over and neither of us are the most patient of souls are we? But we'll muddle through. I'm just longing to get you back home.'

****

Maggie had baked for the occasion, spending a Sunday morning in the kitchen and thoroughly enjoying herself. She had decided on a high tea for their visitors with sandwiches, cakes and scones which they could eat outside if the weather held as it seemed to be doing at present. It was the first match of the football season and Peter had recently subscribed to Sky television and planned to watch a premier league match with Simon while the women caught up on each other's news and Chloe no doubt would entertain them all. Julie and the children arrived at 3.45 pm, just in time for kickoff.

'Goodness me Simon, you are as tall as your Mum now!' Maggie was amazed to see how much the boy had grown. At thirteen, he was possibly an inch or so taller than his mother and his frame had filled out considerably since she had last seen him but in a healthy way with the muscle of a budding footballer and no spare fat anywhere on his body. Chloe too had grown and was a typical chatterbox at four years old, going on fourteen. She had her mother's petite frame with wispy fair hair and eyes the same shape as Julie's but more green than gray. The first thing the children wanted to do was to see Ben and Tara. Simon in particular had always had an attachment to their pets and had loved taking Ben for walks and being in charge of the lead. Chloe had a liking for Tara who patiently allowed the little girl to carry her around like a baby, instinctively knowing not scratch or show her aloof side with the youngster. When the men were settled before the television screen with cans of coke and a huge bag of toffee, Maggie and Julie sat outside with iced tea. Chloe, who had brought her doll's tea set, poured orange juice from the plastic teapot into a saucer for Tara to drink. Mags could wait no longer and while the little girl was busy playing, asked what this 'news' was all about.

'Well, I've started seeing someone.' Julie blushed like a young girl.

'That's wonderful, good for you, you deserve someone nice... and I assume he is?'

'I think so, his name is Craig and he is such a gentle man, so very different from Jim.'

Jim, she thought, had never deserved Julie. A lazy, greedy bully, he had caused his family much pain and suffering. It had always amazed her that this lovely, gentle young woman could have got together with someone so totally self centred as he was, but she had been very young and impressionable at the time.

'So come on then, tell me all the details, where did you meet, how long have you been seeing each other?'

'I suppose I've known him over a year now, but we have only recently been going out and have to keep it quiet really, it's a bit difficult...'

'Why, he is free isn't he?'

Julie laughed,

'Oh yes, it's nothing like that but Craig is actually Simon's football coach at school so you can see the problem.'

'What problem is this? He is single, you are single, and you like each other don't you?'

'Yes, but I don't know if it's right, you know, ethical or whatever, with being my son's teacher?'

'And how does Simon feel about it?'

'Fine actually. I didn't tell him at first in case nothing came of it but after a few dates I felt he should know so I told him but asked him to keep it quiet for a while at school, in case he gets ribbed by the other boys, you know what they can be like.'

'I get the feeling that this is becoming rather serious, otherwise you wouldn't be telling me now?'

Julie grinned, nodding.

'There is something else,' she began then stopped, looking rather sheepish.

'What, come on out with it!'

'Well, he's quite a bit younger than me. I suppose you could call him a toy boy.'

Maggie laughed out loud,

'Oh come on, you are not exactly an old lady yourself you know! What are you, thirty two? And how old is Craig?'

'Twenty seven, twenty eight in September.'

'That's only four years, it's nothing and you certainly don't look anything like your age.'

This was true. When Maggie had first met Julie the younger woman had been so abused and downtrodden that she had actually looked older then than she did now. True she had always had an enviable petite figure and a pretty face but since her husband died and they had been reunited with her family, Julie had blossomed into the lovely young woman of today. It was not surprising that she had caught the eye of Simon's football coach who must be a very special man to have been allowed to get close to her. Maggie wondered if his age and position at the school were the only things worrying her and asked,

'Is it only Craig's age and the fact that he is Simon's teacher which concerns you?'

'Not altogether, I suppose I'm a little afraid that this is too good to be true and maybe he is not really as wonderful as he seems. It's a case of once bitten, twice shy I think.'

'After what you have been through it is quite natural to have such fears but not all men are like Jim. It sounds as if you are taking things slowly which is a good thing and naturally you'll need to be very sure before you trust someone again, for the sake of yourself and the children. What's important now is that you enjoy this time, try not to let your past muddy the waters. Craig is not Jim and you are a very strong and plucky lady, you go for it girl, today is all you need to worry about, face tomorrow when it comes.'

Julie gave her friend a hug, grateful for the sensible, sound advice then the moment was broken by a sudden shout from the lounge,

'A goal do you think?' Maggie smiled but the shout turned into a groan as they went inside to see what the problem was.

'The cat walked over the remote control and switched the telly off and I can't get it back on!' Peter was obviously frustrated as the others tried to keep straight faces.

'Don't laugh. It was a crucial point in the game, if I miss a goal...'

Tara was strolling back into the garden, unaware of having caused such chaos. Mags patted the little cat as she brushed past her legs then they followed the feline miscreant outside, leaving Simon to fix Peter's little technical catastrophe.

When the match was over, tea was served outside, with the table in the shade beside the wall so that the food would not dry out. Earlier efforts in the kitchen were appreciated by them all, the children especially enjoying the chocolate cake and fancy cup cakes.

'I wish you would come more often.' Peter remarked. 'I don't get treated to this every day you know!'

The early evening was beautiful and their visitor admired the stunning view from the house, enjoying the tranquil setting and the company of good friends. Maggie sensed an inner calm which her friend had not possessed before and hoped it was due to this new relationship. It would be wonderful if it worked out well for them all, this young man Craig would be a very lucky man indeed if he could gain Julie's trust and affection.

Chapter 12

'Maggie suggested that what I'm experiencing now is grief at the loss of my sister which makes sense don't you think?' Rae was filling Sean in on her visit to the counsellor. 'I should have recognised it myself, it feels like bereavement but then I have never lost a close family member before, or at least I thought not.'

Her fiancé agreed that this could explain her feelings and mood swings of late. Since finding out about Pattie she had not visited her grandmother again, which was unusual, and had spoken to her father only the once on the telephone, a conversation which was far from satisfactory. Her life seemed to have been completely taken over by this discovery and she was spending a disproportionate amount of time pouring over those old boxes of her grandmothers in the hope of finding more photographs of Pattie. He knew that she'd also been searching the internet for old newspaper articles about the fire, utterly and completely immersed in the past. It was difficult to understand as there was so much to do and plan for their wedding and in the house but Rae was wholly consumed with her quest to the exclusion of everything else.

'I know this has been a huge shock for you but we really need to focus on the wedding plans. We still have to find a photographer and a band for the evening. Have you been looking at any of those whilst you've been on the net?'

'No, you know how it is at the moment. I will get round to it but there's this overwhelming urge to find out anything and everything about my sister.'

'Then don't you think the best thing we could do is to visit your parents as planned? It isn't the same talking on the phone, you really need to see them face to face and you haven't spoken to your mother at all yet. Surely they are the best people to tell you all the facts?'

'I'm not sure if I'm ready to see them at the moment. I don't seem to know them anymore and they are not the people I thought they were.'

'So, what are you going to do, shut them out of your life?'

'Don't you understand? I thought I knew them but obviously don't, how could they have done this to me?'

'Sorry love, I am trying to understand but I honestly think we should go to see them, we'll be together and you can take the opportunity to clear the air and then you will be able to ask all the questions to which you need answers.'

'What is it with you?' The anger was simmering inside her. 'Are you worried about missing your holiday, is it because you've already paid for the ferry?' She plonked down on the battered old sofa and once again the tears began. Sean sat beside her, pulling her close,

'You know that's not true. I simply cannot see how you will find out what you need to know unless we actually visit your parents and hear it first hand from them. I don't care about the holiday or the money for the ferry, I care about you.'

'I'm sorry, that was unfair of me. It's just so confusing and it's the only thing I can think about at the moment. I can't even sleep at night for fear the dream will come back and I'll lose Pattie all over again!'

'Look, we are going round in circles here. Let's go to see your Gran again, do you think that would that help?'

'No, I don't want to see her either. Gran is as culpable as Mum and Dad in my eyes. It's as if the three of them have conspired against me.'

'I'm sure that's not true but maybe when you see your counsellor again you could tell her all this, that is what she's there for isn't it?'

****

Deciding to take this advice and being equally as aware as her fiancé of how this issue was taking up every waking moment of her life, Rae poured her feelings out to her counsellor. She explained how she was becoming even more emotional as time elapsed and it was beginning to affect her performance at work.

'Even the boss has noticed that I'm not myself but I can't explain what's wrong with me. Everyone in the office thinks I'm ill, someone even asked me if I was pregnant yesterday! Sean's adamant that we should go to France as we had planned but I'm not sure that's such a good idea.'

'Do you know why you feel this isn't the way forward?' Maggie reflected her client's words hoping Rae would question these feelings.

After a moment's hesitation, she replied,

'That is actually quite a difficult question... and I don't think I have an answer for it.'

'That's fine, you don't have to answer any of my questions but it can be good at times to stop and ask ourselves where our feelings are coming from.'

'Yes, that makes sense but I seem to be bursting with all kinds of emotions at the moment and it's hard to know where they come from and why.'

'Do you think writing them down might help? Women often seem to be wired with organisational skills and usually benefit from writing lists or journals, but it would have to be something which appealed to you.'

'Oh yes, I'm definitely a list person. I have notebooks for everything, one for the wedding plans, one for the renovations on the house and naturally my endless shopping and 'to do' lists.' Rae seemed quite animated by the idea.

'Do you think you could write your feelings down now?'

'Yes, I think so.'

Moving softly over to the desk Maggie retrieved a pile of blank postcards and a handful of coloured pens. Placing them on the coffee table she suggested,

'Perhaps if you wrote only one of your feelings on each card we can look at them in turn and if we don't make progress with the first one we can move on to the next and return to it later?'

Smiling in approval, Rae reached for a handful of cards and a red coloured pen. She tidied the cards into a neat pile on her lap then wrote on the top one, *angry*. Putting that to the bottom of the pile and tidying it again like a pack of playing cards she wrote, *sad* next and on the third one, *confused*.

'Is 'confused' an emotion?' She asked.

'If that is how you feel then yes, it is.' This answer seemed to give Rae permission to write so much more and very soon there was a lengthy list, including *miserable, let-down, alone, depressed, betrayed*, and *incomplete*. Replacing the cap of the pen, she thoughtfully laid it onto the coffee table but hugged the pile of cards close to her chest.

'Do you want to talk about what you have written?' Maggie asked softly.

'No, not now,' Rae seemed somewhat melancholy as if writing those few words had saddened her and sapped her energy. There was a few thoughtful quiet moments until she spoke again, changing the subject and breaking the reflective silence.

'Do you think I should go to France to see my parents?'

Maggie took the sudden change in her stride.

'Only you can decide that but while we are looking at lists, why not make one of reasons to go and reasons not to go?'

'I don't need to do that, I already know which way the balance would swing. There are so many reasons why I should go but only one why I should not and that is simply because I'm scared.' Her voice had risen whilst speaking this last sentence and her eyes were wide with fear almost tangible enough to see in her expression. Here was a brave young woman who had quite a remarkable understanding of her own emotions and reasoning.

'Would it help to talk about what scares you?'

'It probably would but I'm not sure I can put it into coherent words.'

'You've been doing a great job so far. You express yourself very well indeed but I'm not here to test your skills of oration. What really matters is that you feel better for being here and exploring these feelings. Being scared is a pretty big obstacle to being happy with your life once again and it's you who has identified and admitted this fear, which certainly gains my admiration and sets you on the path to putting your life back together again.'

The words encouraged Rae.

'Well I could try to tell you what I am scared of... I think the biggest thing is no longer knowing who I am any more, followed closely by not knowing who my family are either! From always being a confident, happy person, believing I was an only child and secure in the knowledge that my parent's loved me, it seems to have all been stripped away. They lied to me and it has completely thrown my world off kilter. It's like being in a void, suddenly robbed of everything held dear and I simply do not know how to go on. That sounds a bit melodramatic but it's the only way to describe it.'

'It certainly doesn't seem melodramatic to me, you have expressed it well. I can see the picture you are painting of being alone and confused and you seem to realise that there are decisions to be made but at the moment you don't feel able to make them, is that right?'

'Yes, it is. I almost feel like Alice in wonderland, trying to decide which door to go through.'

'I know you feel very alone in this but what about Sean, where does he fit in? Is he there with you in this void?'

'No, it seems a cruel thing to say but it doesn't feel as if he is with me at all. I know he loves me and cares about me but he doesn't seem to realise what a huge thing this revelation has been. He thinks we can just go to France, sit down to talk with Mum and Dad and it will all go away. How I wish it was that simple...'

****

Alan was now allowed visitors, which was certainly good for his spirits. Although still in some pain he was inactive and becoming bored so visiting times were a much needed distraction. He had been moved from the ICU ward to a six bedded medical ward. This was a move he was initially delighted with until it became clear that the chief topic of conversation revolved around health issues. His education on the finer details of the workings of the human body was most certainly and reluctantly being enhanced. It was Saturday, Maggie and Peter were visiting, declaring on arrival that they would stay no longer than fifteen minutes to allow the patient to rest and spend time with his wife and daughter who were due any time.

'You gave us all quite a fright Alan, it's not everyone who leaves our house and gets shot in the next half an hour.' Peter grinned as he spoke.

'It keeps life interesting though don't you think?'

'That kind of interesting I can do without!' Sue and Rose appeared in the doorway, catching the end of the conversation. Bending over to kiss him, his daughter attempted to launch herself from her mother's arms onto her Daddy's bed only to be pulled back and held even tighter. Alan winced at the thought of the pain he had nearly suffered and Rose was plonked firmly on the floor where, grasping the bed covers, she could only just reach his hand, contenting herself with that for the time being. Sue required the usual updates on how her husband had slept and what he had eaten and received the dutiful responses. Formalities over, she began to share some information recently learned from Paul Madison.

'He said there is a treatment centre in Harrogate where police personnel can recuperate after incidents like this. Paul said that Jack Swanson was quite an advocate of this place and it was mooted as ideal for you.'

'Yes I know it; I visited a colleague there a few years ago. It's a brilliant set up, more like a five star hotel than a convalescent home. The locals call it 'the crippled copper's home' rather a fitting description really.'

'And what's wrong with the five star hotel at home?' His wife was swift to come back.

'Nothing at all, you will never know how much I am longing to get out of here and back with you girls. My brush with mortality has made me appreciate you even more.'

This answer satisfied Sue who rewarded her husband with a huge smile and an affectionate look.

'Should we leave you love birds alone for a while, I could pull the curtains round?' Peter asked, earning him a punch on the arm from his wife.

The light mood was suddenly broken as Alan clutched at his chest, obviously struggling to breathe. Maggie pressed the call bell by his bed then ran into the corridor to speed the assistance he so obviously needed. Peter swept Rose into his arms, taking her to join Maggie. Sue could only stare in shocked silence. Translating the look of concern on Maggie's face, the sister and a staff nurse hurried from their station and were tending to their patient within seconds. As the sister placed an oxygen mask over his face, the nurse ushered Sue into the corridor before ringing for a doctor.

'Is he having a heart attack?' Sue asked.

'We'll have a look at him before we decide that I think. Now could you wait here with your daughter and friends?' Sister had guided them to the day room at the end of the corridor where the women reluctantly sat down while Peter occupied Rose with a box of toys they discovered in the corner.

'He will be alright won't he? I've just got him back, we can't lose him now!' She was naturally agitated, chewing at her nails and unable to sit still. Her friend offered soothing words.

'It's too early to jump to conclusions but whatever it is Alan is in the best possible place so let's not think the worst, it could be something very simple.'

'But he looked so gray! He couldn't breathe and was holding his chest, in such obvious pain!'

'We'll wait and see, I think that was the doctor who just went past so we'll know something soon.'

Soon was a very long twenty minutes until the doctor eventually came to find them.

'Mrs Hurst?' he looked at the two women, Sue jumped up immediately.

'How is he, what's wrong?'

'Your husband's lung has collapsed, pneumothorax to give its technical name, which is not an uncommon occurrence with this kind of trauma. What it means is that air has somehow leaked from his lung and the pressure from this air around the lung caused a collapse. We've inserted a needle and syringe to draw the air out and the lung is already beginning to function again, but he will need to be monitored closely and I've ordered an x-ray for later today. Depending on how things go, we'll consider putting a tube into the area between the ribs which will be in place for a few days or maybe surgery will be the better option, we'll decide when we have seen the x-rays.'

'Not more surgery! He will be all right, won't he?'

'We are taking very good care of him. I don't think this episode is life threatening but Mr Hurst has suffered a severe injury. Let's just see how things go shall we? The nurse will come for you soon but only you please and we'll be moving him to a side ward now because he needs plenty of rest.' The doctor left and Sue flopped down again. Rose came running over to show her Mummy a toy she had found and she scooped the little girl up onto her knee.

'Oh Mags, I thought he was on the mend, I'm so frightened of losing him!'

'He is on the mend, the doctor said it wasn't life threatening and there seems to be a few options which they can consider. Try to hang in there for this little poppet as much as anything. When the nurse comes, we'll take Rose for a walk round the gardens while you see Alan. I've got my phone and you can ring when you come out.'

'Thanks, you're an angel. I don't know what I would do without you.'

Chapter 13

Peter and Maggie were grateful to get home. Putting the kettle on was the first task until Peter suggested a glass of wine might be more appropriate and retrieved a bottle from the rack in the kitchen. Ben came fussing over, his tail wagging the whole rear end of his body and when his mistress sat down he rested his head on her lap, giving one of those irresistibly pathetic looks as if asking what was wrong. Tickling his ears she promised a walk soon so he contented himself with lying across her feet as she sipped the wine and tried to relax.

'Well that was certainly not the visit I was expecting.' Peter remarked.

'Me neither. I thought it would simply be a matter of time now for Alan to recover. This throws up the possibility of all kinds of complications. Poor Sue, she'll be exhausted tonight. I'll ring in a while to check that Ruby is still available to babysit otherwise I can pop over.'

'Okay, but tomorrow you and I are going out for lunch. It's been a difficult week and it's too late now to shop for vegetables, so where do you fancy?'

'Oh, how lovely, what about the new place in Market Street. I've heard good reports about it, silver service but without the hefty prices, could we try that?'

'I'll give them a ring now.' As he left to make the phone call his wife enjoyed the wine and the comforting softness of Ben's coat on her feet. Their home was such a haven of peace and tranquillity but thoughts of their friends lingered in her mind disturbing a little of that peace. Maggie knew a little of what Sue was going through, remembering her own similar concerns over Peter's health last year whilst on their trip to America. They thought he had suffered a heart attack which fortunately was not the case and today the MS symptoms were at their lowest since he had been diagnosed shortly before their marriage. Neither of them however, took this for granted and had learned to enjoy each day as it came, grateful for having each other, their family and their home. Peter returned with the phone in his hand,

'We're booked in at twelve thirty tomorrow and there are two messages on the answer phone for you, one from work and the other from Julie.'

The first one came from the receptionist at the surgery with a message from Molly who wanted her to ring back. Jotting the number down she feared that the news about Lydia would not be good, so turning her thoughts to the second message she decided to make that call first.

'Hi Julie, how are you?'

'I'm really good, thanks for ringing back. I wanted to invite you both for Sunday lunch next weekend? Craig's coming over and I thought it would be a good opportunity for you to get to know him.'

'We'd love to. I'm dying to meet him! Things are still good between you then?'

'Oh yes, he's spending quite a bit of time with us now and the children think the world of him. He's met my sister and her family too, I could hardly keep him a secret when I live in their garden! It seems almost too good to be true and I keep thinking I'll wake up and find it's all been a dream.'

'Enjoy every moment, you deserve it and Craig's a lucky guy. You're quite a catch yourself you know.'

After arranging a time for lunch Maggie found Peter pottering in the study and told him about their invitation.

'What, lunch out two Sundays running? You will be getting spoilt Mrs Lloyd, we can't have that.'

'Why not? I could get used to the high life. But now I have to make another call, it concerns my private client out of town and I think it could be bad news.'

'Can't it wait until Monday love, you are entitled to some time off and today has been difficult enough.'

'No, I need to know, it won't take long and then we'll take Ben out for a walk shall we? Some fresh air will be welcome.'

Molly sounded more than a little flustered and when eventually managing to relate the message, it came as something of a relief. Lydia had gone to stay at the hospice and wanted her counsellor to know that she was no longer at home. Only some very direct questioning eventually drew from the housekeeper the address of the hospice and then she seemed totally unsure of whether Lydia would be well enough to receive visitors. A mental image of Molly's red face and bobbing head came to mind as she thanked her, deciding that the best thing would be to ring the hospice directly to enquire if visiting was appropriate. She hoped this stay in the hospice might only be temporary, for respite care perhaps and that Lydia would be able to return home before too long. Finishing the conversation, she next rang the hospice to be told only that Lady Armstrong was settling in and resting. Visiting was by prior arrangement for anyone other than family and Maggie was asked to leave her name so the receptionist could inform their patient who had called and find out if she was well enough to receive a visitor. Maggie would telephone the following day for an answer, perhaps when they returned from lunch.

Ben waited expectantly in the lounge, head on one side with a look that meant only one thing. Peter was already pulling his shoes on and Maggie too slipped on her comfortable old walking shoes and they set off for an early evening walk. They enjoyed these long walks with Ben, sometimes discussing the events of the day or, like today, in a thoughtful but comfortable silence. After the usual circular route, they returned home to make one more phone call, this time to a rather sombre sounding Sue.

'They decided to put a tube in his ribs and are going to leave it in for a couple of days. It was such a shock after assuming he was on the mend and everything would be okay from now on. It's made me realise that Alan will have to settle down to some serious rest when he comes home. Perhaps that convalescent place isn't such a bad idea after all and Harrogate's not that far away so we could pop down to see him some days.'

'He gave us all a shock but from what the doctor said it sounds as if it's quite a common complication after that type of injury. Anyway, is your mum there or do you want me to come round to babysit while you go back this evening?'

'It's okay thanks, Mum's still here, I know we don't always see eye to eye but she has been a brick throughout all this, as have you and Peter, I don't know what I would do without you all.'

'Well you do have us, so you'll never find that out will you?'

****

Monday morning came around all too quickly and it felt to Maggie as if the whole weekend had been spent on the telephone, some in a good way, some not so good. The hospice had kept their word and when she rang again to enquire about visiting Lydia there was a message waiting to say that Lady Armstrong would be happy to see her on Monday afternoon, the time which had been scheduled for their next appointment. The receptionist had also added a few words of caution from the nursing staff, advising her to be aware that their patient was very weak and any visit would have to be brief. Not a good sign and one which prompted her to wonder how things would pan out, but before that Rae Chapman was due for their third session and she hoped to find out if this young woman had now reached a decision on the trip to France.

****

Rae sighed, taking the usual chair and looking tired and pale which served to emphasize the freckles over her nose and presented a rather girlish appearance. Reaching into her bag she withdrew the cards they had used on the previous occasion and Maggie couldn't help noticing that there was a fair amount of writing on the top card. Smiling she asked,

'Have you been doing homework?'

'Yes, a little, when I should be sleeping or getting on with other things.' Rae managed a slight smile in reply.

'Maybe you need to work through this before you can move on?'

'Try telling Sean that, will you?'

'How are things between you two now?'

'No different really, he's trying to be patient but somehow doesn't quite get how I feel or how this has affected me, which isn't surprising really as I don't even understand it myself.'

'Did you want to work a little more with the cards today?'

'Actually I've started without you.' She flashed a more genuine smile then, picking at the corner of the top card with her thumb nail.

'Good, want to tell me about it?'

'Yes, please. I've been reading them every day, several times some days and trying to work out where it has all come from. I surprised myself last week by writing nine different emotions down, some of which are obviously related to each other, but others must have come from somewhere in my subconscious because I wasn't even aware that I felt like that. Is that possible Maggie?'

'Yes, most certainly. Watching you write on the cards last week, the speed with which you whipped through them was quite surprising, not least because your actions are usually measured and well thought out. Because you wrote so quickly, one word would have triggered another and the feelings you recognise as connected were most likely prompted by each other. Does that make any sense?'

'I think so. What I have been doing is adding to each card, is that all right?'

'Of course it is you can do whatever you wish with them. Some people simply write them down then discard them and others do what you have done and look at each issue separately and in depth. Is that how you feel that you'd like to continue?'

'Yes please, I haven't fully understood why I've written some things but I was hoping that you might be able to help me there.'

'Okay, so where do you want to start?'

'Well, anger was the first one because that keeps resurfacing and I don't really know how to deal with it. I added *'frustration'* to that card and even identified who the anger is directed towards.'

A slight nod encouraged her client to continue.

'The three at the top of my list are obviously Mum Dad and Gran but I've also added Sean and myself. Next to Sean's name is *'guilt'* as I feel guilty about being angry with him when really it's no fault of his at all. And I feel angry with myself for several reasons. Firstly because I did not remember Pattie. She was my twin and we were together for three whole years, I should have remembered her and I'm angry for not doing so. There's also a frustrating kind of anger because I can't seem to move forward and get my head round all of this. I'm usually a very pragmatic, organized person and always thought I could take all of life's knocks with ease, but I'm dithering about here and can't decide which way to turn, no longer the fearless feisty red-head I used to be. You asked me last week if I knew what it was that made me afraid and that's been on my mind quite a bit too. It all seems to boil down to change.' Looking down at the cards in her lap, she stroked her finger over the top card, the '*angry*' card.

'Everything has changed. I'm no longer who I thought I was and nor are my parents or grandmother and it's scary. The future was mapped out but if I don't know my past and who I am now, how can I be certain of making the right choices for my future?' A tear escaped from her eye and landed on the '*angry*' card. Rae sniffed and remained silent for a few minutes.

'Is it better to face your fears Maggie?' her voice was weak and broken.

'If and when a person is ready to face those fears but not before and not necessarily alone either. We will, at some point be looking at your fear of naked flames but I will be here to help you face that and we'll do it in stages, a little at a time, baby steps as it were. Do you think these other fears could be broken down to address them piece by piece? And is there someone in your life who could help you along the way?'

Rae looked up and smiled, the answer was obvious, Sean. As for breaking the fears down, that was perhaps more difficult and she would have to give that one some thought.

'Can I make a suggestion?' Maggie asked.

'Yes please, I need any kind of help on offer!'

'You've written down some very diverse emotions and issues which you want to resolve. What about asking yourself, for each one in turn, who is responsible for resolving this? When you decide who that will be, move on to think about who could help and support with the issue. It may make things clearer and a pattern might develop which could prove helpful.'

'I think I know what you're trying to say, could we do this now, or leave it for this week's 'homework'?'

'Whichever you feel is best Rae.'

'Perhaps that's something to do later and then we can talk about it next time. Can we look today at this one, *'incomplete'*. I really don't know where that came from last week but thinking it over could it be a 'twin' thing?'

'Yes, that's most probably the case. As I said before I'm no expert on twins but it is common knowledge that there's a special bond between them, particularly identical twins. Research into this subject is, and possibly always will be, ongoing, because it's such a fascinating topic. Twins generally see themselves as one half of the other. You perhaps know that they often claim to feel each other's pain and have some kind of telepathic sense of what is going on in each other's lives. You've been denied this and common sense would suggest that you did have this bond for three years, the most formative three years of a child's life. The feeling of being 'incomplete' would have begun when you lost Pattie but obviously you were far too young to understand it at the time and now that feeling is resurfacing with these memories you're experiencing. Sadly it's a bit of a double whammy for you, not only are you going through the grieving process but also feeling the loss of a twin, your other half in many ways.'

Rae listened thoughtfully with the words making sense through this explanation.

'Do you think I will ever lose that feeling?' she asked.

'Maybe not completely but you've already begun the healing process and with time it will become easier.'

Leaving the surgery that morning with plenty to think about and not due at work for another hour, Rae decided to walk, using the time to process some of the things the counselling had thrown up. An understanding of sorts was developing with the knowledge of why certain thoughts and feelings plagued her, which hopefully was the first step to resolving them. Passing the local shopping centre, on impulse she decided to buy some steak for their evening meal and a bottle of wine to go with it. In a lighter mood than expected, some of the tiredness which had dogged her of late seemed to have evaporated. It was time to make some kind of effort for Sean, after all, he had been so loving and patient and she felt suddenly really blessed to have him.

Chapter 14

St. Bernadette's Hospice was a new, purpose built single storey home, standing on land adjacent to the town's hospital with a tarmac parking area stretching the full length of the frontage. Its exterior was totally uninspiring, gray pebble dashed and lacking character or charm, the complete antithesis of Lydia Armstrong's own home. The reception area however was surprisingly bright and welcoming. Maggie made her way to the main desk and was greeted with a warm smile from the elderly lady manning the station, who then proceeded to check her name against a log and rang a bell, explaining that one of the nursing staff would show her to Lady Armstrong's room. The nurse too was friendly and courteous; the pleasantries offered inside certainly made up for the soulless exterior of the premises. The rear of the building however was in complete contrast to the frontage; a spacious and inviting tranquil green area, laid out with flower beds in full bloom at this time of year. On seeing the roses, Maggie hoped that Lydia would be well enough to appreciate them too. The interior continued to impress as they moved along a wide corridor and the chatty nurse pointed out several facilities of which she was clearly proud. Pausing for a moment outside a large airy room, they listened to a pianist in full flow, performing well known Andrew Lloyd Webber compositions to an audience of only four who made up for lack of numbers by their enthusiastic singing.

'One of our volunteers,' the nurse explained. In the next room was a Jacuzzi, unoccupied at the time but readily available for patients who wished to use it. Then came a series of smaller, pamper rooms where a young girl, her head covered by a brightly patterned scarf was having a manicure.

'Hi Jenny!' the girl called out to the nurse, who grinned, waving back to the teenager.

'As you see we have all ages here, our services are not confined to the elderly.'

Maggie smiled, liking what she was seeing. The nurse changed the topic specifically to one patient, Lydia.

'We tried to ring you this morning to warn you that your visit may be wasted. Lady Armstrong had a bad night and has been in considerable pain. When the doctor came he increased the medication with the effect that she's slept all morning.'

'I'm sorry, the number I left was my home number and I was at work but if she's sleeping I won't disturb her, I can come another time.' They had arrived outside Lydia's room and as expected the elderly lady was asleep.

'Could I sit with her for a while?' Maggie asked.

'Of course, there's a bell if you need anything and I'll leave the door open. Perhaps you can ring if she wakes up so that we can see how she is?'

'Yes I will.'

Lydia looked thin and pale under the starched white sheets. Her slim body seemed to have lost flesh almost overnight, making only the slightest of bumps beneath the covers. For the first time since they had met, she thought the older woman actually looked her age and was shocked at how suddenly her condition had deteriorated. Pulling the chair closer to the bed, Maggie took her hand in her own. Again there was a noticeable lack of flesh, the long finger bones and veins visible through translucent skin and her hand cold to the touch. After a few moments,

Lydia turned and opened her eyes a fraction, the sight of her visitor bringing a faint smile. As she tried to speak, Maggie gently squeezed her hand,

'Don't try to talk, rest now. I can come back another time.'

Lydia's eyes closed again but the smile remained giving the distinct impression that her client was at peace. Looking at the frail body, Maggie wondered if she would survive much longer and whether those decisions which troubled her had been resolved. Perhaps she would never know. After twenty minutes had elapsed she rose to leave, meeting the nurse coming in to monitor the patient.

'She opened her eyes for a moment but drifted back to sleep.'

'It's probably the best thing at this stage,' the nurse replied, 'There's no pain while she's asleep.'

****

'Okay, we'll go.'

'What?' Sean was taken aback; did Rae mean that they would go to France after all?

'I said we'll go. That's what you want isn't it?'

'Only if you are going for the right reasons and pleasing me would not fit into that category.'

'No, it's not for you. As you suggested I talked to Maggie and reached the conclusion that I need to go and of course, it would be so much easier if you were with me.'

'That's great. It will be for the best love, what made you change your mind?'

'Well, it was fear that was stopping me from going but I think it's far better to confront that fear rather than run away from it. You were right too, hearing directly from my parents is the only chance I'll have to understand all of this, so thank you for that and sorry that I've been such a pain of late.'

'You don't have to apologise to me. It's been a pretty big shock and I'm probably not the best person to be helping you through it but I love you and you must know I'd happily do anything to help.'

'Coming with me and simply being there is what I need from you now, so you are the best person for the job,' Rae grinned. It was a relief to have made the decision, one she fully intended to stick by. In only five days time they would be on route to France, a journey which usually stirred warm feelings of anticipation but presently left her in a state of dread. Another positive decision was to visit her grandmother again soon, feeling that perhaps she had been too hard on the old lady, who most probably had very little say in the decisions taken after the fire and would have been obliged to go along with her son and daughter in law. She could not go to France without seeing Edith who would have missed her granddaughter as much as she had missed her beloved Gran.

'You don't need to apologise. It was a shock, something that really should never have been kept from you but we are all a lot wiser with hindsight.' Edith Chapman had never been so pleased to see her granddaughter, having worried for the last few days that their close relationship might have been irrevocably ruined by what Rae had discovered.

'None of us meant any harm by not telling you about Patricia. It seemed the best solution at the time and then, as always happens with secrets, it became more difficult to tell you the truth as the years went by. Your mother took it particularly badly and was quite ill for some time afterwards. We pushed the fire to the back of our minds but I see now that we were wrong to do the same with Patricia. I'm so sorry love, can you forgive me?' Seeing the sadness and regret in her watery gray eyes moved Rae to hug her grandmother, kissing her soft powdery cheek.

'I do understand Gran and I know that you wouldn't have had much say in the matter but can you talk about her now? I'm longing to know everything about Pattie. Do you have any more photographs?'

Edith had anticipated this request,

'Sean love, can you pass me that green box over there?' She indicated a place in the alcove where an old box rested on an occasional table. He passed the box to her and she removed the lid.

'Your Mum and Dad don't know that I kept these. I'm not certain where their photographs went but I couldn't bring myself to destroy mine.' Carefully Edith lifted out an album with a faded cover which had seen far better days. Inside were stiff pages with those little adhesive corners designed to hold the pictures in place, most of which had peeled off and yellowed with age. The photographs themselves however were still in a reasonable condition, the colours not quite as vibrant as modern day photographs and the images not as sharp.

'Since your last visit I've been looking at these quite a bit. Some of them are dated and of course they are obviously you and Patricia, but I honestly can't tell you apart on most of them.' She passed the album to Rae who held it as tenderly as if it was a rare and precious treasure which might turn to dust without careful handling. Sean was perched beside her on the edge of the sofa and peered at the images of the two pretty little girls. The first few were baby pictures, side by side on a rug, sitting in a double pushchair or being held, one by their mother and the other in their father's arms. They were indeed identical, dressed in the same clothes except for different coloured bonnets or ribbons as they got older. The same smiles, the same plump little features and the same two front teeth, so alike in every way.

'Gosh, you really can't tell them apart can you?' he commented.

'That's Pattie and that's me.' Rae pointed with certainty.

'How can you tell, are you the one with the blue ribbons?'

'I am, but that's not how I know, it's obvious... we're not really that alike!'

'But you are, identical in every way.'

'Well I don't think so, look at this one, Pattie has a dimple in her right cheek, I used to poke it and giggle at her.'

Edith moved over to look,

'She's right... I had forgotten about the dimple.'

'Do you actually remember that?' Sean was amazed.

'I suppose I must do, but there are differences in them all, look. Pattie is being held by Mum in those pictures and the one on the right in the others.' As she slowly turned the pages of the album, Edith began to nod in agreement, also astounded at such certainty but no more so than Rae herself who tenderly stroked the image of those two little girls with her forefinger.

'Pattie's holding her rabbit there, I remember that. 'Babbit' it was called and she always chewed its ears until one of them came off and she was devastated.'

'That's right,' Edith confirmed, 'you were two then and your mother had to sew the ear back on before Pattie would stop crying. You tried to hug her but she was inconsolable. You are right, I remember too!'

As they carefully turned more pages, Rae had an ache in her chest so acute she could hardly breathe. Her twin was becoming alive again with memories so vivid that it seemed incredible she had never remembered her before. There was silence as they came to the end of the album. It contained not a mass of photographs but enough to bring her sister to the forefront of her mind and with it such intense emotion and pain at the loss. Sean put a comforting arm around his fiancée and the three sat in silence for what seemed hours.

'I am so sorry.' Edith broke the almost reverent quietness, deeply feeling her granddaughter's distress.

'It's okay, it wasn't your fault Gran and it's done now, we can't turn the clocks back.' She no longer harboured any animosity towards Edith. The atmosphere was one of incredible sadness at such a loss and at what might have been. It was time to go home and the two women said a very emotional goodbye.

****

Joyce Patterson had been Maggie's supervisor for more years than she cared to remember. Over time the women had become firm friends and each looked forward to their regular meetings, the former because she had a soft spot for the younger woman and the latter because Joyce was such an empathic, easy to be with person. She had the gift of making her feel comfortable and the knack of reading Maggie's thoughts, or at the very least second guessing what was in her mind. Joyce was now semi-retired, rarely taking clients herself but continuing supervision of two counsellors, ostensibly to keep her mind active. Over coffee in the supervisor's comfortable conservatory they enquired about each other's families and Maggie gave an update on Alan. Joyce had read about the awful shooting in the local paper and knew that he and his wife were close friends of hers.

'I have two new clients since we last spoke.' Maggie began, 'And in many ways there are similarities in their issues. One is an elderly lady of whom I have become quite fond and the other a young girl, about to get married, who has been completely thrown by finding out a family secret from the past. I'd like to tell you about the older lady first, who is perhaps one of the strangest clients I have ever encountered, not as a person but in what has been required of me. At first I was unsure whether we would connect but we did and rather quickly too, which is fortunate as this lady has cancer and probably not much longer to live. In a way I feel somewhat guilty. She's a private client and I don't feel as if I have really earned my money.'

'You always feel guilty about taking money but you give excellent value! Has this lady complained?'

'No, nothing like that, it has been an unusual case in that very little has been required of me except to listen. And you don't need to remind me of the importance of listening! I know it's the biggest part of what we do and a skill in itself. But the visits have almost been too enjoyable. The lady has recounted a fascinating life story and my role seems to have been simply to listen. She's quite a character, so strong and correct yet her life has been blighted by this one issue of having been forced to give up a disabled son, pretending to the world that he had died at birth. She is carrying so much guilt and against her family's wishes has been in regular contact with the boy since he was ten, which if you knew the situation you would agree was an extremely brave thing to do. It seems as if now, as the end of life approaches, past decisions and regrets are coming back to haunt her and the big problem is whether or not to tell her other children about their elder brother.'

'Decisions like that can only be made by the client and it sounds as if you have been needed purely as a sounding board, someone to bounce ideas off. I don't need to ask if you've reflected her words?'

'I have, but our sessions have been rather like listening to a monologue, which made me feel quite inadequate at times. She is a very articulate lady and has put a tremendous amount of thought into the options facing her. Unfortunately she is now in a hospice. I visited a few days ago but she was sleeping and although waking briefly, was certainly not up to talking. The situation doesn't look good, I'll be going again, yet have the feeling that this will be one of those cases when I will never learn the outcome.'

'Frustrating yes, but there will always be clients from whom we never hear the ending to their stories. You really have nothing to chide yourself about here and seem to have done exactly what this lady needed of you, which is nothing short of a job well done. So what about the younger girl, how can that case be similar?'

'Well, I said it was a family secret and strangely enough it also involves a young child. This client has only recently found out that she had a twin sister who died in a house fire when they were three years old. She now remembers the fire and has begun to have nightmares about it, dreams which haven't troubled her since childhood. Recently she came across an old photograph of herself with this identical twin sister and memories have come flooding back. Her grandmother has tried to explain why the family apparently blanked out the twin's very existence, never even mentioning her at all. It would be my guess that this was the only way they could cope with the situation but it hasn't done my client any favours. She is now unsure about seeing her parents who live abroad and also has a phobia of naked flames. It seems incredible to have two cases which both involve young children, one alive whose family pretended he was dead and one who died whose family pretended she had never lived, both such sad cases.'

'They certainly are. Are you going to do any phobia therapy with the younger client?'

'Yes, that's the plan at the moment but for now we're working on this shock revelation. It's been difficult for her to take in but I must admit I find the whole topic of twins quite fascinating. The connection between them is unique, quite complex, but then I'm an only child who often wondered what it would be like to have other siblings, just another of those things in life which will never be known...'

Chapter 15

Linda had changed her mind so often and was still undecided about what the right course of action was. Sitting opposite Maggie for only the second time, her heart was thumping. Could this woman be trusted, was all that was said last time about confidentiality true? The counsellor sensed the uneasiness in this relatively new client. Their first session had not exactly been an unqualified success, with little progress in forming any kind of relationship. Still it was early days and many clients took weeks before they shared what was really troubling them, perhaps this was to be one of those cases.

'Did you mean what you told me last time about not telling anyone what I say?' The question was out resulting in a sense of relief.

'I did, yes, but there are exceptions, would you like me to remind you of them?'

'Yes please.'

'Well, I would only have to break confidentiality if I felt you were going to harm yourself or someone else or if you gave details of a child who was at risk of harm. Is that clear?'

'Yes but, hypothetically speaking, what if I told you about a crime that had already been committed. Would you have to go to the police?'

'I do have a legal responsibility to report any acts of terrorism, committed or about to be committed, but other than that, no.' Maggie was intrigued and a little disturbed, why could this lady be asking such specific questions, unless she or someone known to her had committed a crime?

In her mind's eye, Linda could see Danny. That big hulk of a boy, always confident, in charge, a swaggering, street wise youth, sobbing in his mother's arms! She had been so shocked, unable to imagine whatever could have reduced him to tears. Yes he was still not quite sixteen but had shown not even the least sign of weakness since his father had left. Yet on reflection he had been somewhat subdued over the preceding couple of days, keeping a little more to himself than usual. She had enjoyed the lack of confrontation, thinking it of little significance. Linda had held her sobbing son as if he was a little boy again, anxious but in a twisted way enjoying the sense of need that he had. Being able to comfort him this way gave her a purpose and a role in his life again, other than to wait on him. Eventually he had blurted out the trouble he was in. It was a shock but not altogether a surprise and in a way his vulnerability was touching with the effect of bringing her on-side to share the problem, to which as yet they had come up with no solution. Maggie must hear all kinds of things, would she be able to help or advise? Could she take that risk?

'I have a son, Danny, who is nearly sixteen and for the last couple of years has run a bit wild. I know teenage years are difficult but with his Dad leaving it's been particularly tough and now he's got in with some bad people, well, one in particular, who persuaded him to help commit a crime, a robbery.'

Maggie nodded, possessing information of this kind was an unenviable position to be in, but it was fortunately also rare. She could not judge or give advice, nor even report the crime. A counsellor's role was purely to listen, reflect and assist the client to follow the path which would benefit them the most and to help them make their own decisions with the aim of leading a more fulfilled life. This lady's son could be the root of her problems and she understood the delicate situation the woman was in. Where should a mother's loyalty lie? Hopefully the robbery was on a small scale and the boy would learn a lesson from it and she would be able to support Linda through this difficult time. Her client continued,

'I know plenty of lads go off the rails a bit and in many ways it wasn't a surprise when he told me. He's done things before, but this time it's really serious and I'm at a loss to know what to do. He won't tell me this bloke's name but whoever it was persuaded my Danny to do a job, driving for him... huh, he's fifteen years old! Anyway, it all went horribly wrong and a policeman ended up getting shot!'

****

It was a four hour drive to Dover. Rae had packed with very little thought or enthusiasm but felt obliged to make some kind of effort for Sean's sake. Feelings towards her parents had vacillated between anger and disappointment and the thought of seeing them face to face was not an appealing one. The weather at least was smiling on them and they were grateful to be travelling mid week as a hot August weekend would have meant even more congestion on the roads than there was at present.

'Shall we stop half way?' He broke into her pensive mood.

'Only if you need to, I'm happy to go the full distance if that's okay by you.'

Lapsing into quiet again he turned the radio on, wanting to fill the silent void in the car. On the whole, the first leg of the journey was uneventful and they arrived in Dover with ample time to catch the ferry. Leaving the confines of the car in the port car park, they set off to stretch their legs, filling their lungs with sea air as they walked along the docks.

'I'll be ready for something to eat when we get on the ferry, full English for me, what do you say?'

'A sandwich will do for me.' Her answer was less than enthusiastic.

'Come on love, try to relax a bit, it might not be as bad as you think.'

'How can it be anything other than bad?' She snapped back at him. Holding up his hands in a gesture of surrender he said,

'Fine, it'll be terrible. Sorry, what do I know?'
The reply softened her attitude,

'I'm so sorry Sean. I've got myself all worked up. Gosh, it's worse than going to the dentist, I feel so tense and my head is throbbing.' She took his hand and he smiled, squeezing her fingers.

'Well I think we should try to enjoy at least some of the time in France. We talked about a day in Rouen, are you still up for that?'

'Yes, why not? I think we might be ready to get away by ourselves for a day so let's see how things go shall we?'

The crossing from Dover to Calais took the expected ninety minutes over an extremely calm sea. Sean ate his breakfast with relish whilst Rae nibbled on a sandwich, growing increasingly edgy as they neared the French coastline. It was an eighty five mile drive to her parents' home from Calais, a journey which usually seemed long but today went by all too quickly and the passing landscape held none of its usual interest for her. David and Barbara Chapman lived four miles south of the busy town of Rouen in an isolated spot with only a couple of farms nearby, giving them the peace and solitude they had craved since retiring from their working lives in England. They too were experiencing similar anxieties. Barbara particularly wanted to avoid any kind of confrontation but accepted that this was an unlikely possibility. When the weary visitors drew up outside the converted farmhouse, Rae's parents were waiting in the shade of the veranda, a jug of iced lemonade ready for them. They rose in unison and made towards the car to greet their daughter and her fiancée, a greeting which was usually an exciting occasion but was now overshadowed by the knowledge in all their minds that this visit was not in any way going to be an easy one. Awkward hugs were exchanged and David began to fuss inordinately over helping with the luggage. For the first time ever, Rae was actually lost for something to say to her parents. Talking about the weather or the journey seemed too banal, but to launch into what was really on her mind seemed almost rude, English reserve demanding at least a show of pleasantries. Her mother offered lemonade which they both accepted, ready to quench their thirst after a full day's travelling. It was early evening, they were tired and could happily have made excuses to retire for the night but again, propriety necessitated that they sit with her parents and then share the prepared chicken salad before there would be chance for such an escape.

The meal was welcome and the accompanying bottle of local wine more than acceptable. The young couple had only been alone for a short time before dinner, when they went upstairs to unpack and freshen up.

'Are you going to have the big discussion tonight or leave it until morning?' Sean asked.

'Tonight, I don't think anyone will sleep until the subject is aired.'

'True, you could cut the atmosphere with the proverbial knife, and your mother looks as if she hasn't slept for weeks.'

'The atmosphere is not entirely my fault you know. It's my parents who caused this situation and I think I have a right to some answers.'

'I didn't mean that it was your fault, it was simply an observation which even a blind man could see I'm sure. You're probably right to bring it up tonight though, we all know its coming so the sooner the better.'

Rae sighed and they went down to dinner, still tired but determined to clear the air before the sun went down that evening.

'Shall we have coffee outside? Its cooler now, this is often the most pleasant time of day' David suggested. Sean sat beside Rae on the rattan sofa on the veranda, sliding a protective arm around her shoulders as her parents took the remaining armchairs. There was an awkward silence as coffee was poured and passed around, no one seeming to have any idea how to open the inevitable conversation. Eventually Sean jumped in, addressing their hosts,

'I suppose I'm the outsider here but you know how much I love your daughter and I think you also know how much finding out about Pattie has distressed her.'

Barbara gave an audible moan when he spoke Pattie's name, but he continued,

'Well I don't think any of us will be able to relax until questions are asked and answered, so now that the subject is opened, who will go first?'

Rae wove her fingers through his, squeezing thanks for his efforts. David then took the lead and turning to his daughter began.

'We never meant to deny your sister's existence. I'm sure you can imagine how difficult the situation was. We loved you both so much. You were our whole world but the night of the fire destroyed all of that. In a way you were our salvation as although losing Pattie was devastating, we still had one daughter and over the course of time our world began to revolve entirely around you. It was difficult to know how to explain why your sister was no longer there and each time you asked it opened up the wound and the pain returned. For everyone's sake, or so we thought, we endeavoured to distract you. It was our coping mechanism at the time and we always intended telling you about her but as the weeks and months passed by, you stopped asking. Then it seemed almost cruel to begin to talk about her again, it would only have reopened those painful wounds.' David's little speech came to a stop; his daughter's expression had been unreadable and it was impossible to gauge whether or not his words were helpful. Rae had been looking at him intently all the time but then turned to her mother who had been focussed on a point far into the distance as if oblivious to the conversation. Barbara had barely spoken since their arrival except for making sure there was enough to eat and drink, apparently functioning on automatic pilot.

'Mum?' Rae's pleading expression was almost begging her mother to contribute to the disclosure but she looked away,

'Your father is quite right. I think he has explained everything that needs to be said.' The words were almost dismissive, shocking her daughter so much she could think of nothing to say in reply.

'I'm tired now,' Barbara continued, 'So if you will excuse me, I'll be off to bed.' With those words she stood to go in the house and disappeared up the stairs.

There was a stunned silence until David spoke again.

'I'm so sorry. Your mother has been badly affected by the memories of Pattie and that dreadful time coming up all over again. After the fire, you won't remember, but she became very ill and was hospitalised for a few weeks. She's never fully recovered, so those reasons for not telling you about your sister, although true, are perhaps only part of the story. The other reason was for the sake of your mother's health. Putting the fire and its consequences firmly behind her was the only way that she could and still can, deal with it. That night changed us all forever. Barbara was no longer the carefree young woman I had married. Something died in her with Pattie and I don't suppose she will ever come to terms with it. Don't judge us too harshly please Rae. We did what we thought was best, for you and for your mother but in hindsight it appears we got it wrong. Do you think you can you ever forgive us?'

****

It had been a difficult week for Maggie and on Sunday morning, waking early, knowing that any more sleep would be impossible she slipped out of bed, careful not to wake Peter, pulled on some clothes and took a delighted Ben for an early morning walk. Although only six thirty, the air was warm and still, it would be another hot day, one they would spend with Julie, Simon and Chloe and at last meet Craig. This at least was a pleasant thought unlike the troubling thoughts of Lydia which had plagued her mind during the last few days. A second visit to the Hospice had proved as fruitless as the first, the old lady having slept continually. It was clear now that it was time to let this client go, that this was one of those cases where she would never know if the issues were resolved or not. Joyce had been a brick, reassuring her that she had done her best in fulfilling the role that Lydia had required but she would have loved to do more, a desire which now almost certainly would never come to fruition. Sue and Alan had also given cause for concern. Just as they thought he was out of danger, the collapsed lung brought another scare, making them realise how serious this wound had really been. Sue however appeared to be coping well and would be even more so if someone could give a definitive and positive prognosis on his recovery but that was not going to happen for some time yet. The lung setback had really shaken her, bringing home the full extent of the love she had for her husband and how devastating life would be without him. The tube which had been inserted into his ribs stayed in place for three days until the doctor was satisfied that the lung was functioning well enough to remove it. Maggie and Peter were able to visit a couple of times during the latter part of the week. Thankfully these were uneventful visits which reassured them that Alan was slowly improving at last. Topping everything else that was going on, Maggie was now counselling the mother of the driver of the getaway vehicle from the robbery when he was shot and could tell no-one! Well, that wasn't quite true, after Linda's disclosure, needing to offload she had rung Joyce. As always, her supervisor had a calming effect, giving assurance that no matter how difficult it was, she was in the right and even though screaming inside and wanting to run to the police to tell them what she knew, her client's confidentiality must not be breached. It was an extremely sensitive situation but one which may work out positively in the end. Maggie wondered if being in this position was a good thing in that at least she could be of help to Linda which may possibly have a knock on effect of bringing Danny to his senses. Or was it simply an unhappy coincidence with which she would have to continue to live in order for her professionalism to be maintained?

All these thoughts whirled through Maggie's brain as she and Ben traced their usual circular route. The early morning air felt good and after filling her lungs it seemed as if she was exhaling all the worries and cares of the week, having learned long ago that worrying over anything was invariably counter-productive. Making for home she consciously set her mind to happier subjects, determined to enjoy the company of her husband and friends, to live in the moment and let tomorrow's worries wait for tomorrow.

****

Julie looked nothing short of radiant when her visitors arrived for lunch later that morning. She was dressed in a crisp, cotton print dress, the simple lines of which accentuated her petite figure. With hair tied back and held in place with a slide, she looked cool and elegant; her lightly tanned skin glowing with what was clearly a new found happiness. Both visitors hugged her warmly and then the children in turn, who had come racing to the door, more to see Ben whom they had promised to bring, rather than their two legged visitors.

'He's in the lounge,' Julie whispered unnecessarily as Craig was fully visible from the doorway, waiting quietly to be introduced.

'Hello,' he came forward with an outstretched hand. Peter was first to shake hands, grinning warmly at the young man.

'Good to meet you Craig.'

Maggie greeted him next, looking up into soft brown eyes which reminded her of a cow, in the nicest possible way. She almost laughed at the sudden thought but smiled instead at the tall handsome young man with fair hair flopping over his forehead.

'Hi, I've heard such a lot about you!'

'No pressure then?' The smile was returned and she knew instantly that she was going to like him.

'Can I help with anything Julie?'

'I'm fine thanks Mags, Craig would you get drinks for our visitors please?' Julie was obviously enjoying playing the hostess, particularly with this new man in her life to help. The children had taken Ben into the garden and were throwing a Frisbee for him to catch, the three of them racing energetically around the large open space.

'I don't know who will tire first, probably Ben, he's not as young as he used to be.' Peter commented. Lunch was served after a pleasant half hour of chatting, mainly about football as Craig, being a coach, was every bit as enthusiastic about the sport as Peter. It was a gentle introduction to the couple and he was making a good impression without needing to try. He appeared to be an open, genuine young man who was passionate about his work at the school and seemed to bring out the best in the pupils by sharing his love of sport with them. Over the dinner table it was also clear that he had built a good rapport with the children. Simon chatted easily with him and Chloe insisted on sitting between him and Maggie, quite the seal of approval. All in all it turned out to be a very pleasant visit with good food and good company. Julie's gray eyes held a sparkle Maggie had rarely seen before. Craig was obviously perfect for her, attentive, caring and exactly what she needed. After an enjoyable couple of hours, Maggie and Peter returned home feeling that things were working out well for their friend and looking forward to seeing how this new romance developed.

Chapter 16

'Tell me about the night of the fire Dad?' Rae's request brought a pained look to her father's face but he understood her need to hear the facts.

'It was horrendous, the images from that night will never leave me and I'll always carry the agony of it all. It had been a hot summer, rather like this year. You had picked up some kind of virus and were having difficulty sleeping. I don't know what time you came into our bed, sometime in the early hours of the morning probably and it was easier to comfort you if you slept with us. Your mother had picked up the virus too and had taken a sleeping pill to try and get a good night's sleep having been up with you for the previous two. I remember being restless and throwing off the bed covers because of the heat but then I sensed that something was wrong. There was smoke in the room and you were coughing. I was suddenly wide awake. Barbara was groggy from the sleeping pill so I carried you under my arm and half dragged her downstairs and out into the garden. It was only then that the full extent of the fire became apparent. The back of the house was engulfed in flames and Pattie was still inside... my beautiful Pattie. Going back in, the thick acrid smoke filled the hallway making it almost impossible to see. Feeling my way to the staircase which was hot to touch, my bare feet were burning but there was no time to look for shoes. Climbing the stairs, the intensity of the flames drove me back. The whole of the landing was an inferno by then and impossible to get through. I failed Rae, I just couldn't reach your sister... and she died. I will never forgive myself for that.' David's face was wet with tears, his daughter too was crying as she reached out to hold her father. Sean, deeply moved, felt it right to leave them to comfort each other and went softly inside, making his way to the guest bedroom.

Rae barely slept that night and was up early the following morning sitting on the veranda, her thoughts focussed on the previous evening's conversation. Sean appeared next, closely followed by David,

'Your mother is staying in bed this morning, she slept badly but I suppose you did too?' His face was drawn with dark shadows around the eyes, a reflection of his daughters'. She nodded, not surprised at her mother's non appearance but a little disappointed. It seemed as if once again she was leaving her husband to cope with all the questions.

'We thought we would spend the day in Rouen if that's okay with you?' This was news to Sean as they hadn't yet discussed when they would go, but Rae obviously felt the need to put some distance between herself and her parents and at least it would give them an opportunity to talk. So after a light breakfast they set off on the short drive to Rouen, the clear blue sky promising another hot day, perfect for exploring the busy little town and learn more about its two hundred year history. During the journey Rae related what had happened the previous night after he had gone to bed.

'It seemed as if our roles were reversed after Dad told me about the fire and I ended up comforting him. Not much more was said but he was obviously upset by having to re-live it again. I can't begin to imagine what it has been like to carry that around all these years and he actually blames himself for not saving Pattie! The fire had apparently been caused by an electrical fault, again something which couldn't have been predicted but for which Dad is burdened with guilt.'

'So, do you feel any better about the situation now? Has this answered all the questions you have?'

'I feel better in appreciating what they went through, who wouldn't feel their pain? But I still don't fully understand why they never told me, after all it is part of my history as well as theirs, it is my loss too. To tell you the truth, I don't know how I feel. Dad was open and honest with me but it still seems like I'm missing something, as if there is more that they are not telling me.'

Rouen, like many French towns was dominated by a gothic cathedral, 'Cathedrale Notre Dame de Rouen', one of many churches in the centre of the town which Victor Hugo described as a 'City of a Hundred Spires'. It is divided, like Paris, by the river Seine with a left and right bank offering many places of interest for the summer tourists. Rae was determined to put all problems on hold for the day. They had both only glimpsed the town on previous visits and now she wanted to immerse herself in the history and the continental atmosphere, owing as much to Sean as well as herself. They arrived early enough to find a good parking spot and taking little more than sun hats, bottled water and a camera, they joined the holiday makers who were beginning to spill out onto the streets of the town.

Heading firstly for the cathedral, they made their way along the pretty cobble-stoned street, Rue-Eau de Robec, enjoying the bright pots of flowers along the way. Turning to the left, they passed several pavement cafes and pizzerias where chattering waiters were setting up tables, their smiling invitations to sit for morning coffee were politely declined. Entering the cathedral was the first time Rae had felt cold since leaving England. The thick stone walls kept the interior cool, even with the heavy doors flung wide open to greet the morning sunlight. It was calm and peaceful and she felt almost able to breathe in and capture some of the tranquillity in her own soul. It felt good to be in such an awesome place, the sheer size and history of the building causing her to view her own problems from a different perspective. They spent a leisurely half hour inside letting the unhurried atmosphere wash over them, knowing they did not have to dash away for any reason. Today they were not ruled by the hands on a clock as time was their own. In contrast to the Gothic cathedral, their next destination was a more modern, nineteen seventies built church, 'Eglis Jeanne d'arc'. This was minimalist architecture, beautiful in its own way and much brighter and warmer than the cathedral with its modern angular roof, the 'Roof of Flames' piercing the cerulean skyline. Inside they found stunning stained glass windows which added to the brightness and created a warm friendly ambience as they strolled around the interior. Once outside again, the temperature was still rising and the streets becoming busier. Sean suggested finding a shady spot for coffee. There was plenty of choice and they soon found a welcoming cafe where they sat beneath a candy striped awning with a view of the Place du Vieux Marche, bursting with life as mid day approached. Narrow streets led off the square, begging to be explored. Their four and five storey buildings were crowded together like dominoes supporting each other with the threat of toppling over seeming a likely possibility. The strong black coffee was welcome as were the croissants with thick raspberry jam. This vantage point offered a tranquil oasis in the midst of the busy town and Rae's troubles were thankfully pushed to the back of her mind as the holiday atmosphere took hold and she relaxed in Sean's company. For the first time in weeks she was able to talk about things other than the family.

'When we get home, I'm going to throw myself into our wedding preparations with a vengeance!' She smiled at her fiancé, seeing his expression mirror his delight.

'I have a list somewhere of flower suppliers and photographers, I'll set up some meetings and we can get some of the loose ends tied up.'

'Great, focussing on the wedding really appeals. It can't come soon enough for me!' Paying for their coffee they next headed, hand in hand, towards 'Jardin des Plantes', the public gardens in the centre of the town. Before entering, they noticed a small museum dedicated to the life of Joan of Arc. From the outside it looked rather dark and dingy but on venturing inside it proved to be surprisingly interesting. It was a rather cramped space with exhibits depicting stages of the heroine's life with wax models and interactive storytelling attempting to capture the imaginations of visiting children. Inevitably the scene of Joan being burned at the stake proved somewhat poignant, so they moved swiftly on, determined to sustain the current good mood. Exiting the museum they bought ice creams to take into the gardens seeking a bench on which to rest. The heat of the sun seemed to permeate right through to Rae's spirit. Lifting her face to the sky and smiling she squeezed Sean's arm, for the first time in weeks daring to hope that happiness was once again within her grasp.

The mood was broken by the shrill tone of Rae's phone. The caller ID displayed her father's number.

'Hi Dad, are you coming to join us after all?' She asked brightly, thinking that her mother might be feeling better and they were coming to Rouen to meet them. Listening silently, her face suddenly drained and she leaned heavily on her fiancé for support.

'We're on our way!' Closing the phone and turning anxiously to Sean, she gasped,

'It's Mum, they're at the hospital, she's tried to kill herself...'

****

Alan was heartily sick of his enforced incarceration. Admittedly the care was great but the meals only served the purpose of making him appreciate Sue's basic attempts in the kitchen and he longed to be home with her and Rose. Having now returned to work, there were days when she only managed to pop in late afternoons, sometimes picking Rose up from nursery to visit too. Most evenings after bathing and settling their daughter, she came again, relying on her mother or Maggie to babysit. It was not an ideal situation but there was no choice in the matter until he was well enough to be discharged. It was now over a week since the setback with his lung collapse, two weeks in all that he had been in hospital and being discharged couldn't come soon enough. The physiotherapists had begun their work as soon as the tube was removed from his ribs, a painful process which was necessary for him to re-gain the use of his right arm and shoulder in particular. He worked hard, not daring to allow his thoughts to stray to what life would be like if he did not make a full recovery, a subject which was also taboo during visiting hours, the word 'when' rather than 'if' being the preferred choice.

On returning from a physiotherapy session, he was surprised to find Detective Chief Superintendent Jack Swanson waiting by his bed. He stood as Alan was pushed in a wheelchair through the door by a hospital porter.

'Hello Alan,' the Chief Super smiled.

'Hello sir, this is a surprise.'

'I had intended visiting before but have received regular updates on your condition from Paul Madison.'

'I'm sorry sir, I didn't mean anything by that...'

'Don't worry, no offence taken. I've really come to tell you about some recent developments.' Alan's eyes widened with interest.

'We're fairly sure we've got the shooter,' he continued, 'It's a chap we interviewed pretty soon after the event who apparently had an alibi. That's not holding up under scrutiny and we've managed to pull enough of a case together to bring him in. He's our man alright and we are throwing everything we've got at him. It's only a matter of time before he gives up the identity of his accomplice.' Paul Madison had mentioned this suspect earlier in the investigation when they had initially been confident that they had the right man, but at the time his alibi seemed genuine although obviously it was not.

'That's good news sir. I am pleased and thank you for coming to tell me personally, I really appreciate that. How is the woman from the shop, Iris something isn't it? Is she getting over it?'

'To a point yes, although the poor woman's still on medication and I can't see her returning to work there again. It was a tremendous shock. Iris is, however, full of admiration for your bravery, thinking that you somehow took the bullet for her.'

'I certainly didn't intend taking a bullet for anyone. It all happened so quickly and she probably saw more than I did. Mercifully things went blank for me after the gun went off but I can understand how witnessing a shooting can be equally as traumatic as being shot.'

'Well, maybe not quite but it will stay with her for a long time to come, as it will with you. Is there any word as to when you will be discharged?'

'Not yet and not for the lack of asking. It's possible that I may be home in two or three days, or that's the indications I've picked up from the doctor. Are you missing me at work then?' He grinned.

'I would have to say yes to that, you're a valuable member of the team but there is no way I want you back until you are fully fit. And regarding that, I've taken the liberty of inquiring about a place for you at St. Stephen's in Harrogate, no time scales or anything but it would be worth considering as the next phase in your recovery. They have some excellent facilities and I'm sure you would benefit greatly from a few days in their care.'

Alan nodded in agreement, he could see the sense in going but his immediate desire was to be at home with his wife and daughter. Other arrangements could be made in due course. Reluctantly the patient was beginning to accept that recovery was going to be a long process.

Chapter 17

To Alan's great delight his discharge came at the weekend, three full weeks after the shooting, which he reckoned was pretty good going. Sue was equally thrilled as the days had dragged endlessly and the nights alone proved to be the most vulnerable of times. Sleep only came due to the exhaustion of trying to fit in all her usual duties as well as visiting the hospital as often as time would allow. The ward sister insisted that the patient leave their care in a wheelchair which she herself pushed, with Rose sitting on her Daddy's lap delighting in the wonderful new game. Alan could not thank the nursing staff enough, they had been excellent, but couldn't resist telling them there would be no recommendations for a stay there to his friends and colleagues. With goodbye's said and gratitude expressed the family drove home in high spirits singing along to the nursery rhyme CD playing in the car. Pulling into the driveway, he was choked with unexpected emotion at the familiar sight of their home and stepping out of the car into the bright sunshine seemed like the most wonderful experience in the world. It was a feeling which could not be expressed in words but one which Sue instinctively understood as her own emotions were running parallel to his. Inside, she insisted that he rested while Rose had a nap and he dutifully complied, enjoying the way she was fussing over him, thinking how he could easily get to like it.

'Rose is worn out. It must be the excitement of having Daddy home and she'll probably sleep all afternoon.'

'And what about you, are you excited at my being home?' There was a wicked twinkle in his eye.

'Of course...oh hey, no, there'll be none of that hanky-panky stuff until you are fully recovered!' Sue laughed at his disappointed expression. 'But perhaps a little cuddle won't hurt?' She moved to sit beside him, relaxing into his arms, enjoying the closeness and the feel of his lips on hers.

'I've missed you.' She said, drawing away from him, 'We're going to have to be very careful though, I don't want you to have another relapse.'

'Neither do I, I promise to be a very good patient, but come here, a hug and a few kisses shouldn't do any harm, in fact it's just what the doctor ordered.'

****

Molly was barely audible on the telephone, a difficult lady to communicate with at the best of times but today she was attempting to speak whilst holding back a wall of emotion which was threatening to gush out at any time. Maggie had guessed the reason for the call on recognising the voice.

'Lady Armstrong...last night...it was peaceful tho', she'll be at rest now.' Molly eventually gave way to her emotions and could say little more. Taking over the conversation, Maggie asked the distressed housekeeper to let her know when the funeral would be and Molly made affirmative noises before replacing the phone. Lydia Armstrong was dead and Maggie felt a deep sadness, wishing there had been time to do more for this lovely lady. Now she may never know what would become of her first born son, James and whether his siblings had been told of his existence or not. Sitting motionless in her office, her thoughts reflected on Lydia with affection. Her life had appeared to be one of privilege and position with wealth and until latterly, good health too, the sort of life which many would envy. But she had carried a burden and been consumed with guilt, unable to see the right way forward. If only there had been a little more time, Maggie felt sure her client had been close to resolving many of the issues which troubled her. Had it been purely a matter of Lydia's own reputation, it would have been so much easier to reveal the secret to her children. But salving her own conscience in that way would have sullied the memory of their father and grandmother. This had been her stumbling block and having come so close to making decisions, tragically time had run out. Maggie would never forget this client, a lady in every sense of the word, remaining loyal to a family into which she had married, the family who had readily accepted a farm girl into their midst to share a life of privilege at a cost the young girl could not have foreseen and now their secret would be buried with Lady Lydia Armstrong.

****

Driving through the unfamiliar and increasingly crowded streets of Rouen in search of the local hospital and following directions that David had hurriedly given, Rae's head was spinning with all kinds of terrible scenarios. What if her mother died? Had she driven her to this by insisting on raking up the past? How she wished the last few weeks could be blotted out and they could begin again.

'This is my fault. I had to insist on them telling me everything! Why couldn't I have let it be?'

'It's nobody's fault. People do these things, it's impossible to see them coming and you are not to blame.' Sean spoke with a deliberate firmness intending to focus his girlfriend on the facts rather than apportioning blame.

'Let's see how things are before we panic shall we? We don't know the circumstances yet so best not think the worst.'

Staring into her lap she remained silent for the rest of the journey, an unreal feeling pervading her body, a shutting down of all emotion. At this stage nothing could persuade her that she wasn't at fault here and she believed herself to have handled the whole issue of Pattie badly from the start. Entering the emergency wing they soon found David anxiously pacing the corridor and Rae held him as if a little girl again. After a few moments, pulling away and looking into his tired face, she asked,

'How is she Dad? Is she going to be alright?'

'I really don't know yet. They took her into theatre to pump her stomach out. It was tablets, sleeping pills which I didn't even know she had.' Concern was etched into his features as they moved to a row of fixed plastic bucket chairs where they sat anxiously waiting for news. Rae wanted to know more details. Did he know when the pills had been taken, how many and how long was it since he'd found her? But her lips would not form the questions, certain that it had been this kind of incessant questioning that had driven her mother to such a desperate act. Fear and guilt washed over her and she dearly wished they could turn the clock back and approach this whole issue in a completely different way. David had apologised, both on the telephone and in person yesterday, why was that not enough? Had she really been so wronged? They had obviously thought their decisions had been for the best, why did she have to put them through the pain of losing Pattie all over again?

Forty minutes later a young doctor appeared from the lift at the end of the corridor, obviously seeking them out. The three stood, their expressions asking the question to which the doctor smiled, surely a good sign.

'Your wife is going to be fine Monsieur Chapman. The stomach pump is not a pleasant procedure and she will feel quite ill for a while. In cases like these we like to admit the patient for a couple of days of evaluation. I am sure you understand, yes?'

A nod of relief replaced David's concern, understanding what the doctor was saying. Barbara had tried to kill herself. They would not simply treat the physical symptoms and would need to be sure that this attempt would not be repeated and perhaps find out the underlying cause. Barbara was in the best place and obviously needed some kind of therapy.

'Can we see her?' He managed to ask.

'Of course, but she is sleepy due to the medication which entered her system and the physical trauma in surgery and may not feel like talking, which is probably for the best.'

'I understand. We'll only stay for a short while.'

The doctor directed them to the third floor and asked them to check in with the ward sister first.

'Cinque minutes, five minutes only.' The sister held up one hand, her English not as good as the doctor's. They nodded in agreement before going into the side room near the nurses' station to be confronted by a pale, sleeping Barbara. David took her hand and as her eyes opened to see him, she turned away, embarrassed.

'It's alright love, you are going to be fine. Whatever it is we'll sort it out so you mustn't worry.'

She nodded then looked at Rae standing beside the door.

'I'm sorry Mum. I shouldn't have made such an issue out of it all...'

'No, don't be sorry.' her voice was hoarse, 'It is me who should apologise, it's time to face up to the past and stop the pretending.'

'Mum, we don't have to have this conversation now. You are tired and need to rest and we promised the sister we would only stay a few minutes.'

'Will you come back this evening? I need to tell you something, to explain things to you.'

'Of course I'll come back, but there's no need to explain anything. I've been selfish and am so sorry. We can put all of this behind us now.'

'No.' Barbara's voice although weak was emphatic, 'It's putting it all behind us that has got us into this situation. I need to explain, please?'

The sister appeared in the doorway, frowning disapproval and the visitors had to leave. All three kissed her goodbye and promised to return later during regular visiting hours. Any explanations would have to wait until then.

Chapter 18

'I had a call today to say that one of my client's has died.' Maggie wanted Peter to understand why she felt a little down.

'Oh sweetheart, I'm sorry. Was it expected?'

'Yes, it was the private client I've been seeing so regularly of late. She had gone into a hospice and died quite peacefully but even though it was anticipated my time with her did not seem entirely finished. There was more to be done and now I will never really know if she made her peace with the world or not. I wish we could have had a little longer together.'

'Ah, you are not going to dwell on the 'what-ifs' are you?' Peter grinned. Not playing the 'what-if' game was something she always advocated. History cannot be re-written and the present can be wasted with regrets and 'what-if' thinking. She laughed softly,

'You are, of course, completely right. Someone with great wisdom must have taught you that!' The subject was closed. Peter knew he would never be privy to any details about clients and he admired his wife for this professionalism.

'I popped over to visit Alan today.' He moved the conversation on to other things.

'Oh good, how is he settling back in?'

'Well really, but a little bored perhaps. I took him some paperbacks that we've finished with so he can lose himself in those and work on his tan. Its okay on the days Sue and Rose are home, but he's like a bear with a sore head when left alone. I suppose he has such an active job and loves sport but he won't be playing squash for a long time yet, which sort of lets me off the hook, and goodness knows when he will get back to work.'

'Sue hasn't said as much but she seems a little worried about him going back, not because of getting shot again, they are more likely to win the lottery than have that happen twice but whether he will ever be fit enough to return to active service. I don't think they have discussed it fully as yet, it's still early days but it would be a blow if he never regains complete fitness.'

'Weren't they talking about him going to some convalescent place in Harrogate?'

'Yes, I think that's still going ahead but for the moment he is just happy to be home and needless to say Sue is delighted to have him there as well. We're going to try the water aerobics class again tomorrow. She's a little concerned about leaving him for longer than necessary although I think it will do her good to have time for herself. Life has been totally consumed by hospital visits for the last month. She needs some routine mundane activity in her life for a change.'

'Well I can always ring to see if he's okay but it is probably much easier for him to relax when Rose and Sue aren't about.'

'I agree, but don't let her hear you say it or you'll be toast!'

****

Danny had not left the house since the day he had broken down and admitted his wrongdoing to his mother and in fact had barely left the bedroom. On returning from shopping, Linda decided that it was time to make another attempt at reasoning with him.

'You can't hide away here forever you know.' The words barely registered, Dan was concentrating on a video game, a rather violent one judging from the portion of screen which was visible.

'Come downstairs for a cuppa and we'll talk about it, try to sort something out eh?'

He swung round scowling.

'Talking's not going to do anything, I don't want to talk!'

'Burying your head in the sand won't do any good either. We have to do something and quickly too.' She was exasperated but even if he did come down to talk what on earth would she say? Maggie had very gently suggested looking at each and every option and considering whichever one appeared to be the best but what were the options? Turning him over to the police? Allowing him to stay put and hoping it would all blow over? It was impossible to decide and she didn't even have all the facts.

'Please, you have to tell me everything. There could be a knock on the door at any time and how would I be able to help you if I don't know who this man is or when this robbery took place?' This was not quite true as since the bombshell had fallen, Linda had spent time on the internet reading through recent back copies of the local papers and did know more than she was letting on. There was really only one incident that it could be, the attempted robbery of a small post office cum newsagents, when an off duty police officer had been shot. It had been a massive relief to read that the officer was still alive and hopefully it was not going to be a murder charge.

'Come on down love and I'll put the kettle on. I've brought fish and chips in for dinner, they'll be getting cold.' Turning to go back downstairs she busied herself with the mundane activity of making a pot of tea and buttering bread. Soon the sound of Danny clumping down the stairs made her heart skip a beat.

'Good!' She thought and began to set the table.
After eating in relative silence, it was time to grasp the opportunity of her son being somewhat subdued and attempt to begin the 'what can we do' dialogue.

'We have to do something love and I've given it a lot of thought. If we went to the police and explained that you were coerced into driving, it could work out okay. You're only fifteen still...' Linda was really speaking off the top of her head, true she had given it plenty of thought but was now making the only suggestion which came to mind to test Danny's reactions.

'Yeah, and they'll get me for driving uninsured and without a licence too, not to mention nicking the wheels, great plan Mum!'

'Did you steal the car?' She was stunned having not even considered where the car had come from.

'What, do you think that Ron borrowed it from his sister or used his own car? Get real!'

'So its Ron is it? What's his other name?'

'I can't tell you that, it doesn't matter what his name is!'

'Of course it matters, do you think he'll protect you if the police get him? It's you that needs to get real. He shot a man and a policeman at that! They'll be pulling out all the stops on this one and will keep at it until they find both of you! Look, we can go and see a solicitor in the morning to get some advice. If you turn yourself in and tell the police about him they'll take it into consideration. You have to show some remorse, surely you do regret it don't you?'

'Of course I bloody regret it! He said nothing about a gun, I'd have never agreed if I'd known that.'

'You don't have to swear at me. If you're telling the truth then prove it by going to the police before they come to you and they will you know, probably very soon too.' Although not expressing it, she was hugely relieved to hear this admission of regret. It had occurred to her that her son was turning into a hardened criminal, a most unpalatable thought but one that niggled at the back of her mind. Voicing regret and saying that he wouldn't have had anything to do with it if he had known it involved a gun was balm to his mother's ears, a sign of hope that they might just somehow come through this and despite the way he had behaved over the last few years, there was still a chance to make something good out of his life.

Danny remained subdued; a mood his mother hoped meant that he was thinking about seeing a solicitor and then the police. Surely this was the best, the only, way out of this mess. She would leave him to think it over and put the idea to him again the next day. In the meantime she had better get back on the computer to find a local solicitor and hopefully one that wouldn't charge the earth.

****

Alan received another visit from Jack Swanson only a week after the Chief Superintendant had been to see him in hospital.

'There's a place available at St. Stephen's in Harrogate from Monday should you want it. Occupational health has made all the arrangements and an initial two week period has been provisionally booked for you.' Jack smiled as if handing his detective sergeant a gift.

'Two weeks? I've hardly been home from hospital a week and I don't know how well this will go down with Sue. Could we defer it sir?'

'Not really. I'm not sure of the medical point of view but I would have thought the sooner the better, don't you think?'

Alan nodded his head thoughtfully, recognising the sense in his Chief Superintendent's words. Although it was brilliant to be home with his wife and daughter, life was becoming a tad boring. Physiotherapy was available at the hospital three times a week but at St. Stephen's there were facilities for this to be stepped up with more intensive one to one support. A swift recovery appealed and he was itching to get back to work, knowing that his fitness would be monitored rigorously before even a phased return was allowed.

'Can I discuss it with Sue and get back to you on this? I appreciate the offer and the trouble you've gone to in arranging it but she's had a tough time of late. I'm sure she'll see the benefits but I would like to consult her first.'

'There's no problem with that, I understand how difficult it's been for both of you. Perhaps you could go as a resident during the week and come home, say, Friday night until Monday morning?'

'That would be great sir, thank you! We'll have a chat about it tonight and I'll ring you first thing in the morning.' The compromise appealed and he was pleasantly surprised that it had been Jack Swanson who had made the suggestion. Showing his visitor out he resumed the arduous task of resting, reading the latest James Patterson novel that Peter had brought him while waiting for his wife to come home.

As expected Sue wasn't entirely thrilled at the idea of him going away again so soon but the knowledge that this would enhance his recovery took precedence and getting him back to full health was currently their one single aim in life. The idea of returning at weekends however, did appeal and she introduced the possibility of a mid-week visit from herself and Rose to which he could see no objection. It was not some kind of a lock down facility after all and lunch in Harrogate with his family mid-week would be a pleasant diversion. They agreed that he would ring Jack Swanson in the morning and accept the place for the following Monday.

Chapter 19

'Angry, sad, confused, miserable, alone, betrayed, incomplete...' Rae, needing to be alone, sat in the bedroom at her parent's home sifting through the cards written during her counselling session which now seemed to be eons ago. Reading them now brought such very different feelings to mind. 'It's all about me, how utterly selfish I've been,' she whispered into the silence. Her mother was in hospital having tried to kill herself, how disconsolate she must have felt to do such a thing. Had it been her stubborn insistence to know the truth about Pattie's life and death which had prompted such desperate action? The unreliable reasoning of her mind said it was. The day had started so well, with the confrontation of the previous night seeming to have spent some of the tension between the family even though Barbara had 'run away' from the situation once more. And then, only mildly perturbed at her mother's non appearance at breakfast, Rae had pushed it all to the back of her mind thinking a day in Rouen would give them as well as her parents the space to re-group and talk over what had been said before deciding what else, if anything, could be done. Immersing themselves in the history and atmosphere of the beautiful French town had seemed the right thing to do. Surely the worst of the confrontation was over. The words had been spoken and now needed to be reflected upon before they could move forward. Unfortunately she was wrong and the worst was not over. Her mother had attempted suicide and Rae felt culpable. This desire to be alone concerned her father and fiancé as they reluctantly allowed her hide in the bedroom. Sean made far more visits to the bathroom than necessary, checking up on her which was something that under normal circumstances would have brought a smile to her face. Hearing his footsteps in the passageway outside the door, she made deliberate noises in an attempt to reassure him. A cough, a sigh or walking over the creaking floor board in the bay window was her way to let him know that all was well. Again it was probably selfish but an hour or so alone to gather her thoughts was what she needed most. The ache in her temples had developed into a full on headache. Shortly she would go down for some water and an aspirin and join the two men who were clearly concerned for her welfare and later she would visit the hospital as promised. It had already been decided that only she and David would go that evening and that her father would remain outside to give Barbara the chance to tell their daughter what it was that lay so heavily on her mind.

The hospital was buzzing with activity unlike earlier in the day when they had left. Visitors arrived with arms full of fragrant summer flowers and smiling faces, anticipating seeing loved ones who were there to be made well and return home once again. The night sister on the ward spoke much better English than the day sister and told them that Madame Chapman had slept most of the afternoon and eaten a little of the meal served to her. Again caution was advised to ensure they did not tire the patient and impede the recovery process. David found a seat not far from Barbara's room and after a reassuring hug for his daughter sat down to wait, for how long he had no idea.

Barbara was lying on her back beneath the crisp sheet which was neatly folded up to her chin and with eyes closed although not asleep. Her face was pale and expressionless. Aware of Rae's presence, she opened her eyes and attempted to shift position to sit up and talk. Her daughter plumped the pillows on the bed, feeling the need to do something practical and aid her mother in some small way.

'How are you feeling Mum?'

'Tired, but I brought it on myself didn't I?' Barbara's voice sounded a little stronger than earlier in the day, with a judgemental tone purely self directed.

'You mustn't say that. Circumstances have been difficult and we've all made mistakes.'

'No, please don't blame yourself. The mistakes were mine, not yours or your father or grandmother's. I've been a coward and have let you all down.'

'I don't think blaming anyone is very constructive. I'm the one who has been so incredibly selfish in pushing this whole issue, but after much thinking and worrying I want to put it behind us and start afresh. I thought knowing about Pattie would create a permanent wedge in our relationship but it doesn't have to does it? I love you and Dad and want things to be right between us again.' Her expression was one of such concern, for her mother's health and ultimately for their relationship with hope that the negative impact of the last few weeks would not cause a permanent rift.

'Rae, I need to tell you something...'

'There's no need to tell me anything. I've learned all about Pattie that's necessary to work through this Mum, honestly.'

'It's not just your sister you need to know about. There's something else I'd like you to know but not in any way to excuse my handling of events but to help you understand my actions. Will you just listen, please?'

Pulling the chair a little closer to the bed until her eyes were level with her mothers, she gently took hold of the pale hand which was resting on the sheet.

'Sorry Mum, of course I'll listen.'

'I was a twin too and had an identical sister just as you did but my sister died at birth.' The statement was spoken softly yet hit Rae as hard as a physical blow. Unconsciously she gripped her mother's hand tighter.

'My sister was called Grace, but of course growing up I had no real memories of her. I say 'real memories' because there were times when it felt as if I had known her and that there was a part of me which was strangely missing. It was like being only half a person. It could have been from the nine months we shared a womb or perhaps because Grace remained very real to my parents. She was talked about regularly, a very present but invisible member of the family, so much so that at times it would not have surprised me if she had turned up at the dinner table one evening. Grace inhabited our home every bit as much as I did. Every milestone, birthdays, achievements at school, dancing class or whatever, my sister was always brought into the event. Grace would have been a good scholar, a brilliant dancer, a loving daughter. It reached the point where I was almost jealous of my twin. She could do no wrong, made no mistakes and set the benchmark at perfection, a standard I could never hope to attain. Adolescence was difficult enough without being constantly compared to someone who was perfect. There were times when I wanted to scream that Grace might have made mistakes too, that she might have let them down and perhaps not be top of the class in every subject! But inevitably those thoughts brought guilt and shame, so much so that I knew my parents were right and that Grace would have been a better daughter than I ever could, which only served to multiply the guilt. It was a never ending circle which dogged my entire childhood. It never seemed to occur to my parents what they were doing. In their minds they were keeping her memory alive which I understood better the older I grew. But it wasn't a dead baby they were remembering, it was pure fiction. They projected their image of what they wanted from a daughter, an unattainable standard for me, and Grace won every time. I became jealous of my twin, a sister I had never known but who grew up beside me every day of my life.' Barbara sighed and reached for the water beside the bed then turning to Rae, offered a weak smile,

'Don't ever let anyone tell you that parenting is easy. In retrospect its understandable why my parents behaved that way. Perhaps seeing me was a constant reminder of the daughter they had lost, a fact I translated into me being not good enough for them. There were of course faults and misunderstandings on both sides but the saddest part is that I have let my childhood reflect on my relationship with you. I didn't consciously decide to cut Patricia out of our lives, it somehow evolved over time. Not wanting your life to be overshadowed by the loss of your sister as mine had been, I failed to take into account your own memories of Pattie. You would think that I had learned from my parents' mistakes yet it drove me too far in the opposite direction, never finding that middle ground, the right way to go. As time passed I found that pretending Pattie had never existed was easier on me too. It was easier to cope with pretending that you were an only child, so you grew up believing the lie. I am so sorry Rae. I hope you can forgive me and that Pattie can too. I adored you both, my beautiful girls and losing her was devastating, I over compensated by trying to focus all my love on you. It was wrong and now you are suffering for my mistakes, I am so very sorry love.'

Rae was stunned by this revelation. Her mother had spoken from the heart and with a clarity which brought the understanding she had been seeking. Having never known her maternal grandparents she felt no animosity to them or to her parents. It was what it was. Human nature is such that everyone makes mistakes. Her family had never intended to hurt each other and had acted in the way that felt prudent at the time and unable to predict the effects of their actions on future generations. This moving story explained most of what she needed to know but there was one more question to which Rae needed an answer,

'What about Dad and Gran, did they know about your sister?'

'Your father found out before we married. When I took him home to meet my parents, Grace was still very much a part of our family. I think your Dad found it rather weird but accepted the situation and at some point told your Gran who kept her own counsel on the matter. When Mum and Dad died it was finally time to let Grace die with them, which may sound cruel, but in some ways she had never been able to 'rest in peace' and it was a relief to eventually let her do so. After the fire and Pattie's death it all came flooding back and I was thrown into a despair which is painful even to think about. Hospitalization was necessary for a while and it was a difficult time for us all. Your Gran was brilliant then. Although grieving for Pattie too, she took over your care at a time when we needed her help and when I was incapable of doing so. I owe so much to Edith for the support and kindness she gave us. When I came home, to Gran's house until our own was rebuilt, they were very conscious of my mental state and we all tiptoed around each other on eggshells as it were. The pretence had begun, not intentionally, but it was in those early difficult days that the seeds were sown. I like to think we continued it for your sake, so that you would not live under the shadow of your sister as I had done. But to be honest, it was to help me as much as anything and the pretence simply grew until we too almost believed that you had always been an only child.

Chapter 20

'Great looking place!' Sue observed pulling into the drive at St. Stephen's in Harrogate.

'I wouldn't expect anything else in this town. It's a lovely area but buying property here must cost a bomb and it's not somewhere I would choose to live.'

'Me neither but mainly because I don't want to leave our own home town, it suits me well enough and I love our life there.'

Alan nodded in agreement, Fenbridge suited them both. Sue had driven on their trip to Harrogate, something else that her husband would have to get used to for some time yet. Rose had been dropped off at nursery on the way, unable to understand that she wouldn't be seeing her Daddy for a few days but enjoying the fuss he made when saying goodbye. It was Sue who carried the case into the reception hall too with Alan being under doctor's orders not to lift anything until the physiotherapists gave the okay. The couple were welcomed warmly into an establishment which appeared to be some sort of hybrid, not quite a hospital but obviously a medical facility of some kind. They were shown to his room, which resembled a four star hotel and in Sue's opinion was a tad too comfortable and her husband might grow to enjoy this lifestyle. Coffee making facilities were available of which they took advantage, sitting by the open window to enjoy a last drink together before she had to leave for home.

'You'll be back on Wednesday then?' Her husband attempted to be chirpy, 'With Rose, and we'll find somewhere nice for lunch in town.'

Adopting the brave face she was becoming heartily sick of, she linked her husband's good arm as they walked back to the car. During the drive home the silence was filled with a Chris de Burgh CD and she purposely steered her thoughts to planning the rest of the day before it would be time to pick up Rose. Making a mental list she decided to use the time to get round to some much needed cleaning in the house. Curtains could be washed while the weather held and there would be time to complete all those mundane little tasks she had let slip while Alan had been so ill. The following day would pass quickly at work. She was still putting in only half her usual hours which would have to increase in a couple of weeks. Yes, keeping busy would get her through the next few days and hopefully with some good results to show for it.

Alan's first task was to complete the paper work for his stay at St. Stephen's fulfilling the endless bureaucracy which needed to be adhered to in all walks of life, even illness. He was then introduced to a member of staff, Robin, who showed him round the facility and answered any questions prompted by their tour. It was pretty impressive; a well maintained building which was more than comfortable. He was shown into the communal area which consisted of an L-shaped room which had at one time been three separate large lounges. A television was at the top of the room with another round the corner at the other end, presumably to accommodate more than one channel. There were more facilities for tea and coffee here and he found himself wondering if the patients needed regular caffeine boosts for a reason. Next door a smaller room with a snooker table was being used by two men engaged in friendly rivalry. Everywhere was beautifully furnished, comfortable with a relaxed atmosphere throughout the whole building. Several other police officers greeted Robin, with witty comments flying through the air parried between men who obviously had a good rapport with each other and the members of staff. He liked the informality of the place. There were no uniforms to delineate ranks, they were all simply police officers who for one reason or another needed the support on offer to help them back to physical and mental fitness. The gym was pretty impressive causing Alan to wish he was fit enough to take full advantage of its facilities and finally he was shown the indoor pool. It was not a large pool, about fifteen metres by ten, but the clear water looked so inviting and gave rise to an optimistic hope that swimming would be part of his treatment. Finally Robin took him back to the foyer to make a quick telephone call and find out if the assigned physiotherapist was available to see him.

The physio charged with the task of restoring Alan's fitness was a middle aged woman named Leah. She was sprightly, friendly but her bright and intelligent green eyes suggested she would accept no nonsense. After introducing herself, Leah began to outline what was to be his daily routine for the next two weeks. If he had thought this was going to be some kind of holiday he was soon disillusioned but happily so. A more strenuous routine would be welcome after the weeks of inactivity in hospital with only occasional physio sessions. Each morning would incorporate a two hour session with Leah in the gym, which, she explained, would be shared by another three recovering officers and one other therapist. There would be ample time for lunch before another one to one session, after which, if it was considered suitable, he could make use of the pool. On two of the evenings he was booked in to see a counsellor for an hour each time which could then be repeated the following week if required. It was all quite satisfactory and flexible enough for him to meet his girls on Wednesday as arranged and return home for the weekend too. He would ring Sue later to outline his routine and see how she was coping with being left alone yet again.

****

Maggie welcomed Linda with mixed feelings. Although, as always, wanting to give the best possible help to this client her position was proving difficult in that she was aware of the crime committed from the victim's perspective as well as from the clients. When Linda had disclosed the information about Danny, Maggie knew it would have to remain confidential yet wondered if possessing this knowledge constituted a conflict of interest due to her relationship with Alan and Sue. Seeking advice from the ever sage Joyce Patterson, she was encouraged to stay with the client who most certainly needed support and was reassured that as long as she herself felt no animosity towards this woman then it would not be construed as a conflict of interest. Maggie would never discuss a client outside the bounds of professionalism and her feelings were certainly positive with no resentment whatsoever. She could barely begin to understand how Linda herself must be torn by this dilemma and once reassured by Joyce was determined to see her through this difficult time.

'Danny's begun to open up a bit.' Linda began the dialogue with this snippet of good news. 'We had a long chat last night and after sleeping on it he's agreed to see a solicitor with me today. We have an appointment this afternoon.'

Maggie felt almost as relieved as her client having learned from Sue that the police were holding a man for the crime but were still seeking his accomplice which was news that Linda seemed to be unaware of. Perhaps the solicitor would persuade the boy to turn himself in which would be far better in the longer term than waiting until they found him. She nodded and smiled at this more positive news as her client continued relating the emotional conversation of the prior evening and how her son had appeared at breakfast time, penitent and ready to accept advice.

This was her only client for the day, having kept the rest of the day free to attend Lydia's funeral. As the session ran its course there was a much more optimistic atmosphere in the conclusion than at the beginning. Linda Johnson was also in a much better place emotionally accepting that there was nothing which could be done to alter the fact that her son had been involved in a serious crime. She was, however, more content that he was at least showing some regret and was willing to face up to the consequences of his actions which would potentially stand him in good stead as the outcome unfolded.

****

'Oh Tara, no!' The little tortoise shell cat was comfortably curled up on the black jacket Maggie had left on the bed intending to wear for the funeral that afternoon. Opening one sleepy eye, she stretched out her front paws, yawned and went straight back to sleep. Maggie smiled, lifting the cat off the jacket and laying the purring bundle of fur back in the same warm spot. Then leaving the bedroom she went in search of a clothes brush to rid the jacket of cat hairs.

'Are you sure you don't want me to drive you there?' Peter asked as she vigorously brushed the coat.

'Thanks but no. I can park in the town centre and walk, it's only a couple of minutes.'

Lydia Armstrong's housekeeper, true to her word, had rung with the time and venue of her employer's funeral even though it had been well advertised in the local paper.

The afternoon seemed prematurely dark considering the glorious weather they had been having of late but it was somehow fitting for a funeral and a burial at that. Maggie hated funerals and intended to pay her respects at the Church service then leave before the interment. It was not as if she had been close to Lydia after all.

Slipping into the back of the Church half an hour later, she looked around the cavernous interior. The high ceiling and grey stone walls made the place feel cold and rather unwelcoming despite the lavish arrangements of flowers in several strategic places. The organist was playing what sounded like a dirge which might seem appropriate to some but not to Maggie who preferred funeral services to be a celebration of the deceased's life which should be reflected in music and the spoken words. Maybe Lydia had planned this herself, something else which was not uncommon these days. As the pews began to fill up it looked as if she had been right to arrive early and settle inconspicuously at the back. Even though it was a large Church, it would probably be quite full. Looking forward across several already assembled mourners Maggie recognised Molly, more from the constant bobbing of her head than anything else, a head that today was swamped with a large black hat, more fitting to a wedding than a funeral. From the movement of her shoulders the housekeeper appeared to be crying. She had been a loyal servant to Lady Armstrong and would probably miss her employer greatly. Thoughts of Molly prompted questions pertaining to the beautiful home she had helped to maintain and what would become of it now. Perhaps one of Lydia's children would take over running the estate. Maggie hoped so as it would be sad to see it sold off to become a country hotel or some other commercial venture. As the Church filled up, the volume of the organ playing became louder building to a crescendo which stopped abruptly when the vicar stepped inside the porch followed by the coffin carried by four pall bearers. Familiar passages from the Bible were recited as the family followed the coffin to the front of the Church. Maggie was to get her first glimpse of Lydia's family although she had seen their images smiling from the silver photograph frames dotted about the Armstrong drawing room. Elizabeth Armstrong was unmistakable, a mirror image of her mother, tall and slim with the same aquiline nose and soft brown eyes, holding onto the arm of a good looking man in a black suit, presumably her husband. After studying Elizabeth for a moment, her attention was taken by a slightly older man, most probably Patrick. He was behind his sister and pushing a wheelchair in which sat the unmistakable older sibling, James. Maggie gasped as a wave of emotion swept through her and she gripped the pew in front of her for support.

'Good for you Lydia!' she whispered into the echoing chamber of the Church. In that one moment so many of the questions which had remained niggling at the back of her mind were answered, bringing a most inappropriate grin to her face. Lydia had told them, and by James's very presence it would appear that his younger brother and sister had accepted him into his rightful place in their family and included him today in saying goodbye to their mother. There was no doubt in her mind that if Lydia could somehow see them gathered there, she would be delighted. The service progressed and Maggie learned more about Lydia's public life as the vicar commended Lady Armstrong's charitable works in the community and applauded her efforts for the many committees she chaired and causes generously supported by the giving of her time and money. The service was fitting, both of the lady and the occasion and within the hour the family were retracing their steps down the aisle in the opposite direction to take their mother to her final resting place.

In order to give the funeral party time to leave, Maggie sat for a few moments breathing in the scent of lilies which pervaded the atmosphere. Molly edged into the pew beside her.

'She would have been glad you came Miss.' the housekeeper nodded.

'Thank you, I wanted to come. Although we only met in the last few weeks of her life I became very fond of Lady Armstrong. I appreciate you keeping me in touch with what was happening. But what about you now, will you be kept on at the house?'

'Oh yes, they've got big plans for the house and they want me to stay on to help. I'll even be getting a girl to help with the heavy work and things.' Molly spoke with pride and Maggie couldn't imagine what such plans might be but was pleased that the housekeeper would still have a job.

'That's such good news and I am so glad for you. I think they should be gone now so I'd better get off home, it was nice seeing you again.'

'Oh no, don't go Miss, please! That's what I have to tell you. Miss Elizabeth wants you to go back to the house. She said to tell you she'd really like to meet you so please come. I've done lots of baking, there's plenty to eat.'

'I'm sure there is and I can vouch for how good it will be too but surely it's just for close friends and family?'

'No, Miss Elizabeth was very insistent that you come. We can wait outside and get a lift with the family if you like.'

'Thanks but I have my car not far away. Perhaps I can give you a lift, you must want to get back quickly?'

Molly smiled. This was obviously the solution she had hoped for and the two women walked briskly to the car park before making their way to the beautiful house which Maggie had never expected to enter again.

Chapter 21

Molly bustled off to the kitchen as soon as they arrived at the Armstrong family home. Water was to be boiled and the business of refreshments set in motion. Maggie was left to wait in the grand hall where she settled into a wing backed chair and took out her phone to ring Peter.

'I feel somewhat out of place but it seems that the family want to see me so I felt obliged to come. I'll try to slip away once I've met them and offered condolences but they're not back from the burial yet. I just didn't want you to worry.'

Peter appreciated the call and told his wife not to hurry for his sake as there was a football match due to kick off in half an hour. She ended the call on hearing the crunching of tyres on the gravel drive announcing the return of the family. Feeling suddenly awkward and not wanting to be found waiting alone in their hall, she made her way to the kitchen in order to tell Molly of their arrival and in the hope that the housekeeper would introduce her to Lydia's children. This she did and Maggie was shown into the drawing room to be introduced firstly to Patrick and then to his sister. James had been settled near the window with a plate of food on his lap which he was tucking into with relish and Maggie hoped she would have the chance to speak to him before leaving. Elizabeth proved to be as gracious a hostess as her mother had been, ensuring that their guest had coffee and was offered something from the inviting selection of dainty sandwiches and homemade cake.

'It was only in the last week of Mother's life that we learned of your relationship with her,' Elizabeth began to explain. 'And although I appreciate that you didn't meet until she was already ill I am sure you helped her enormously in preparing herself for the end, in fact I know you did, Mother told me so.'

This was somewhat of an embarrassment but she was given no time to respond as Elizabeth, with the same straight forward approach as her mother, continued.

'Naturally Patrick and I would like to thank you for your ministrations to Mother and we felt that perhaps you would have an interest in knowing about the grand scheme she concocted in the last months of her life, unless of course you already know?'

Maggie shook her head, somewhat puzzled so Elizabeth, taking her arm, led her to a sofa in a quiet corner of the room where they could talk more privately.

'It came as a shock to find out that we had an older brother. I have learned over the years never to be surprised by my mother who was a woman of many parts as it were, fulfilling several roles, always with skill and enthusiasm. In short, we have always been proud of her yet obviously it seems that we did not know everything there was to know. Mother told us about James three weeks before she died, on one of her more lucid days when we were able to push her chair into the garden. In fact I think it was probably the last time she went outside, her last breaths of fresh air on a beautifully warm day. At the time she appeared to be quite young again. She spoke fluently and confidently, ignoring our shocked expressions and forbidding us to interrupt or ask questions until the story was finished. The strength of her younger self was visible that day and that is how I shall always remember her.' Elizabeth's tender expression spoke volumes, obviously Lydia's fears that her children would think badly of her had not materialised. If anything the older lady seemed to have risen in their esteem. How Lydia must have loved that. It would have come as such a relief.

'Oh I'm not saying that we have taken it all in our stride and that it hasn't given us both some anxious moments. Of course there has been disillusionment about the role of some family members and their part in the whole affair but it is what it is and we have a brother! It would have been good to know about him sooner but history cannot be changed so we will simply have to make up for lost time from now on.'

Elizabeth's pragmatic approach to the revelation was both a surprise and a delight and there was little doubt that Lydia would have been comforted at how well they accepted the rather unorthodox situation.

'I have to go and do the hostess thing now and circulate among the other guests. Please stay as long as you like and do have some food. Molly has over catered as usual. I haven't time to go into Mother's plans now but I would like to tell you if you are interested?'

'Well yes, I am. It's wonderful that you are reunited with James and I'd really love to hear your plans for the future.'

'They are Mother's plans actually and I think you will like them. Could you come for coffee tomorrow? I shall be here all day sorting through mountains of paperwork. What time would suit you?'

'The afternoon would be good. I have clients in the morning.'

'That's settled then, about two thirty?'

Once this was agreed, Elizabeth left to move amongst the other guests accepting their condolences and re-living memories of happy times gone by. Finishing her coffee, Maggie moved over to speak to Patrick who was tucking a linen napkin into his brother's collar and laughing at a shared joke.

'I wanted to say goodbye before leaving,' she began. 'Although I didn't know your mother for very long I do know that she was a truly remarkable lady.'

'Ms Sayer isn't it? I saw you talking to Lizzie. I don't think any of us knew Mother as well as we thought we did. Have you met my elder brother James?'

Maggie smiled at the man in the wheelchair. His plump face and almond shaped eyes beamed back at her but he did not stop eating his food.

'Hello James. I'm pleased to meet you.' Her words prompted James to reach for her hand with his own claw like fingers and as he held on firmly, she instinctively bent to kiss his cheek. This man, who was still very much a child, had unintentionally been at the centre of an ongoing family dispute. Oblivious to the heartache his mother had borne and the bitter feelings of other family members, James was a complete innocent. In his own way and limited perception he would miss his mother but in that loss he had gained an extended family, opening up a whole new world to him. Maggie hoped to learn more of what would become of him when she met with Elizabeth the following day. But it appeared to be obvious from the solicitous way Patrick looked at his brother that the relationship would continue.

****

Danny's mood was still repentant even if a little solemn, true to his word and looking smarter than he had in a long time, he was ready for his mother when she arrived home.

'I've made a pot of tea.' The words were flat, a statement which made Linda's heart skip at this simple but pivotal gesture. Seeing her son's pale face and watching him move to pour the tea brought a new resolve to Linda's mind, a seed of hope and a determination that together they would get through this terrible time no matter what the outcome.

'I love you Danny!' She spoke on impulse, the words a surprise to them both, prompting a spontaneous hug, much needed by both mother and son.

The solicitor's office was housed in a large Victorian terraced property which occupied a prominent position close to the centre of Fenbridge and was only a short walk from the bus station. Arriving early for their appointment, they were shown to a comfortable waiting area where they watched a large clock on the wall, its hands moving painfully slowly before eventually striking the hour. Mr Burdock appeared to his new clients to be very young for a solicitor but he greeted them with confidence and showed them through to his office with a smile. He must have had some idea of why they were there as when the appointment was arranged over the telephone Linda had been asked about the nature of her business in order to be directed to the right partner in the firm. The solicitor however was not going to make things easy for them now.

'How can I help?' were his only words, leaving the ball firmly in the court of mother and son. Jumping straight in Linda proceeded to tell him what Danny had done, without excuse or embellishment and making it clear that they intended to go to the police and therefore needed the services of a solicitor. After listening carefully and scribbling a few notes, Mr Burdock turned his attention to the boy, who was yet to speak.

'I need to hear your side of things now. We'll take it slowly and from the beginning but I want you to understand that your best chance of coming out of this mess without a long sentence is to tell the truth. Don't think you can fool the police or protect the man who got you into this situation. A full and honest confession is the best way forward. I should tell you now that because you went willingly to commit a crime, even though you did not know a gun was involved, you will almost certainly get a custodial sentence.'

Linda gasped, raising a hand to her mouth. It sounded so terrible, Dan was only fifteen. Yes, it had been a dreadful mistake but to be locked away with hardened criminals was an unbearable thought. Her son too had gone pale, suddenly looking so much younger than his years despite his physique. A nod of understanding preceded a few moments silence with Mr. Burdock waiting to hear directly from his client who eventually began to speak.

'Ron Harrison's his name. I met him a couple of months ago and let him talk me into 'helping' with a couple of jobs. Nothing that I thought was illegal at first. He wanted me to store a few things for him and said it was because he didn't want his wife to know he had them. I got a few quid for my trouble but then he began to talk about us working together on other jobs. It sounded exciting at first and I honestly didn't think anyone would get hurt...'

'Let me stop you there Danny. I'd like to ring the police now and see how quickly we can get someone to see you, is that okay with you both?'

Mother and son exchanged glances then both nodded and the solicitor made the call there and then. Asking to speak to the lead detective in the case, he was put through immediately. After a short conversation he ended the call with the words, 'Thank you, we'll be there.'

The solicitor replaced the telephone and stunned the anxious pair by announcing that they had an appointment for six o'clock that very evening.

'It's important to do this as soon as possible.' He began to explain. 'We don't know how far the police investigation has progressed and it's likely that they already have your name as a person of interest. If that's the case, the sooner we act the better. Now, I need you to tell me everything about your relationship with Ron Harrison, what he's asked you to do and what you have done together. If there are other crimes you have committed, it's far better to tell the police now and ask for them to be taken into consideration as well as the robbery.'

His mother listened ashen faced as her son began to reveal the full extent of the activities he had been involved in during the last few weeks.

****

Barbara Chapman was allowed home after three nights in hospital. During that time she had received two visits from a psychiatrist. Dr. Reynard was a fatherly figure with an owl like face and thin lips framing a tiny mouth. He had kind eyes which crinkled at the corners with laughter lines. Each movement was slow and deliberate as if he was afraid to startle the fragile patient. His voice was soft and she had to concentrate hard to hear the words. Although his English was excellent, the accent impeded their clarity. He had spoken to her with great compassion, making her feel valued, as if she truly mattered and it suddenly became easy to open up to this kindly man. Gentle questions drew from her those thoughts and feelings with which she had wrestled for years. The whole sorry story was recounted and Barbara felt certain that this gentle Frenchman understood every word she said. Occasionally a simple question was posed, questions which were designed to help him understand how his patient was feeling and more specifically, to probe the likelihood of a repeat attempt at suicide. She accepted the need for this but still felt the psychiatrist was an ally and on her side. His quiet wisdom and unshockable nature impressed her and she knew with certainty that she would be able to talk to him again if necessary. Towards the end of their second meeting, Dr. Reynard offered the option of returning to his clinic as an outpatient over the next few weeks, to be reviewed at the end of the month. The phrasing of the offer made it clear that this was not a mandatory condition of discharge, simply a suggestion, a possibility for continued support should she need it. Barbara readily accepted knowing that it was probably the best course of action at the present time.

David came alone to collect his wife from the hospital, their daughter thinking it best to allow them time together rather than make a big fuss of the homecoming. Rae used the time to prepare a meal, a simple salad with poached salmon which they could share with a glass of white wine. Hopefully they could then relax and put the last few days behind them. Barbara was remarkably calm and appeared genuinely pleased to be home. The meal went well and the conversation became easier as the evening wore on. There was another week left of the couple's holiday and Rae broached the subject of them returning home earlier if it would make things easier for her mother.

'No, that's not necessary. I want you to stay and for us to be able to discuss things openly, to talk about Pattie and Grace. I've made so many mistakes in the past but want to learn from them. The pretending is over. Do you think we could possibly start again?' Barbara sounded determined and sincere, prompting Rae to hug her mother, both women with tears in their eyes but a great dollop of hope in their hearts.

'And what could be better than celebrating a new start with preparations for a wedding?' David beamed at the little group around the table, feeling happier than he had dared to think possible in the last few strained weeks. Pulling herself away from her mother Rae said,

'I'll go and get my notebook shall I?' and headed for the stairs. Sean rolled his eyes but grinned at the welcome change of subject. When she came back with the book the men escaped to clear the dishes while mother and daughter poured over the notes and magazine clippings which she had been collecting.

'We need to decide on invitations Mum. It's really time they were sent out, any ideas?'

'Absolutely, the French have great style with such things. There are a couple of little shops in Rouen, one an amazing stationary shop you wouldn't believe! I'm sure we'll find something really original there and the other, a bridal shop. How about we go tomorrow to look at invitations and dresses? You haven't chosen your dress have you?'

'No, not yet and that sounds wonderful Mum. Sean and Dad can help to choose the invitations and then we can banish them for coffee while we look at dresses. It will be fantastic!'

Chapter 22

August had transmuted into September with the mornings decidedly cooler than of late, a sign of things to come. But the afternoon was warm as Maggie set off to once again return to Lydia Armstrong's house. Having absolutely no idea what the plans could be which Elizabeth had alluded to at the funeral, her mood was one of excited anticipation. These mysterious plans were apparently Lydia's own 'grand scheme' but she could recall nothing from her final visits to the old lady which provided a clue. Molly showed her in before bustling off to make the inevitable coffee whilst Elizabeth greeted her visitor enthusiastically, her mother's warm eyes smiling at Maggie.

'I should have asked you yesterday but it didn't seem quite appropriate, are there any outstanding fees due to you? I would hate for you to be out of pocket.'

'Oh no, not at all, everything was squared up by your mother.' She was a little embarrassed at the question but straight talking Elizabeth obviously was not.

'Good' she continued, 'I must admit to being rather taken aback when mother told me she had been seeing a counsellor. It seems so modern for someone of her generation, rather 'American' even, but good for her. I have to say she was full of admiration for you too Maggie, you certainly helped her considerably.'

'I wish I could have done more, our time seemed so short and was limited from the beginning.'

'Yes, but your therapy obviously worked.'

Molly appeared with the tray. The two coffee cups, the pot, cream and sugar were almost buried under a huge selection of homemade biscuits and cakes.

'Good heavens, there are only two of us!'
Molly blushed,
'But there's such a lot left in the pantry from yesterday Miss, I didn't know what to do with them.'
'It's okay, we'll do our best.'
Left alone, Elizabeth poured the coffee and as Maggie watched she was struck by the similarities to her mother, little nuances and movements which were identical to Lydia's and caused a wave of sadness to pass fleetingly over her.

'Well, I think you are going to be surprised by what my dear mother had been planning in those last few months. Strange as it may seem when she became ill it was the first time we, that is Patrick and I, had ever considered that she would one day die and it was only then that we began to wonder what would happen to the estate. Mother was always so capable and even after Father died needed no assistance from us in the financial side of things. We presumed that she would somehow go on forever which perhaps is the way most children perceive their parents. Of course most of the land is tenanted and there is an estate manager who looks after that side of things. However, Mother was shrewd, in the best possible way of course, that is not a criticism I might add. Naturally when she told us she had cancer and it was terminal we could hardly ask about money but knowing Mother we assumed that things would be left in an orderly fashion, so this all came as quite a shock. The plan is all due to James of course and I am so glad! Please, come over here, I want to show you something.'
Maggie followed an animated Elizabeth to a table beside the window where unrolled and anchored at the corners with glass paperweights was a set of plans. Even though

married to an architect her knowledge of plans was limited and these were of a very large building of two storeys with at least a dozen rooms on each level. Putting on her reading glasses she looked closer finding a clue in the external wall pattern.

'It's this house isn't it?' She gawped at the plans, not fully understanding their significance.

'Correct, and look at this tiny writing here in each of these rooms.' A well manicured finger tapped on several spots of the plans.

Peering closer Maggie read the words 'en-suite bedroom' printed neatly in most of the boxes.

'I still don't really understand.' Feeling a little uncomfortable now and worried that she appeared foolish she asked, 'Is it a hotel of some kind?'

'Almost, but not quite. These are the plans for a complete overhaul of this house which will turn it into a residential care facility for children and adults with disabilities, inspired, I'm sure you have guessed by James!' Elizabeth spoke triumphantly, obviously enthused with the project and with a sense of pride in her voice.

'That is so wonderful!' was the only response she could manage, relieved that nothing more was required as her hostess continued to speak, so very like her mother.

'The place where James lives at the moment is brilliant in its ethos, care and atmosphere. The staff are excellent too but the fabric of the place is crumbling. It was probably tip top thirty or more years ago when my brother first went there yet now it would cost an absolute fortune to bring it up to standard. I believe Mother looked into doing just that with a view to leaving a bequest for that very purpose but the architect she employed suggested it would be more economical to pull the place down and build a new one; a suggestion which seemed to be the catalyst for this scheme. Patrick and I would never want to live here, it's far too big. We are both extremely comfortable where we are and so are a hundred percent behind the project. And really, when you think about it, this is true poetic justice. James is the first born son and the title should really have been his. Daddy sorted that out years ago with his solicitors. There is apparently provision for the next in line to take over as heir if the elder son is incapacitated in any way. And this is so fitting! James has a right to be here and I will make sure he gets the best of everything. I am quite excited about the whole scheme.'

Maggie's head spun with myriad thoughts, not least of which was surprise at both brother and sister being prepared to give up their inheritance. A slow smile crossed Elizabeth's face, almost as if she had read her visitor's mind and knew the question which politeness decreed would never be asked.

'Patrick is as keen as I am,' she explained. 'The money is not an issue to either of us but we will still have the income from the tenants who remain unaffected by the proposal. The new home will only require the gardens immediately surrounding the house therefore nothing will change regarding the rest of the estate. It is all so perfect. James will be able to enjoy his inheritance in this house and Mother's beloved gardens. The tenants keep their livelihood and everyone is happy. Of course we need to get the necessary planning approvals but as we are not changing the exterior of the premises we've been told that there should be no major problems and any trivia can easily be resolved. The local council will almost certainly be flexible. They are benefitting too of course as they currently fund most of the residents so are receiving upgraded facilities at no cost to themselves. Patrick or I will have a seat on a board of trustees which will be appointed to administer the private funding and charitable donations. Mother certainly put a great deal of thought and effort into this idea and I'm only glad she shared it with us before her death. It would have been even more of a shock if had she not done so, although her will did stipulate that in the event of our disagreement with the plans, a sum would be bequeathed to the current facility and the fate of this house left with Patrick and I as expected. I honestly think this is such a wonderful plan. Inheriting the house as it is would have left us with the problem of how to dispose of it in a fitting way and one which Mother would have approved of. So you see, Lady Lydia Armstrong has eventually got her way. She told me that she felt this plan was, in some small measure, making up for past injustices. Her delight that we had no objections was obvious. She was thrilled that we shared her enthusiasm and died very peacefully having done everything possible to make amends. James may have lost his mother but he has gained a brother, sister and a nephew and if as yet he doesn't fully understand it, we will always be there for him from now on. We are his family.'

Driving home later that afternoon, Maggie felt almost dizzy at what she had learned in the last couple of hours. Elizabeth's enthusiasm was a credit to her and to Lydia who had never forgotten her roots as a farmer's daughter, a humble upbringing which taught her the true value of money and how it could be used for the good of the community. They were a remarkable family with an altruistic nature which had been passed on from mother to children. It was a pleasure to have known them and she would always remember her client whom it seemed had finally found peace before leaving this world; a knowledge which contented Maggie, bringing a satisfactory ending to Lydia's story, one of which she would never have guessed.

'God bless you Lydia,' she whispered into the silent confines of her car.

****

The boutique style stationary shop in Rouen stocked an incredible number of wedding invitations, far surpassing Rae's expectations. If anything there was perhaps too much choice and they were in danger of spending the whole morning in that one shop. After the initial delight and in deference to Sean and her father, the bride-to-be disciplined herself to choose only ten possible invitations for them all to consider, the three favourites then to be left with Rae and her mother to make the final decision. Eventually they selected a gatefold opening card in cream, with two entwined hearts pearl embossed on the front beneath which the happy couple's names were inscribed in gold with matching script inside. It was simple, elegant and different from any others they had previously seen. To their delight the shop also stocked matching place cards, table confetti and thank you cards. David and Sean left the women to place the order, eagerly escaping in search of coffee and a quiet place to sit and enjoy the atmosphere.

Rae felt they were making progress, not only in the wedding plans but also in the relationship with her mother who seemed now to be relaxed, incredibly so taking into account that only a week ago Barbara had been so low that she had attempted suicide. This improved disposition seemed genuine. Rae felt sure she would have picked up the vibes if her mother had only been making an effort to please her. Events seemed to have taken an extraordinary turn for the better with the whole family was so much more at ease, a far better outcome than the young couple had expected when they decided to make the trip. Barbara had even shared some of the things previously discussed with the psychiatrist with which her daughter could identify due to her own relationship with Maggie. A new, deeper alliance was developing between the two bringing them both so much more hope for the future. Rae now knew that when they left for home in a few days time she would be in a much better place emotionally than she had been since learning about Pattie. The rest of that day was to be devoted to enjoying the hunt for the perfect wedding dress. They were on a roll and once again her mother proved to be right about the French penchant for style, the bridal boutique was amazing with at least a dozen dresses which Rae simply had to try on. It was going to be an extremely long days' shopping.

Later that evening as the foursome sat outside to watch the sunset, Barbara surprised them once more by introducing the subject of Patricia.

'For years I've blocked memories of your sister from my mind.' She addressed her daughter in particular but the men were suddenly alert at the unexpected shift in conversation.

'I have become something of an expert at avoidance or distraction. There are so many ways to evade unpleasant thoughts and I've probably mastered the majority of them. When you found out, even before you came to France, I was forced to re-think my strategies and possibly even face reality for the first time. The doctor at the hospital suggested that I still use some of those strategies but instead of avoiding the subject of Pattie altogether I should pursue the train of thought, channelling it to happier memories. Since coming out of hospital I have tried to do this. You could call it a little experiment I suppose and it really seems to work. There are so many good memories which have been neglected because they inevitably led to unhappy ones but concentrating on the time before the fire, those precious years when we had both our beautiful daughters, has actually brought me comfort. Do you remember David how we dressed them, not exactly alike but similar? The ribbons of course had to be different but sometimes Rae, you would change them with Patricia and laugh at Gran when she got you mixed up. And I remember those pretty dresses we bought at

Easter, the first summery clothes of the year. They were gathered at the bodice with little puff sleeves in such a soft delicate fabric, I can almost feel it now. You both cried when I wouldn't let you play in the garden with them on. They were to keep for best but you pleaded and promised not to get them dirty so I gave in and Pattie ripped hers at the hem on a branch.'

'I remember that! We were both so heartbroken that you couldn't be cross with us could you?'

Barbara nodded at the bitter sweet memory and they were all silent for a while.

'I've been so wrong haven't I? I should have thought more about you instead of my own pain, I am so, so sorry!'

'No Mum, don't say that! What's done is behind us now and we can get over this together. It is so good that you can talk about Pattie now too! I want to know everything about her and now I'm able to ask without it causing you the pain it has previously. Is that okay?'

'Yes my darling it is. We'll celebrate Pattie's life and the short time she was with us which is what we should have done all along.' Turning to her husband she continued, 'I've been so unfair to you too David, you should have been able to talk about your daughter and I denied you that. Can you please forgive me?'

His answer was to hold his wife close, smiling at the thought of the new chapter which appeared at last to be unfolding in their lives.

Chapter 23

'This is such an extravagance, but I'm not complaining!' Sue looked into her husband's smiling eyes as they sat in the famous 'Betty's Tea Rooms' in Harrogate on Wednesday lunch time.

'You deserve a little spoiling and yes, perhaps it is extravagant but good don't you think?' He replied.

She nodded then began to study the menu, quickly deciding on a Salad Nicoise while Alan opted for Betty's Welsh rarebit with potato wedges. The children's menu included spaghetti bolognaise, currently Rose's favourite meal so they were all happily catered for. It seemed longer than two days since the family had been together and true to her plans Sue had begun a thorough spring clean of their home to keep occupied while her husband was away. He had thrown himself wholeheartedly into the physiotherapist's program, determined to get back to full physical fitness as soon as possible.

'So tell me what you've been up to?' she asked even though they had spoken at length on the telephone the evening before.

'Nothing terribly exciting. Another session in the gym this morning, Leah seemed to be pushing me a little harder today and my shoulder was quite painful afterwards.'

'Well tell her!'

'She knows what she's doing love. I think pushing me to the limit will help to see how the healing process is going. I must admit to a niggling doubt in my mind as to whether I will ever be a hundred percent again and I'm not sure what the options at work will be if that's the case.'

'Of course you'll be a hundred percent, that's why you're here isn't it?' The terrible events of the last few weeks having a permanent affect on her husband's future, was something she did not wish to think about.

'It's still too early to know,' he softened his tone, 'The doctor at the hospital said it would take time before they could give a longer term prognosis, you know that. They are certainly good here but not quite miracle workers.'

'Well I think it's just a matter of time.' She didn't want anything to spoil their lunch together and Alan knew that her way of coping with unpleasant thoughts was to deny them until confronted with no other alternatives.

'And what about my beautiful daughter, what have you been up to?' He changed the subject, ruffling Rose's soft golden wisps of hair, causing her to grin at him through a mouth covered with tomato sauce from the pasta. Mercifully the little girl had been too young to understand most of the difficulties her parent's had faced recently and had generally been her usual cheery self. Now she generously offered her Daddy a spoonful of spaghetti which he pretended to eat enthusiastically. Rose chuckled, kicking her chubby legs in the high chair and attracting smiles from fellow diners. After their meal there was time for a short walk in Valley Gardens which was nearby and not too far from where the car was parked. All too soon their time together was at an end. Sue drove her husband back to St Stephen's, leaving him at the doorway as Rose was already fast asleep and snoring softly in the back of the car.

Alan had first seen the counsellor at St. Stephen's on his second day, an awkward meeting which he admitted was mostly due to his attitude. Always having been self sufficient and capable, whether at work or in jobs around the home, he usually felt in control of every aspect of life. It was not a feeling of relinquishing this control to the counsellor but rather that he was uncomfortable talking about his experience of the shooting and exploring subsequent feelings. Now as he was due for a second contact he was trying to work out some kind of strategy, ostensibly to make the hour pass smoothly and reassure the professional that he did not need his help. He had convinced himself that any after effects of his injuries were purely physical, or had he? If he was truly honest the episode had left him to some degree shaken but he felt it was nothing he could not handle and having a good relationship with Sue, they were able to talk freely about any topic. There was Maggie too, a counsellor and a pretty good one at that. But would he talk to Maggie if the need arose, or would it indeed be ethical to talk to a friend and expect them to help in a professional manner? No, the more he thought about it the clearer it became that he should take advantage of the counselling available to him at St Stephens. Swallowing his pride he entered the comfortable office at the appointed hour to give this second session a better chance of success than the first one had had.

Jeff Dickson stood to greet him with a wide smile,

'Hello there, good to see you again, have a seat.'

Alan returned the smile and sat in the only other vacant chair in the room, unsure if he should begin the dialogue but saved from doing so by Jeff's honesty.

'I wasn't sure we got off to a brilliant start on Tuesday. Perhaps I didn't stress that these sessions are intended for your benefit only. I did mention that everything said here is confidential but it occurred to me afterwards that you may have had some notion about my reporting back to the Chief Superintendent on your state of mind, so I'd like to begin today by reassuring you that this is not the case. The only time I would be obliged to breach any confidence would be if I had concerns for your safety or the safety of others and in that unlikely event I would discuss it with you before approaching another professional. I'm not a snitch.' This last phrase was said with a grin and Alan had to smile at the joke.

'Yes, I know that Jeff but thanks for making it clear. It was really my fault that we didn't quite hit the mark last time. I was uptight and perhaps not in the right frame of mind to have come to see you. Since then I've done quite a bit of thinking, this place is certainly ideal for that and I want to give it a shot... gosh that's worse than your pun isn't it?' They both laughed, the ice was broken and the beginning of a relationship was emerging. Once Alan began to talk about the shooting he found he wanted to tell Jeff everything, something he had only done as yet with his colleagues in his official statement.

'In many ways passing out after being shot made it easier, certainly regarding any pain. All I remember was a terrific burning sensation in my right side and then everything went black. Before that things happened too quickly for me to actually take anything in. I was acting on instinct and running on adrenaline, planning to work my way round the shelves before the gunman was aware of my presence. His accomplice sounded the car horn which was probably a pre-arranged warning and he turned round and saw me. I suppose I felt some degree of fear but the hours of training took over with my first concern being for the woman shop assistant who was clearly petrified. Although attempting to diffuse the situation, I obviously need to hone those skills as the bastard shot me!' Alan's face had paled and his hands felt clammy. He realised that he was actually shaking which was a surprise for an instant. Jeff too had noticed and said,

'Just take your time Alan. Only tell me what you are comfortable with. Do you want to go on?'

His client nodded,

'Waking up in the hospital was the first time I realised how close I had come to being killed. Despite what people think, the shooting of a police officer isn't an everyday occurrence, particularly when in a relatively quiet town like Fenbridge. Seeing the look on my wife's face brought home to me what a narrow escape I'd had which is quite surreal thinking how easily I could have been killed and then what would have happened to Sue and Rose?' Alan's eyes stung with the tears he was holding back and he remained silent for a few moments in order to compose himself. Lifting his head once again he was ready to continue,

'Perhaps I wasn't scared at the time but I've certainly been scared thinking about what might have been since. Look, I'm actually trembling, silly isn't it?'

'Not at all. Fear is a protective emotion, making us wary and alert in dangerous situations. For example, a child being scalded is harsh, but a way of learning to avoid hot substances. Your experience may cause you to exercise greater care in your work in the future which can't be a bad thing can it? How are you feeling about starting work again?'

'Strangely enough I'm quite keen. You may be right about being more wary, all experiences can be learned from and I can honestly say that I want to get back out there and do the job I trained for and love. My biggest fear is that if this shoulder doesn't fully heal, I'll be consigned to some type of desk job and that is something I would loathe.'

'It's probably early days to anticipate that yet. Has the physiotherapist been able to give you any indication as to whether you'll achieve full fitness?'

'No. After my two weeks here I'm due to see the surgeon who stitched me up back at the hospital. X-rays and a scan will be taken to see how things are healing but even then it could take more time and I'm not the most patient of souls.'

The mood was set and Alan found it easy to continue talking about his feelings, the depth of which he had barely understood until he began to verbalise them. An hour passed swiftly by. It had been like physiotherapy for his soul and he readily booked two more sessions for the following week convinced now that this time at St. Stephen's was proving invaluable.

Chapter 24

The interview room was little more than a box with a pervasive smell of disinfectant which didn't quite succeed in masking the odour of vomit. Danny wanted to cry. He realised he was in deep trouble and sitting here with a solicitor and his mother seemed like the lowest point in his entire fifteen years. Of course he didn't cry. Tears were reserved for those moments when he was alone in his room with the horrors of what he had done keeping him awake night after night. Although he dearly wished it was possible to go back in time, it simply was not and now he must face the consequences. His mother was talking softly to the solicitor, asking questions which she had already asked before, in a voice clearly filled with anxiety. Danny should have been paying attention but as they waited for the detective to join them his mind swirled with thoughts of his own stupidity. Yes, he had known that the stuff Ron had given him was stolen but if he thought of it as 'knocked off' it didn't sound so bad, even rather cool. He hadn't asked questions and gladly accepted the money and expensive software which Harrison had been so generous with. He had never thought of himself as an accomplice and did not even realise that he was being used and in turn using his mother and her weakness in not standing up to him. With hindsight Danny knew he had been a fool, acting tough since his Dad had left home, even to the point of imitating his father's behaviour towards his mother, actions which shamed him now. He hadn't meant it to turn out like this. Mum just seemed to respond to that kind of behaviour and he had taken advantage of it. The stupid thing was that he had always hated the way his father had treated her but within months of him leaving he was no better himself. Now he felt so ashamed, particularly as she was being so supportive and standing by him, which was a complete surprise as well as being totally undeserved.

The door banged behind the two police officers and Danny winced as the chairs scraped on the linoleum floor when they pulled them out. A tape recorder was switched on by the taller of the two men and the other one began to introduce himself as Detective Inspector Aiden Greaves and his partner, Detective Constable Paul Madison. Five solemn expressions created an almost tangible, tense and unfriendly atmosphere in the tiny room but why, wondered Danny, would they be anything other than solemn. DI Greaves had taken the seat directly opposite the table and looked into Danny's eyes with his own steely blue ones.

'Would you like to tell me what it is you wanted to say to us?' His tone was as steely as his eyes. Danny remained silent as instructed and Mr Burdock began to answer the question.

'My client has come here voluntarily and wishes to admit to his part in a recent crime. He is prepared to answer all your questions and will assist your investigation in any way that he can...'

In a similar room in another part of the police station, Ron Harrison was seated at an identical table and had been for over an hour since being brought there again for further questioning. His solicitor was apparently on route so he was accompanied only by a silent PC who seemed bored with his baby sitting duties. So far Harrison had remained silent apart from an occasional 'no comment' which, accompanied by a smug grin, was designed to annoy the officers who were conducting the interview. He had been formally charged the day before with robbery and attempted murder yet maintained the silence in the hope that he would eventually be released, being mistakenly confident that the police could not possibly have any concrete evidence to tie him to the crime. It came as a shock when DC Paul Madison entered the room, sat in the opposite chair and casually asked,

'Do you know Danny Johnson?'

****

Sue had picked her husband up from St Stephens to bring him home for the weekend. It wasn't a long journey so she took Rose knowing how keen he would be to see her. He greeted them both enthusiastically. Although the week had been beneficial to Alan, emotions were still raw for them both and the security of being together and enjoying some degree of normality was what they craved the most. Rose slept throughout the journey, allowing her parents the opportunity to catch up on each other's news, every mundane detail exchanged with enthusiasm. Alan's favourite homemade steak pie was prepared and waiting for him on arrival and the family ate an ordinary meal with such extraordinary pleasure at being together. Even the usual bedtime routine of settling their daughter with a bath, followed by a story, was a delight. The little girl's laughter sounded like the sweetest noise on earth to her Daddy. When Rose was asleep, the couple settled down to watch something undemanding on television, their evening going according to plan until the doorbell rang at seven thirty.

'Who on earth can this be at this time on a Friday night?' Sue was resentful of the interruption even before knowing who their caller was, yet managed a polite smile when opening the door to find a grinning Paul Madison. Inviting him in she hoped his visit would be brief.

'We've got the driver now as well as the shooter!' Paul launched straight into his news, conveying the details of how a fifteen year old youth had been the getaway driver and how he had turned up at the station with his solicitor to confess.

'We had enough on the shooter to make a case, even though he's not talking but the kid's evidence makes it watertight and the CPS are delighted! It seems the lad was coerced to some degree and says he had no idea about the gun which I'm inclined to believe. He genuinely seems shaken up by the gravity of it all and is answering every question we ask him.'

'That's great Paul, thanks for letting us know. With help from the lad it should be fairly straightforward now. Fifteen years old... incredible isn't it? Does he realise he'll go away for this?'

'I think so. His solicitor seems to have laid the facts down and we've given him the speech about not running with the hare and the hounds. The mother's quite a sensible sort. I think they see this as the only way to turn things around and prevent the lad from turning into a career criminal if it's not already too late.'

'Perhaps this could be a chance for instigating restorative justice? I know it's all a bit experimental at the moment but I'd be willing to talk to the youngster at some point. Mention it to the chief will you Paul and we'll see how it goes?'

'Yes, will do. Now, I can see I'm a gooseberry here so I'll not take up any more of your time, enjoy the weekend and I'll keep in touch.'

The following day was Saturday with nothing more important for the Hurst family to do than to enjoy each other's company. Sitting in their garden and enjoying the unusually warm September sunshine, Alan began to talk about the case.

'There must have been only the two of them involved. The lad's solicitor has obviously advised him to be as helpful as possible, hoping the shooter will take the full rap and his client will get off lightly if he acts ignorant.'

'I suppose it's difficult to prove whether he knew about the gun or not, but they should both get locked away forever in my opinion. You have to live with this, the physical and the mental injuries not to mention the knock on effect it's had on all of us. And look at that poor woman in the shop. I should think she'll have nightmares for the rest of her life!' Sue was angry, the tension of the last few weeks rising to the surface. He stroked her hair in a soothing manner.

'I know love, it doesn't seem fair but it goes with the job. The perpetrator appears to get all the attention and a disproportionate sentence while the victims and witnesses have to live with the consequences, often re-living events for years to come, if not forever.'

'Exactly, they might eventually be locked up, at the tax payers expense I might add, but it's no real deterrent, quite a cushy number even, and you... you could have been killed!' Suddenly she burst into tears, angry frustration and fear catching up, as huge sobs wracked her body. Alan held and comforted her while at the same time shielding his wife from Rose who was happily occupied in picking daisies from the lawn. He had witnessed similar outbursts from victims of crimes he had come across in the course of his work, never thinking for one moment that his own family would one day be affected in the same way. When the tears subsided and she was calmer, they sat as close as possible, fingers linked together as Alan turned the conversation to their little daughter.

'Hopefully she'll never remember this time. You've done such a brilliant job. We've got it all Sue.' He looked at his wife with such happiness in his eyes that she couldn't disagree. Rose skipped towards them with her offering of a fist full of daisies, completely oblivious to how close she had come to losing her beloved Daddy.

'It's been difficult but we will get over it. You'll never know how good it feels to have you back here with us now.'

Later that evening the couple made love, slowly and gently, savouring each moment of physical closeness which had been denied them of late. Afterwards, as they lay entwined in each other's arms, Sue, whose mind since the shooting had often dwelt on what would have happened if the trajectory of the bullet had been a few degrees to the right, thought now about Alan's earlier words, echoing in her mind that the worst of it was over and yes, contrary to what she had initially thought, they did have it all!

Chapter 25

Rae Chapman rang her counsellor almost as soon as they were home from France, hoping to make an early appointment. Without going into detail it was obvious to Maggie that things had gone well for the young woman who now expressed a desire to move on to confront her fear of fire. The request prompted Maggie to prepare a cognitive behavioural therapy session over the weekend, with the specific aim of tackling the phobia. Having addressed several of the most common phobias in her career, such as fear of spiders, heights and snakes, she had built up a box file of useful aids which unfortunately did not include anything about fire. The file contained documented information on spiders, snakes, aeroplanes and other such objects of phobias together with illustrations and also her one rather grim trophy, a dead spider enclosed in a sealed glass box. These were used in exposure therapy when clients were introduced to the object of their fear in a safe, controlled environment, with small acceptable doses and the support of the counsellor. It was usually referred to as corrective learning therapy and in most cases brought about a significant change in the client's attitude to whatever it was that they feared. Maggie had gathered some new tools to add to the file, pertinent to Rae's case. These included pictures of candles cut from Christmas cards and magazines, a box of small birthday cake candles, a larger household candle and a box of matches. There were other pictures too which might not be appropriate and may not be used, including images of a house fire and a bush fire, both being tackled and brought under control by fire-fighters. Feeling well prepared after the weekend, Maggie greeted her young client warmly noting the general glow of health and dare she think it, happiness?

'It was so awful at first,' Rae began to relate details of the trip, 'There was an atmosphere from the moment we arrived, so completely unlike anything I've experienced before, as if we were meeting strangers not Mum and Dad! We were all so stiff and polite, pussy footing around the issue, which made me want to turn around and run straight home. Instead I decided to jump right in on the first night and ask them directly about Pattie. Sean was wonderful, in fact he was the one who actually started the ball rolling and initiated the 'big' conversation. At first I thought it had been a mistake to go there at all. Dad tried to answer my questions while Mum seemed as if she was somewhere else entirely and the conversation had nothing at all to do with her. I couldn't believe it! We made some progress that first night and I actually felt sorry for Dad who was so apologetic but there was no way he could turn the clock back. Mum disappeared off to bed, so after going as far as we could with the discussion, we went to bed too. The atmosphere the next day was only a fraction better. Mum didn't even put in an appearance over breakfast and Sean and I decided to go into Rouen for the day to give us all some space. Sorry Maggie, I'm rambling on here aren't I?'

'Not at all, if it helps, please tell me as much or as little as you like.'

Rae went on to recount her mother's suicide attempt and how eventually she had revealed how her own childhood had been lived in the shadow of a dead twin. It was clear to Maggie that the attitude of Rae's parents and the concealing of her own twin sister now made sense to her client. An intense and emotional few days had ended well with many issues resolved and the family now able to resume their previous close relationship. Perhaps the experience would create an even stronger bond than before.

'It's incredible isn't it that Mum had also lost a twin? It explains so much and I'm glad she's seeing someone who can help her as well.' This concern was touching.

'It sounds as if your mother was suffering from some kind of survivor's guilt which probably started when she was very young. Her parents unwittingly fed this, thinking they were only perpetuating the memory of their lost child and completely unaware of the effect it had on the surviving twin. Everyone deals with grief differently. That way of coping probably worked for your grandparents but at the expense of their daughter. And of course at that time very little was known about psychology and thought processes, with such topics certainly not openly discussed. So, you are obviously feeling much better but are you sure you want to go straight into tackling this fear of fire?'

'Absolutely, I feel ready to take on the world now! No, seriously, its well into September and I would love to have all this behind me before the wedding in December which isn't very long. Perhaps if you explained what you have in mind to tackle this issue? I found working with the cards previously so helpful in overcoming all those negative feelings, so I'm hoping for another good result with this stupid phobia.'

'It's not so stupid when you think about it. Most fears are rational, such as a fear of snakes. They can be a very real danger and our fear makes us aware of this and therefore we rightly become wary. Fire too should be respected. It can also kill and cause unlimited damage, so again our fear makes us act in an appropriate way, with caution. So you see it isn't totally irrational, particularly with regard to your history. Even though you can only remember a little about the fire at your home, there are so many more memories stored in your subconscious. I even think it's quite possible that your subconscious mind equates the fire with the separation from Pattie. It seems logical to link the two together. Although at the time you didn't understand they were connected, your brain stores those two traumatic incidents together. Taking all this into account it certainly isn't surprising that you have a fear of naked flames. The therapy I have in mind is a technique called cognitive behavioural therapy, a method of retraining the brain by changing the way you think about and understand fire. We can try exposing you to fire in a controlled way, beginning with the two dimensional, pictures and photographs and then moving on to fire on a very small scale. I have some birthday cake candles and matches but I won't even show them to you until you're ready.'

Rae smiled,

'I feel rather silly when you explain it all!'

'There's no need to feel like that. Perhaps the things you have learned in France have already prepared the way for this to be addressed? Are you sure you feel ready?'

'Yes.' She remained emphatic, so Maggie opened the box file, removed the pictures of candles and placed them in view on the coffee table. Rae looked at the Christmas card images and took a deep breath.

'Do you know, candles on Christmas cards have never bothered me too much? I suppose I've grown up with them being around and somehow don't equate them with fire.'

'That's a good start. Let's just talk about candles for now. When are they a problem if they are okay on Christmas cards?'

'In the flesh, or should I say in the wax? I have visions of a lighted candle toppling over, setting fire to curtains, clothing or something. When we were looking at wedding venues I was quite rude to the event's organiser who was really pushing candles as romantic. They might be to most people but not to me. I'd like to be able to see candles without getting that panicky feeling and becoming upset and angry.'

'That's a very reasonable aim. Tell me, how did you cope as a child when you went to birthday parties and friends had candles on their cakes?'

'Ahh, I was the awkward child who hid in the corner or under the table when the cake came out! I could usually get away with it as everyone was so excited and busy. If I was lucky I didn't even get noticed.'

'How would you feel if I brought a box of those little candles out now?'

'Have you got some in there?' She nodded towards the box file.

'Yes, but they can stay there if you like?'

'No, take them out. I really don't think they are going to worry me that much.'

She was right, the candles were very small and there was no suggestion of lighting them at that time. After talking more about candles and before the hour was over, Rae actually picked them up, holding them with confidence as they spoke. Maggie decided they had made significant progress and it was probably a good point to finish. The photographs of house fires stayed in the box, as did the matches and larger candle, perhaps next time her client would move on to looking at these. Rae left in a buoyant mood having had no adverse reactions to the sight of candles or talking about them. Perhaps her counsellor was right and all the issues so recently resolved in France had strengthened her in some way, preparing for this last assault on the phobia. This thought was certainly encouraging and Rae couldn't wait to see Sean and tell him how well things had gone.

Chapter 26

Leah laughed out loud, her green eyes twinkling with mischief as Alan tried again to grasp the bars and lift himself up by his arms.

'It's okay for you just giving orders, I suffer all the pain!' His complaint was spoken with good humour as he dropped down onto the rubber mat, massaging his shoulder to ease the stiffness.

'You're doing fine really, sorry for laughing but your face was a picture!' The physiotherapist certainly put patients through their paces but with such enthusiasm and a sense of fun that made her a popular member of staff at St. Stephens.

'I know it's painful but the muscles have healed sufficiently to begin stretching them. If you give up now it's possible you'll never gain the same movement in your shoulder as you had previously.'

'I know and I have no intention of giving up. You've certainly chosen the right career though, have you always been a natural bully?'

Leah feigned taking a swipe at her patient but he jumped straight up, grasping the bars again to continue the regime, delighted that he was healing so well and determined to put in the effort to attain the same level of fitness he had before the shooting. He knew that she was as pleased with this progress as he himself and the next attempt to lift his own weight succeeded although most of the strain was on his left arm. It would be some time before he was confident enough to really test the right shoulder, but it was still a good achievement and there was a spontaneous round of applause from Leah and another patient who was working in the gym, to which he took a bow, bestowing them with his best cheesy grin.

This was his third week at St. Stephen's. Initially he had been booked in for only two but when told there was a vacancy for another and the Chief Superintendant signed off his approval, Alan readily accepted the offer, delighted with the progress they had helped him achieve. Sue was content as long as they still had their Wednesday lunchtimes and weekends to look forward to. She had also noticed the improvement in his health and was keen see him back to his former self. It was a fantastic place for a convalescent home with pleasant grounds where he had spent time in the peaceful setting, walking or reading in the autumn sunshine. Alan had benefitted considerably from the facilities, enjoying use of the pool and gym and also grateful for the hours spent with the counsellor. It had not been easy to open up initially but when he did, the benefits were great and it had been suggested that the counselling could continue even after he had left St. Stephens. He did not think this would be necessary but it was always good to know the offer was in the background. Of course, he could talk to Sue and friends and colleagues but he was aware that an incident like this could return to haunt him at a later date. He also knew that the reports from Leah would be crucial when he wished to return to work. Occupational Health would collate all medical details before allowing him to return to duty, a goal which was at the forefront of his mind. He had had enough rest to last him the duration of his career. Alan was anxious to return to the job he loved.

****

To say that the week had been traumatic for Linda Johnson was most certainly an understatement. Her son had been charged for his part in a serious crime and according to their solicitor he would undoubtedly receive a custodial sentence. She had not thought herself a bad mother but with hindsight perhaps there were times when she should have stood up to Fred more, in defence of Danny as well as herself. It had however always been easier to allow Fred to bully them both and perhaps in trying to appease him she had somehow neglected her son. Now they were paying the price but in a weird way Linda felt a sense of relief, not that he was going to prison but that he regretted the crime and his involvement with Ron Harrison. Could this be an opportunity for a new start? She certainly hoped so. Perhaps when it was all over they could move away to another town and begin again where no-one knew them. A strangely peaceful feeling momentarily washed over her only to be replaced once again by those feelings of guilt. What a strange week it had been.

Maggie greeted her warmly despite being in the unusual and rather unpleasant position of knowing about the recent happenings in her client's life before being told. Such knowledge had prompted assumptions which she determinedly suppressed reminding herself that her client's feelings may be totally different to what her own would be in a similar position.

'What kind of week has it been for you Linda?'

'An eventful one for sure. We went to a solicitor and from there to the police station where Danny confessed everything. They have formally arrested him but he's been given bail and has to report to the police every day with a curfew of seven o'clock each evening.' She spoke rapidly, almost tripping over the words, which was understandable since there was no one else for her to share this difficult time with. 'The solicitor says he will almost certainly go to prison, well some kind of young offenders institution anyway, as he intentionally set out to commit a crime even though he didn't know that a gun would be used. He looked so young and sad. I know he's nearly sixteen and a big lad at that but he's still a little boy at heart who's just made a couple of bad decisions and got in with the wrong sort.' Such concern was touching and this boy was fortunate to have a mother who would stand by him.

'The strange thing is that I feel almost pleased that it's happened. Well, not that that poor policeman got shot of course, but that Danny's been found out and is going to be punished for it. Does that sound odd? It's a kind of release, a second chance for him really and I've never felt so close to him for years.'

'It's not odd at all. From what you've told me before, your relationship with your son has been far from easy and it is a difficult age for a boy, thinking he's grown up but still needing support and guidance, which is hard to admit. Perhaps this will be a wakeup call for him and if as you say he is sorry for his actions, having to pay the price for them will hopefully set things straight. At his age, in a young offender's institute there will be a lot of support and even training which could help to set him out on a more responsible path. With your love and support too, things may turn around eventually. As for feeling happy, I can understand that. It's been a huge shock but you did the right thing in persuading him to go to the police which has resulted in the best possible outcome from your endeavours. You are bound to feel a sense of relief that Danny has made the right decision and much of the conflict you have been living with is now at an end. I think you should be proud of yourself for the way you've coped with this whole situation. Has he opened up to you much since the arrest?'

'Well he's never been much of a talker but we have had a few chats. He's frightened about the trial and going away and everything else that may happen but still sees that it was the right thing to do. Fortunately that Harrison man has been remanded in custody. We would both have been terrified if they had let him out on bail. Dan's subdued at home and the curfew is no hardship as he doesn't want to go out, too ashamed and embarrassed I think but it's making for a quieter life. He even sits and watches telly with me now during the evening instead of spending all the time in his room.' She continued to talk about her son and her own feelings of relief that things were working out and probably for the better in the long term. Maggie nodded, understanding her need to talk about all the details and having no-one else to share these thoughts with. But her client needed to think about her own well being and what it was she wanted for her future too. Perhaps in further sessions she could explore her own needs but it was early days and she would probably find the immediate future difficult to cope with. As the hour drew to a close Maggie felt relief that the usual empathy and desire to help Linda was not tainted by her closeness to Alan and she could happily continue this relationship as long as it was considered to be beneficial.

Chapter 27

Alan was home to stay and an excited Sue invited Maggie and Peter round for coffee on Saturday morning, a welcome diversion after an extremely busy week. Initially she had asked them to come for a meal on the evening, an offer which they declined feeling it was too soon and their friends needed time alone and so the coffee date was a compromise. It was reassuring to see Alan after his time at St. Stephen's rather than simply hearing progress reports second hand. His recovery had been quite remarkable considering that it was not yet three months since the shooting and even the doctors were surprised, having anticipated a much slower recovery. He put it down to positive thinking and hard work, his wife called it pig-headedness. Whatever it was it was wonderful to see the three of them so relaxed and happy and the frivolous mood they shared, with ridiculously tall tales of St. Stephens coupled with Sue's witty responses was a tonic for their friends. Peter laughed until there were tears in his eyes, Maggie laughed at him and little Rose ran around them all, giggling and screeching without understanding a thing.

It had been a delightful visit but one which they were not going to prolong and the Lloyds found themselves on their way home by about eleven thirty, in good time for a walk with Ben before lunch. As they pulled into their drive, a small blue Mini was already parked outside with Julie sitting in the driver's seat. They all exited their cars and Maggie went to hug her friend.

'Where are the children?' she asked, as the three usually did everything together.

'With Mum and Dad. Have you got a few minutes Mags?' Julie looked rather sombre.

'Of course, come in and I'll put the kettle on.'

Ben was as usual beating the wall with his tail in welcome, looking hopefully from one to the other.

'Okay boy, I'll take you eh?' Peter realised his wife had other things to attend to now.

'Sorry, I don't mean to drive you out...' Julie protested.

'You're not, he needs a walk and so do I! I'll leave you girls to your chat.'

The women headed to the kitchen where, after making coffee they sat around the kitchen table with the late September sun warming the room and Julie began to reveal the reason for her visit.

'Craig's asked me to marry him.' The words were devoid of emotion and although Maggie's reaction was a desire to jump up and down and hug her friend, it was obvious that she didn't share the excitement.

'Isn't this cause for celebration? I can't say it's a surprise, it was obvious when I met him that he's crazy about you.'

Julie sighed,

'Oh Maggie, if only it was that simple.'

'And why isn't it?'

'You know why, surely?'

'No, I don't think I do.' She wasn't making things easy for her friend but intuition suggested that the only problems Julie had were a lack of self confidence and a fear of trusting another man after such a horrendous experience in her first marriage. 'Do you love him?'

'I think so, yes, I'm pretty sure I do.'

'Then what's the problem? Is it Jim?'

'I suppose so. Marriage is such a huge commitment, for Craig as well as me. He'd be taking on Simon and Chloe too, that's extra pressure for him.'

'But he knows that surely? When we met him he appeared to be very fond of the children and must realise you come as a package.'

'Yes, he really does seems to enjoy being with them and they love him too.'

'So, don't you think you should be asking yourself about your own feelings and trusting him to make his own desicion? If he has asked you to marry him it must be because he loves you and wants to spend the rest of his life with you. Do you feel that way about him?'

'Yes, but I'm afraid he'll get bored with me after a while, my track record isn't very good, perhaps I'm not cut out to be married?'

'That's absolute nonsense. You were a good and faithful wife to Jim in spite of the way he treated you. It was him that wasn't cut out to be married. You are a born homemaker if ever I met one and a brilliant mother.' Maggie's words were firm but spoken gently as she continued in the same vein, 'You can't judge marriage by your one bad experience. Take this chance of happiness for yourself and Simon and Chloe, I think in your heart you want to, don't you?'

Julie sipped her coffee, thoughtfully considering her friend's words.

'Yes I do, but I'm so afraid it will all go wrong...'

'There are never any guarantees with the future. Why not try to imagine how you would feel if you turned him down and never saw him again?'

'Oh Maggie, that would be awful! We see each other every day now and the children love him, they would be devastated too.'

'Well, it's your choice but I'm sure Craig will be happy to wait a while and not rush things.'

'I don't know about that. He was so excited when he asked me and just expected me to say yes and we would all live happily ever after. He went very quiet when I hesitated and asked if I could have time to think about it.'

'And when was this?'

'Yesterday, last night after the children had gone to bed. I didn't know what to say as there were so many thoughts swimming around my head. He must have been so disappointed and did look as if I'd slapped him in the face! Do you think I've blown it?'

'And how would you feel if you had?'

'I couldn't bear it! Oh Mags, do you think he'll still have me?'

Her reply was to fetch the telephone and a tissue for her friend's damp face.

'There's no time like the present.' She handed her the phone and then moved into the lounge to allow some privacy, turning on the radio to make sure that she would not overhear the conversation. After five very long minutes, a beaming Julie came to find her.

'I think I've just got engaged!' she grinned. Now Maggie could hug her and they both laughed together as she repeated some of the conversation.

'He thought I didn't love him enough. I've been really stupid haven't I?'

As Maggie reassured her that it was natural for someone who had been through such a bad experience to be cautious, Peter arrived home with Ben. He was told the good news and after more hugs and laughter, Julie left to go and meet her husband to be.

'He wants to see me straight away, then we're going to Mum and Dad's to tell them and the children!'

'Well, what a great day.' Maggie sighed when they were alone, 'Alan home and well on the way to full fitness and Julie getting married, she deserves some happiness and I couldn't be more pleased! I wonder when the wedding will be?'

****

The box file was on the coffee table, the contents still inside, as Rae entered the room. After an initial enquiry as to how the week had been and if there were any thoughts on their last meeting, Rae nodded at the box to which her eyes kept returning to during the conversation.

'Have you got anything different in there from last week for me to worry about?' She asked.

'No, it's exactly the same, pictures, birthday candles, a larger candle and a box of matches. And there are also the two pictures of actual fires, a house fire and a bush fire. Would you like to see any of them?'

'You can take the pictures of the candles and the birthday candles out.' She nodded and Maggie did as asked placing the items on the coffee table between them. Rae lifted the pictures up, studying them again and smiled,

'No problem!'
She then took the tiny candles from their box and held them in her palm.

'I've had no dreams about fire or candles at all and knowing what else you have in there has prepared me I suppose, so can I see the other pictures now?'

'Of course.' The counsellor slowly lifted the picture of the bush fire and placed it on the table, turning it so it was fully visible and then paused for a moment before bringing out the image of a house fire and placing it beside the first. There was a barely perceptible gasp from Rae as she gazed at the second picture, otherwise her face was solemn and unreadable. Maggie picked up on some slight tension from her body language but generally her reactions were very controlled.

'What are you thinking when you look at these?' She asked quietly. The answer took a few moments to consider.

'I was looking for Pattie, but common sense tells me that this isn't our house fire. My next thought and concern was if anyone was inside.'

Maggie nodded, waiting as her client continued to stare. Obviously the bush fire did not have the same effect and eventually Rae touched the picture, tentatively, as if she might be scorched from it. Drawing back her hand quickly, she averted her eyes. Her counsellor moved to put the images away.

'No, leave them there, I'm okay.' She reached out to stop Maggie. 'I'm waiting for a reaction which isn't happening.' A smile began to form as she spoke. 'I expected something, although I don't know what, and it isn't there. Does that sound silly?'

'Not at all, I think you've been well prepared for this, both in our previous sessions and by what happened in France. If we had begun with this therapy before you had faced your other issues, you would probably have had a very different reaction. You are ready now and doing brilliantly but we still need to go slowly, at your own pace. You told me what you were thinking, can you also tell me how you are feeling?'

'Surprisingly fine. Seeing the house fire was a bit of a shock and I felt a flutter or two in my chest but after a really good look I can be quite objective. As I said, I know it isn't our house and from what I can see there's no-one trapped inside or anything awful like that. I feel as if things are in proportion so perhaps you could get the matches and the other candle out now?'

'Are you sure, we could leave that for another time?'

Rae glanced at her watch, noting that they were only thirty minutes into their allotted hour.

'Yes, I'm sure, we have the time and honestly, I'm feeling fine.'

Taking out the candle and placing it unlit on the table, Maggie moved to the desk to fetch a saucer. Sitting back down, the matches were brought out next and very slowly she struck one and lit the white candle, carefully allowing a few drops of molten wax to drip onto the saucer before anchoring the candle to it. Rae sat back in the chair, mesmerized but not afraid. Maggie too sat back and they watched in silence as the candle burned in front of them. It was controlled, it was safe and Maggie was watching her client for the slightest adverse reaction of which there was none.

'You can blow it out if you want to, any time.' The invitation was given but not accepted and Rae eventually took her eyes off the flame to focus on her counsellor and smiled. She would never have believed it possible to sit so close to a naked flame without feeling a constricting of her heart and tightness of chest which would have made her want to bolt.

'When we were in Rouen...' She wanted to share one more thing with Maggie, 'We visited a tiny museum which was dedicated to Joan of Arc. There were several tableaux depicting stages of her life, the very last one being a reconstruction of the fire in which she died. A model of the young Joan was tied to a stake and the fire was represented by coloured cellophane with a hidden fan giving the appearance of movement and burning flames leaping about. I didn't have any kind of panic attack as it was so obviously unreal but I was moved by the look on the girl's face. She was serene, unafraid of her fate with her face tilted towards Heaven, ready to meet her maker. Looking at the tableau made me think of Pattie. Perhaps she's peaceful now, with God maybe and I'd like to think that one day I'll see her... I'll be with my Pattie again.'

As Rae spoke, Maggie could visualise the poignant scene and long after her client had left, the image remained in her mind.

Chapter 28

It was the day of the plea hearing at York Crown Court, a day which Danny had been dreading and wishing it could be over and done with. It would be the first time he had seen Ron Harrison since the actual robbery and shooting, a prospect not to be relished. Mr Burdock, the solicitor had coached him on what to say and even how to say it. He had stressed to both his client and Linda that the hearing was a chance to make an impression. It was important that Dan should appear remorseful, even ashamed of his actions and vital that his mother should also be visible in her support of the boy. How on earth he would manage to show regret was something of a puzzle as the only word he would be required to speak was 'guilty'. Having been fifteen years old when the crime was committed, he was somewhat worried that the fact that he had now reached the age of sixteen would affect the sentence and more particularly, where it would be served. The solicitor was able to reassure him that because the crime happened when he was fifteen, he would still be dealt with accordingly and his incarceration would certainly be in a young offender's institute. This knowledge came as a huge relief. Danny's main concern was that he may end up in a prison with Harrison, a thought which gave him nightmares, woke him up in a cold sweat and to his acute embarrassment brought tears to his eyes. Linda had been incredibly supportive for which her son would always be grateful. Their relationship had changed over the last few weeks becoming a much closer one, out of need perhaps but a more satisfactory relationship for them both. Coming downstairs for breakfast, Dan was touched by the sight of his Mum polishing his shoes.

'I was going to do that, there's plenty of time before we need to set off,' he said.

'Oh, its okay, I need to keep busy son. You look very smart, Mr Burdock will be pleased.'

'Thanks Mum, for everything I mean, not just the shoes. I know I've been a pain to live with but I'm going to change, honestly!' He even managed a thin smile which touched his mother's heart more than he would ever know.

'You don't have to keep apologising you know. I believe you and I'm sorry too. We both made mistakes but when this is all over, things are going to be different, we can start again, build a new life. I love you Danny... so get some breakfast into yourself before you have me blubbing!'

'The condemned man's last breakfast!' he joked and amazingly they laughed together.

Ron Harrison glared at his co-defendant from narrowed eyes, a look designed to intimidate but the boy refused to make eye contact just as the solicitor had advised. Harrison was hand-cuffed to an officer and sitting opposite Dan who was now also under the watchful eye of a prison officer. The time seemed to drag until at last they got the nod to enter the courtroom and were ushered up a short flight of stairs into a wooden box with Perspex on the top half creating a barrier between the accused and the rest of the court. Fortunately, as Mr Burdock had said, there were not too many people present. His solicitor acknowledged him with a nod and Danny moved to stand where the prison officer steered him. It was comforting to be able to see his mother who smiled at her only child, a knot causing her stomach to constrict and ache but a gritty tenacity helping her to swallow back the tears. The warmth from Harrison's body and the smell of sweat pervaded Danny's space but he resolutely stared forward determined not to look at the older man. Proceedings went almost exactly as Mr Burdock had predicted and when asked to plead Dan quietly and respectfully said 'guilty' hanging his head with genuine shame. Ron Harrison tutted loudly earning a yank back a step from his escort. It was all mercifully short although certainly not sweet. Dan was oblivious to what was said, he tried to concentrate but was awed by the severity of the occasion and had to bite hard on his tongue to stem the flow of tears. Within an hour of arriving at the court, mother, son and solicitor were leaving, the latter reciting instructions and information as to the next court appearance when Danny's fate would be decided. The young man took nothing in. He was in a trance and allowed himself to be taken home in a taxi by his mother who fussed over him with such love and concern that he eventually gave way to the tears.

****

'I think it's too soon!' Sue knew she was fighting a losing battle. Alan was single minded in his determination to return to work as soon as possible.

'Oh come on love, I'm feeling almost completely well again. The physio thinks it's time and the doctor's have given the okay. I'll be on light duties at first and a phased return, so you'll still have me hanging around here for much of the time.' He was keen to make an appointment to see someone in the Occupational Health department at work to discuss returning to work. They were always cautious especially after an officer had been injured in the course of duty and he knew he would initially be assigned to desk duties. But time dragged, he was bored and longed to be useful again.

'Well it had better be phased over a long time and only desk duties at that.' Sue was understandably afraid for his safety but knew how important this was to him. It was a good thing she wasn't the jealous sort and had long since accepted that policing was more than just a job to her husband. He cupped her face in his hands, kissing her gently.

'Thanks love, you have to let me go sometime.' He laughed, she was like an over protective mother but he wouldn't have it any other way. Leaving the house looking happier than he had for a while, Alan headed for Fenbridge police station to pay a visit to his colleagues and make an appointment with Occupational Health.

'Hey, look what the cat dragged in!' DI Aiden Greaves shouted out seeing their visitor approaching.

'And why aren't you out catching the bad guys?' Alan replied.

'It's all under control, the bad ones are locked up downstairs and the really bad ones left the country when they heard you were back on your feet!' Aiden slapped his friend on the back and shook his hand.

'Is this purely a social call or are you coming back to pull your weight at last?'

'Bit of both I hope. I feel ready to get back into work now but I know I'll have to get the okay from the powers that be.'

'Rather you than me, but seriously we have missed you and I for one will be pleased to have you back. Great day to visit too mate, the Chief Superintendent's around somewhere that's why there's only a few of us in the office.'

Alan rolled his eyes although he had to admit that Jack Swanson had been really good with him throughout his recovery. Bumping into him would not be a problem.

Aiden went on to update his colleague on the plea hearing for Harrison and the lad who had driven for him.

'The youngster pleaded guilty as expected but Harrison's sticking to his story, probably hoping the lad will be too scared to testify against him.'

'Talk of the devil!' Aiden whispered, nodding towards the doorway where the Chief Superintendent was just coming in.

'DS Hurst, good to see you!' Jack Swanson made his way over and shook his hand vigorously.

'Thank you sir, I've popped in to see about an appointment with Occupational Health to discuss returning to work.'

'You're sure it's not too soon?' The concern was genuine.

'Quite sure; a phased return would be no problem at the moment and we can take it from there. Actually, there is something I wanted to have a word about, have you got a minute sir?'

The Chief Superintendent led the way to a screened off corner, hardly private but it would suffice with so few in the station.

'What can I do for you Alan?'

'Well, it's about the lad who was the driver when I was shot. He's just fifteen or sixteen I believe and DI Greaves has been keeping me up to speed on the case. I believe the lad's quite remorseful for his part in it all and I know they all say they didn't know a gun was involved but Aiden seems to believe him. What I'm trying to say is that I think he could be an ideal candidate for restorative justice, what do you think sir?'

Swanson rubbed his chin as he thought for a few moments.

'Yes, Paul mentioned that you'd raised the subject. I presume you're thinking of yourself doing this and not the woman from the shop? I don't think she's up to a face to face with the lad even if he was only the driver.'

'That's right sir, I'd be happy to meet with him. I know it's still a fairly new approach but if he does go to a young offenders' institute it might be a good case on which to trial the scheme. With the victim being a police officer too, it makes sense to set up a meeting. It's something we could use to gauge the effectiveness of the new restorative justice scheme.'

'You've obviously had too much time on your hands to think Alan.' Jack smiled at his younger colleague, 'But perhaps you might have something here, leave it with me to mull over and I'll let you know. It's early days yet.'

Thanking the Chief Superintendent, he then disappeared upstairs to make the appointment with Occupational Health. Jack Swanson may well agree to an attempt to engage the perpetrator with a view to showing him the consequences of his actions, but it would certainly be a more difficult task to persuade Sue.

Chapter 29

The lounge looked amazing. True, the furniture was dated but a few brightly coloured throws and cushions made all the difference. Rae and Sean had stripped off the old wallpaper, painted three of the walls and chosen an extravagant but very elegant paper for the fourth. With fresh paint brightening up the woodwork the whole room seemed larger and brighter than before. A new carpet and modern lighting added the finishing touches. In contrast, the kitchen was a mess, albeit a clean mess. The builders had ripped out the existing units completely then knocked through into the obsolete pantry area so the space appeared much more open and airy. It was now freshly plastered and ready to accept the new, modern units. That was as much as the couple had achieved, not a bad effort considering they both worked full time. With only Rae living in the house it was manageable, at least until the next couple of pay cheques gave them the means to complete the task. They were both delighted with the progress so far and with still nearly three months to the wedding they hoped to have a new kitchen installed and operational by then. Until that time, Rae was becoming imaginatively adept at creating simple meals with a microwave and an electric kettle. The last push to complete the lounge was motivated by the imminent arrival of Barbara and David from France. They would not be staying with their daughter mainly due to the lack of a kitchen and an upstairs which was best not mentioned too often and would be in a nearby hotel, close enough to see their daughter and her grandmother daily. Phone conversations had been long and frequent of late but Rae longed to see them in person, anxious to see for herself how her mother was and to ensure that their new close relationship was still viable and not something they would lose sight of again. There was also the excitement of the wedding plans. This would be her parent's last visit until December when they would arrive during the week prior to the big event.

'You've worked miracles!' Barbara Chapman enthused as they toured their daughter's home. 'I would never have known it was the same house that Edith lived in for all those years.'

Rae beamed, enjoying the compliments though knowing they were a little biased. It was wonderful to have both parents here in her home. She had known from the minute they stepped out of their car that things were still good between them. Her mother looked so well, tanned and with a little more weight than the last time they had seen her. Previously she had appeared gaunt and drawn but a little more flesh on her bones suited her and conveyed a much healthier impression. The aura of tension was no longer evident either, enabling them all to revert to former happy times and enjoy each other's company. Barbara and David had settled in at their hotel and paid a brief visit to Edith before seeing their daughter, after which they were all meeting for dinner that evening. A grand family get together which Rae anticipated with girlish delight. For the moment, coffee and bought in biscuits would suffice as they chatted eagerly, catching up on each other's news.

'Are you still seeing anyone Mum, you know, medically I mean?'

'The psychiatrist? Yes, I am but probably not for much longer. I do find it helps to talk things over with someone without boring your poor Dad all the time. How about you, do you still see that counsellor you told me about?'

'Maggie, yes. Like you I probably won't need to keep going much longer but we've been working on my fear of fire lately and with more than a little success I think.'

'That's great, how about the nightmares, do you still have any?'

'Not for ages now, it's wonderful to be able to go to bed not expecting to be plunged into a place I don't want to go. The counselling has really helped and I feel better than I have in a long time.'

The hotel was excellent and the food unbelievable. It was 'The Bridge', the venue for their wedding and chosen for the opportunity to show Rae's parents the place and to sample the food. David insisted that it was his treat and Sean was somewhat relieved when his father-in-law-to-be would not allow him to share the bill. Conversation flowed freely and the Chapman family were relaxed and happy. Edith, a little tipsy after indulging in one too many glasses of sherry, smiled throughout the whole evening delighting in the company of those she loved the most in the world. After desert David filled everyone's glass and began to propose a toast.

'To my beautiful daughter Rae and her fiancé Sean. May they have a long and happy marriage ahead of them and be blessed with everything they need.' Rae liked the word 'need' instead of 'want' which was her wish too. She blushed slightly before asking if she also could propose a toast. Given permission by smiles and nods, she raised her glass and said,

'A toast to my wonderful family, thank you for everything! And of course to Sean, my soul mate. But also...a toast to Pattie and Grace...always with us.' Words which only a short while ago would have brought such pain were now welcomed as perfectly natural. They raised their glasses and drank the toast with genuine warmth and pleasure at the memories which not so long ago had been strictly taboo.

****

Danny had again been briefed by his solicitor as to what to expect and the fact that it was his second visit to the court in as many weeks had taken some of the fear and mystery out of the situation although his stomach still churned and his hands trembled. Another plus for the young man was the fact that Ron Harrison would not be appearing this time. His case would be heard at a later date due to his insistence of innocence. Mr Burdock would be doing most of the talking and had discussed what he would be saying with Danny to ensure that his words would be an accurate reflection of his client's thoughts. The sentence was expected be anywhere between two and four years or even something outside those boundaries depending on how the judge viewed the misdemeanour. Once again the court was relatively quiet with little interest shown by the press. The solicitor explained that most of the media attention would be on Harrison's trial and Danny was thankfully thought to be only a minor player. It would not be easy giving evidence against Harrison but he was determined to do so. It would be a relief when it was eventually all over and he perceived this as the last difficult hurdle before serving his time and putting the whole disastrous episode behind him. Dan had learned his lesson and would never again do anything so stupid, owing that much to his mother as well as himself. As the judge entered the courtroom, Danny stood beside his solicitor. Proceedings were as predicted and before the sentence was given, Mr Burdock spoke on his client's behalf, stressing the troubled background which had affected the boy and slipping in the fact that he had never been in trouble before. He moved on swiftly to an apology on his client's behalf, eloquently describing the remorse and regret Danny felt at the injuries and distress caused to the victims. Linda sat close by, anxiously awaiting the verdict on her only child's future. Wringing her hands in her lap and absorbing every word as she scrutinised the face of the judge trying to gauge his reactions and read his mind, which was of course impossible.

'Two years and six months, with six months commuted due to the defendant's confession and co-operation.'

The words, although expected, hit hard at both Danny and his mother. They exchanged a look, both faces filled with apprehension, sadness and a fear of the unknown. Just as their relationship was blossoming, they were to be torn apart. Linda attempted to smile at her distraught son, silently mouthing the words, 'I love you' as he was taken from the courtroom. Two years! It seemed an eternity even though Danny knew the sentence could have been much longer. He comforted himself with the fact that, with good behaviour, he could reduce this time by a third which was a far more palatable prospect. Already the days, weeks and months rolled out in his imagination as something to be endured, hours which would crawl at a snail's pace, taking a huge chunk out of his teenage years. Danny had come to accept that he deserved this punishment which he would take without complaint believing that only then could his life begin again.

Sitting in the public area of the court, Sue had listened to every word spoken on behalf of the boy who had conspired in the crime which almost killed her husband. Picking out his mother was easy. There were so few people in attendance and the expression on her face was of such anxiety and concern that even before she turned to her son, Sue knew her identity. She had gone to the hearing knowing it would be over in a matter of minutes but compelled by a desire to see the face of the youth who had helped to cause her such pain and was completely thrown by the remorse and regret apparent in that face. Having expected to feel something akin to hatred, her actual feeling of unexpected compassion for the boy and his mother came as a complete surprise. Whether it was the eloquence of the solicitor who had done a convincing job, or if the contrite appearance of the boy was genuine, she could not tell but found herself simply saddened that such a child could become involved in a crime of any sort, let alone one which involved a firearm. The solicitor had spoken of the boy's previous good character and some of the problems he had faced in his short life, words she had often read in newspapers and scoffed at. But there, in that court of law and justice, she saw a different side and silently left with much to contemplate.

Chapter 30

Linda had not seen her counsellor for two weeks mainly due to attending court and the arduous task of travelling to visit Danny in the Young Offenders Institute where he had been taken after sentencing. Maggie had learned of the sentence from Sue and a column inch or two which had been reported in the local newspaper. It appeared that the judge had been fairly lenient.

'How have you been since we last met?' Maggie asked.

'I honestly don't know how to answer that. If you ask me one minute it will probably be a different answer than ten minutes later. I've been really busy but when I stop I feel so low.'

'There have been so many things going on in your life lately.'

'Yes, the pressure is easing off now and in some ways Danny is settling in and I'm learning not to worry about him too much.'

'Ah, but I think it's in a mother's job description to worry about her child.' The counsellor smiled gently and her client responded in the same manner.

'Do you want to talk about the hearing?'

'I think that would help. It's been on my mind continually. It was short, not much longer than the plea hearing and Dan's solicitor did a really good job of expressing his feelings. I was grateful for that. The judge still gave him two and a half years but with six months off for pleading guilty and if he keeps clear of trouble, Mr Burdock says he could reduce that by a third as well. It was hard seeing them take him away. He looked like a little boy again and he is really so sorry!' Pausing to compose herself for a few moments, she continued.

'I was allowed to visit him the third day that he was there and again a week later, which was yesterday. It's such a long journey on the bus, but I only have to change once. Anyway, on the first visit, Danny was really down. I should have expected that as it was all so new and confusing. He has a support worker assigned to him, a nice chap called Graham who had a few words with me before I left. It's not really what I expected prison to be like, well I know it's not really prison but you know what I mean.'

Maggie nodded encouragingly.

'Graham said that he could probably take his GCSE's while he's there. He missed quite a bit of school over the last couple of years but there are teachers who go in daily and because of his age he'll get tuition and maybe take the exams next year. The second visit was much more positive. Dan had begun some lessons and appears to enjoy them, particularly technology studies. He always loved the computer and his games and things. There's only a dozen or so in the class and I suppose there are no distractions and no opportunity of bunking off is there? One of my worries had been that he might get in with a bad crowd and get into trouble, but so far he's made a couple of friends who are about his own age and seem fairly okay. He shares a room with one of them and told me it's quite a nice room with a desk for studying and bunk beds. The supervision seems good too which has relieved some of my worries and he sees his support worker a couple of times a week. On the whole I feel quite encouraged. If he could settle down to study and get some qualifications and skills, he could have a future to look forward to when he comes out.'

'And what about you Linda, how have you been coping on your own at home?'

'It's quiet that's for sure and I miss having him around, particularly as we had become so much closer of late and were having real conversations, you know? But I keep busy. I'm working any extra hours I can get which fills the time in and gives me the chance to save up a bit so when Dan does come out we can move away somewhere where no one knows us. There's not much to tie us here so I'm planning a fresh start for us both.'

'How have you been sleeping, any better?'

'Strangely yes, I know I just wanted medication when I first came to see you but I'm so glad not to have gone down that route now. Sleep's perhaps a little better because I'm so exhausted at night and in a better routine now and it's been such a help having you to talk to. Before I felt so alone but being able to tell you anything and everything has been great and I'll probably have more conversation with Dan during weekly visits than we ever did before at home! The more I think about it the more I am sure that we can really turn things around. Yes, he did a terrible thing and I almost wish I could apologise to that poor policeman and his family, but that's not possible and it's great that he's recovered all right.'

Linda appeared to be making good progress and may not need the counselling services too much longer. She was now able to accept the present, making the most of it within her limitations and means but more importantly, planning for the future. The distressing situation with her son had somehow made her stronger, bringing the pair closer together which was a positive outcome all round. It had been a strange case for Maggie who had an insight from both sides, although of course she would be the only one to ever know that fact. Sue had confided about her visit to the court and it was a relief to see that her friend could view things from a different perspective now and even had a degree of sympathy for the boy and his mother. Perhaps being a mother herself had softened some of her edges, allowing a glimpse of those things which were not always simply black or white and accepting that people were often victims of circumstance. Whatever the reason, she too seemed to have moved on and her friend couldn't be more pleased.

****

Danny had been in Boulden Young Offender's institute for two months. In a surreal kind of way it now seemed like home, not that he wouldn't be glad when eventually he was released as the time often dragged. Keeping busy helped, with studying and using the gym and he had made a couple of friends too. They were both in for drug related offences and appeared to be benefitting from the rehabilitation programme they attended as a condition of their sentence. Neither were of bad character but had simply gotten in with the wrong crowd, something he could identify with, often wishing his path had never crossed that of Ron Harrison's. Testifying against Harrison had been the hardest thing he had ever had to do. Ron's solicitor was relentless in his questioning, obviously trying to confuse Dan, who, as advised, stuck only to the facts, knowing that answering each question truthfully was the way forward to help put Harrison behind bars and regain a degree of badly needed self-respect. But another ordeal was looming now. His support worker, Graham had asked him about participating in a restorative justice session which entailed meeting with the victim of the shooting, a scheme designed as a means of getting prisoners to understand the impact their actions had on the victim. It wasn't compulsory but Graham strongly recommended that he should participate as it would be taken into consideration when he was nearing a release date. In itself that was only a minor incentive. Dan had often thought about the policeman who had been shot and although he was not the one who pulled the trigger, he had accepted culpability for his part in the crime. The policeman would be coming to Boulden the next day and Danny would be excused algebra to attend the restorative justice session. Algebra would be preferable but he had agreed, a little reluctantly perhaps, to participate in the scheme.

Alan had been back at work for the past six weeks, initially for only three days a week and strictly on desk duties with the hours to be increased gradually over the next month. In himself he was feeling good, his shoulder generally behaved itself and there was very little pain. It only seemed to bother him if he attempted too much lifting in the garden, something he only dared to do when Sue was not around to see. The whole incident had been a salutary lesson in reminding him of his mortality and the frailty of the human body. As a comparatively young and active man, he had never previously given much thought to health and strength, taking it as given. Now he was much more aware of his good fortune and also the fact that he was not invincible. He even found himself sounding like his grandmother. Had he really said that his shoulder played up in damp weather? The Chief Super had been most encouraging about the idea to meet with Danny Johnson and that Monday morning found Alan making the forty-five minute drive to Boulden instead of the usual short trip to Fenbridge police station. Even Sue had not put up the expected resistance and his mood was positive as he anticipated meeting with the youngster.

The interview room was bright and airy, far superior to the box rooms used for such purposes at the police station and Alan was offered coffee on arrival, decent coffee at that. The boy's support worker was to be present at the meeting together with a prison liaison officer, both men already waiting and eager to have a few words before Danny was brought in.

'How are you DS Hurst?' Graham opened the dialogue.

'Much better now thanks.'

Introductions were made and the liaison officer, David Banks, outlined how they expected the meeting to proceed.

'Johnson will be here in about ten minutes. Obviously, because of the lad's age, we'll want to keep things as simple as we can. He knows he's meeting you and will be learning something of the wider implications this incident has had on you and your family. Graham here tells me he's a bright lad and so far has been no trouble at all and will hopefully benefit from this meeting.'

'Yes,' Graham chipped in, 'He's expressed remorse to me on more than one occasion. We certainly won't need to be heavy handed in any way.'

'I have no intention of being heavy handed.' Alan responded.

'No, of course not, I'm sorry I phrased that badly. I've only ever sat in on one other RJ session where the victim ended up becoming quite angry and we had to cut it short. Naturally with you being a police officer, that's not going to be an issue. No offence intended.'

'None taken, don't worry. It was me who suggested this case as appropriate for RJ. I don't hold any grudges or harbour any thoughts of making him suffer and simply thought that due to his age and co-operation so far, he seemed to be an ideal candidate.'

'I'll be making a report afterwards and would certainly appreciate feedback from both of you and eventually from Johnson in due course, is that okay?' Dave asked.

Both men nodded and Graham left the room to see if Danny had arrived.

For his height and large frame Johnson appeared to have a very boyish face but then he was only sixteen, awash with adolescent hormones, pimples and by the expression on his face, terrified of meeting this man who had been shot in his bungled effort to break the law. In an attempt to put him at ease, Alan stood and offered his hand as the boy came into the room. Dan responded with a limp effort of a handshake before sitting beside Graham, the only familiar figure in the room. David Banks seemed to be the self appointed chair of the meeting and began by reminding the boy why they were there.

'DS Hurst has very kindly offered to meet with us today to explain the wider impact of your actions. Graham is here for your support but there's no reason for you to feel in any way intimidated. I'm sure if there is anything you don't understand, between us we'll be happy to try and explain, so I'm going to hand over to DS Hurst but is there anything you would like to say first?'

'I'm sorry DS Hurst, really I am. I didn't know Ron had a gun...honestly!'

'I believe you and that's why we are all here today. We are certainly of the opinion that you are not a bad person and hopefully through our little chat you'll have a better understanding of the implications of wrong doing and make a determined effort to live a law abiding life when you get out.' As he talked, the boy nodded his head, keen to make a good impression. Alan continued,

'Have you ever broken an arm or a leg Dan?' he asked. The nods changed to a negative shake of his head.

'Well I did when I was about your age, my arm, playing rugby. It was excruciating and I could have burst into tears except that I was on a rugger field with all my mates watching! Anyway, being shot is ten, maybe twenty times worse. All I remember was a searing white hot pain then nothing. The next thing I remember was waking up in hospital. Perhaps I was fortunate in blacking out. I do know that the poor lady who was working in the post office that day was scared out of her wits. The gun had been pointed at her face and she was ordered to hand over money from the till. She saw me being shot and bleeding all over her nice clean floor and thought I was dead and that was going to be her fate too. The last I heard about her was that she was unable to return to work and now lives a very reclusive life, dependent on medication for her nerves. When I woke up the pain was much worse than a broken bone and my fear was that I would never be able to use my right arm again. Medication helped to ease the pain and the regime of the physiotherapists coupled with some very hard work eventually sorted my shoulder and arm out. I spent several weeks in hospital, during which time I suffered a collapsed lung and thought I was dying. Then there was a three week stay in a convalescent home. The shoulder is still not quite as good as new but getting there. And then there's my family. I have a wife and a baby daughter. They too have gone through hell, firstly thinking that I would die and then worrying about my long term recovery. Admittedly the baby isn't yet old enough to understand all the implications but she has felt the effects having been passed around to different people to care for her so my wife could be with me. She also knew that Daddy wasn't around to play as usual but did not understand why. I could continue Danny. There are my parents, I'm sure you know how they can worry, friends and colleagues, the ripples spread widely. Being a policeman I could also go on about the cost of investigations, the criminal justice system and of keeping you in here, but I'll leave it at that, I'm sure you get the picture.' Alan paused, searching Danny's face for a reaction and noting how hard the boy was struggling to fight back the tears. Hoping he hadn't gone too far and not intending to heap unbearable guilt on the boy, he tried a different tactic.

'You're an intelligent lad Danny and I can see that you feel bad about what I've told you but that isn't my purpose in doing this. What I really want to happen is for you to make a conscious decision never to engage in criminal activity again. I see so many lads of your age starting out on a life of crime and thinking it makes them big or smart. It doesn't. It makes them a drain on society and a menace to those around them. That's not what I want for you. If you are really sorry then the best way you can prove it is to turn your life around and be an asset to your family and community. There's not much more I wanted to say but I'm happy to answer any questions you might have.'

Danny swallowed hard.

'I really am sorry and have already decided to change. My Mum says we're going to move away when I get out and start a new life where no one knows us. I admit to being scared by all this and I have certainly learned my lesson.'

'That's great and I'm pleased to hear you've got plans. It's good that your Mum is supporting you too!'

'He's knuckling down to studying while he's here and doing quite well according to the teachers.' Graham spoke up on the lad's behalf. Alan smiled, genuinely pleased and only wishing that Danny's reaction could be echoed by the many other youngsters who so easily fell into criminal activities, but unfortunately it was not.

Eventually Dan was led away and after a few minutes discussing the value of the meeting, Alan left to go home satisfied that, in his opinion this attempt at restorative justice had been an unqualified success.

Epilogue

It was over a year since Lydia Armstrong's death. Another winter had passed and another spring and summer were once again fading into memory. The invitation to the opening of Armstrong House had come as a surprise to Maggie but a delightful one for herself and Peter. It was inscribed on the reverse of the card with a few personal words from Elizabeth, encouraging her to accept and saying how thrilled the family would be if they could attend. Fortunately Peter asked few questions where his wife's work was concerned and showed only mild curiosity as to how she came to know such an influential family. Shrugging it off as all in a day's work, they gracefully accepted the invitation in the same manner it had been offered.

Turning into the gravelled drive evoked that familiar feeling of entering another world but it was Peter's turn to gasp in awe of the scene before them. Apart from the installation of a long, wide ramp to provide easy access to the main entrance, the house had changed very little from the outside. A few new potted shrubs stood like sentinels along the ramp and someone had tied yellow ribbons to them, the ends of which fluttered in the cool autumn breeze, giving a celebratory feel to the old house. The doors stood wide open, framing the smiling staff who were poised to greet the visitors and usher them into the drawing room which Maggie remembered so well.

Naturally the proportions of the room were the same, as were the French windows at the far end, dressed now with rather modern blinds which strangely fitted the room well adding a splash of contemporary colour which was more appropriate for its new occupants. Lydia's writing desk had been moved, tucked away into a corner now, presumably more for decorative use than any functional purpose but Maggie was comforted to see it. Somehow it symbolized Lady Armstrong's presence in the room that she had loved the most. Modern, comfortable seating was positioned around walls, pushed back to accommodate the high backed chairs arranged in the body of the area for the use of guests at what the invitation described as 'a short dedication and opening ceremony.' Choosing seats on the end of an aisle, close to the back, the Lloyds settled into the almost full room with only a few minutes to spare before proceedings began.

Elizabeth and Patrick, pushing his brother's chair, made their way to the front of the gathering closely followed by two men and a lady whom Maggie did not recognise. As they turned to face the guests the identity of one of the men became apparent due to the Mayoral chain of office around his neck. The smartly dressed lady beside him was presumably the Mayoress and the third man was only noticeable due to the rather absurd toupee he was wearing, so obviously a wig that the couple exchanged glances and then turned away from each other for fear of laughing out loud. Elizabeth acted as chair, introducing the small party as the Mayor and his wife and toupee-man as Mr Earnest Snow, the chief executive of the Armstrong trust, the body which would oversee the management of the home. After polite applause and thanking everyone for their attendance, she handed over to Mr Snow to say a few words. Unexpectedly, his speech was brief and even amusing with the usual round of thanks, particularly to the Armstrong family who had made the project possible. He then paid tribute to Lady Lydia, who had been the one with the vision and generosity behind the scheme. From the reaction and approving murmurings of those assembled, it was clear that Lady Armstrong was highly thought of and dearly missed. Maggie caught sight of a misty eyed Molly at the side of the room, head nodding in agreement and a face which beamed with obvious pride and love for her former employer. The Mayor was up next and spoke equally appropriate words of thanks before declaring Armstrong house to be officially open!

Elizabeth was busy posing for press photographers with her siblings and the local dignitaries so Maggie steered Peter through the French windows into the garden which was still vibrant with colour even though most of the shrubs and flowers were past their best. What she was looking for was the rose garden where late blooms clung to their stems despite having lost petals to the sometimes wild autumn weather and early frosts; petals which were strewn over the beds like a fragrant blanket. Finding the large orange blooms she was seeking, she told her husband that the rose was named after Sir George Armstrong and had been his wife's favourite flower.

'Maggie!' a voice from behind called. 'I thought you had left, I'm so glad I haven't missed you.' Elizabeth was approaching, slightly out of breath but still with the same poise and elegance inherited from her mother.

'This must be your husband?' It was both a question and an assumption as, keen to engage the visitors, she shook Peter's hand warmly and grasped Maggie's with her left hand.

'Please come in for some refreshments! You know Mr Sayer, my mother thought very highly of your wife, we're all so grateful to her for the help she gave Mother in those last weeks.'

"So much for client confidentiality" Maggie thought.

'Please call me Peter.' He decided not to correct Elizabeth as to his surname being Lloyd, not minding in the least about being identified with his wife who still used her first husband's name for work. 'We'd be delighted to stay for refreshments.'

Realising what it was that the couple had been admiring, Elizabeth asked,

'I expect mother boasted of her lovely roses, particularly this one, named after my father?' Maggie smiled, nodding as her gaze was directed to an empty flower bed beside the George Armstrong Roses.

'We're preparing this ground for the latest new rose, one named after mother which will be planted here in the spring. I like to think that she would be pleased to have a rose too, a fitting tribute don't you think?'

'Absolutely, a lovely idea and one I'm sure Lydia would approve of!'

Their hostess then led them back through the house to the library which was full of heavily laden tables of food. Molly's handiwork was certainly in evidence. Some of the new residents were serving guests, carrying trays of canapés, dainty sandwiches, cakes and biscuits, their beaming faces bearing testimony to the delight they had already found in their new home. Elizabeth praised the young man who was quick to offer them sherry or wine with their food, then when all proprieties were attended to, she excused herself to circulate among the many other visitors. The Lloyds moved on to another large reception room, greeted there by Patrick and his brother James. After introducing her husband, Maggie remarked on how well and sympathetically the renovations had been completed.

'We're certainly delighted with the way it's turned out, aren't we James?' Patrick agreed. James waved his arm towards Maggie who took his hand and squeezed it in both of her own.

'I really don't think there could be a more fitting tribute to Lady Armstrong than the home you have created here. It's magnificent and I am certain she would be delighted at how it has all come together. I hope you and your friends will be very happy here James, it's what your mother wanted.'

****

The autumn also brought a wedding and one which had been much anticipated in the Lloyd household. Julie was to marry Craig after an engagement of just over a year. The two couples had met on several occasions during that time and come to know Craig well and were convinced that this was a perfect match. Julie's cautiousness in the beginning was understandable. Her only experience of marriage had been one of violence and abuse which had naturally left a legacy of insecurity. Craig's patience and love had won her over and it was obvious how much he cared for her. Simon and Chloe were excited at the thought of having him for a new father and they had very quickly taken to calling him Daddy or Dad in Simon's case! It was not very often that Maggie had the pleasure of seeing a client right through their most difficult times and on into a new and very positive life. And so it was with elation and anticipation that they made their way to the Church to witness the marriage of Julie and Craig.

Walking slowly down the aisle on the arm of her fourteen year old son, the bride was a vision of happiness; beautiful, confident and radiant. In the packed Church all eyes were on her, particularly the groom's. The service was everything it should be and everything Julie deserved but had missed out on in her first disastrous marriage. Chloe was living every little girl's dream of being a bridesmaid, second only to her mother in capturing attention and carrying a miniature version of the bride's bouquet. The parents of the bride could not have been happier. Those painful years when their daughter was alienated from them were most certainly at an end and they held hands at the front of the Church. Her father was delighted to let his grandson have the privilege of giving his mother away, knowing that he would be making the speech later and only worrying that his words would seem totally inadequate to express how they were feeling.

Maggie's mind slipped back in time to the last wedding she had attended, a December wedding, that of Rae and Sean. Sitting near the back of the same Church they were in now, she witnessed another young couple declaring their love openly and enthusiastically. Rae too had looked stunning, as all brides do. It was a large gathering, a euphoric occasion but what stood out in her mind and something the majority of the guests would not have understood the significance of, was the lighted candles on the windowsills! At each side of the Church in the recessed stone windows, large white candles had burned brightly adding warmth to the already festive atmosphere. Hugged by holly and ivy wreathes they symbolized a new beginning for Rae, one without fear, with the man she loved and the loving support of her family.

Witnessing Julie and Craig declaring their love now, evoked so many personal memories for Maggie too as she reflected on her own first marriage to Chris and his loss three years later, the nadir of her young life. But now Peter stood beside her, the man who had brought her a new love and joy which she thought she would never experience again. Julie too was getting a second chance at happiness and her friend felt honoured to share these celebrations with her. Life predictably rolls on with each new day totally unpredictable in what it might bring. She would enjoy the weekend with Peter and her friends and on Monday morning there was a new client booked into her diary for Maggie to meet.

The End

If you have enjoyed 'Pretence' the first two books in the Maggie Sayer series are also available at Amazon and other on-line retailers.

Book 1 'The Counsellor'

Book 2 'Maggie's World'

Lightning Source UK Ltd.
Milton Keynes UK
UKOW05f1916281113

222055UK00001B/18/P